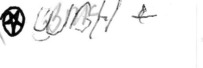

W9-CET-147

LIBRARY-NEWARK, OHIO 43055

Large Print Gor
Gorman, Edward.
Trouble man

STACKS

WITHDRAWN

TROUBLE MAN

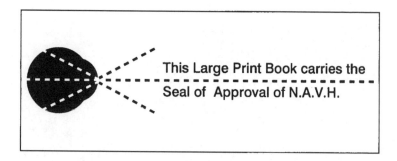

This Large Print Book carries the
Seal of Approval of N.A.V.H.

TROUBLE MAN

ED GORMAN

Thorndike Press • Waterville, Maine

Copyright © 1998 by Ed Gorman

Published in 2004 by arrangement with Leisure Books,
a division of Dorchester Publishing Co., Inc.

Thorndike Press® Large Print Western.

The tree indicium is a trademark of Thorndike Press.

The text of this Large Print edition is unabridged.
Other aspects of the book may vary from the original edition.

Set in 16 pt. Plantin by Al Chase.

Printed in the United States on permanent paper.

ISBN 0-7862-6124-2 (lg. print : hc : alk. paper)

To my editor, Don D'Auria,
Who's making it fun again —
the way it used to be.

NEWARK PUBLIC LIBRARY
NEWARK, OHIO 43055-5054

Large Print Gor
Gorman, Edward.
Trouble man

7814099

As the Founder/CEO of NAVH, the only national health agency solely devoted to those who, although not totally blind, have an eye disease which could lead to serious visual impairment, I am pleased to recognize Thorndike Press* as one of the leading publishers in the large print field.

Founded in 1954 in San Francisco to prepare large print textbooks for partially seeing children, NAVH became the pioneer and standard setting agency in the preparation of large type.

Today, those publishers who meet our standards carry the prestigious "Seal of Approval" indicating high quality large print. We are delighted that Thorndike Press is one of the publishers whose titles meet these standards. We are also pleased to recognize the significant contribution Thorndike Press is making in this important and growing field.

Lorraine H. Marchi, L.H.D.
Founder/CEO
NAVH

* Thorndike Press encompasses the following imprints: Thorndike, Wheeler, Walker and Large Print Press.

Part 1

Chapter One

Doc Tompkins looked at the corpse and said, "What's this?"

They were in the back room of the combination house-and-office the doc owned. This was where he dealt with the corpses. He liked to joke that if he couldn't make money healing you, he could make money burying you. The back room was not known to smell very good, especially on a blistering August night like this one.

"What's what?" Sheriff Jim Graham said. "It's a dead man, Doc. What the hell you think it is?"

"This. This cut on the right side of his forehead."

"How the hell would I know? The only other witness was Jimmy Clinton, and he's Bob Trevor's best friend."

"Did somebody cut him with something?"

"Cut him?" Graham said. "Hell, no, they didn't cut him. Bob Trevor shot him. Look right there. The bullet wound in the man's chest."

Doc snorted. The forehead cut bothered him and he wasn't sure why. As a frontier doctor, he'd developed instincts. He knew when to use leeches and when not to, when yellow bile signified a cancer and when it did not, and when to use mercurous chloride, which was so rough a purge that it sometimes caused internal bleeding. For all this, the doc charged twenty-five dollars a year to take care of each family, no matter how many children were added, and took as payment fruit, vegetables, meat, and cutting wood from those who couldn't afford his annual fee. One man had traded him for the new coat of paint on the house.

Doc was so old, his bones made noise even when he bent over a little bit.

He wanted a closer look at the dead man's forehead.

"I'd still like to know what the hell this wound is."

"Wound? It's just a little cut, and it don't mean nothing, Doc. It don't mean nothing." Then the sheriff started fanning away the noisy blackflies that had collected around the waist of the dead man's trousers. The man had fouled himself, as men often do in death. The flies had declared a national holiday.

Doc said, "If it was a fair fight, it was the first fair fight Bob Trevor was ever in."

"You're too hard on the boy."

"No, I'm not. He's a loudmouth good-fer-nothin' and someday somebody's not going to give a damn about his old man, and they're going to give it to Bob just the way he's got it coming."

"You want me to tell old man Trevor what you said?" Graham laughed. He'd liked the old man ever since Doc had helped him get rid of a stubborn case of crabs a couple years back.

"You think I give a damn? If Ralph Trevor wants to kill some sixty-eight-year-old sawbones with arthritis in every bone in his body, that's up to him."

Graham grinned. "I wish I had your balls, Doc. You say just what you feel."

"You can do that when you're the only doc for one hundred miles in any direction."

Graham looked down at the dead young man. Nothing special about him. Nice-looking kid of maybe nineteen, twenty, in a dusty plaid shirt, dusty black trousers, and dusty black boots. Around his neck he wore a chain with a St. Christopher medal hanging from it, signifying that he'd been a Catholic.

"Anybody know anything about this poor bastard?" Doc said.

"Not so's you'd notice. Apparently rode into town tonight and was staying over at

11

the Adams Hotel. He was drinking at the Red Rooster when Bob come in pretty drunk and started crowding him right away. I got there right at the end of it, just before they went outside."

"You could've stopped it."

"Uh-huh, and if I'd *tried* to stop it, it'd be me with flies all over him."

"Damn flies, anyway," Doc said, as if he'd just noticed them. He shooed them away. "Anybody look in his pockets?"

"I didn't. I just had my deputy, Harley, give me a hand and carry the kid straight over here."

Doc rolled the kid over on his right side, then patted his front and back pockets. And felt nothing. Then he rolled the kid over on his left side. He had some luck.

The letter was in the back pocket, a small white envelope, big blue scrawl, addressed to Mike Coyle. Doc dug the letter out and read it and said, "His old man."

"Kid's old man?"

"Yeah. Listen to this: 'I hope you're spending an hour a day practicing the way I taught you. I know you get bored with it, but it's something you've got to do, son.' "

Doc's eyes skipped down the letter to the signature. "Well, I'll be a sonofabitch."

"What?"

"You know who his old man is?"

"Who?"

"Ray Coyle."

"The gunfighter?"

Doc nodded. "Now that makes sense, what he wrote about practicing and all. Practicing his shooting is what he was talking about."

"Ray Coyle," Graham said. "I'll be damned. He was about the best there was for a long time."

"A long, *long* time," Doc said. "I was in Cheyenne one night when two men picked a fight with him at the county fair. They both drew down on him at the same time, and he nailed 'em both." Doc smiled. " 'Course, by the time the newspapers ran an account of it, it was *four* men he had to kill. But he was one mean sonofabitch." Doc stared at the envelope in his hand. "I wonder where he's been the last ten years or so."

"I thought he was dead."

"Not according to the date on this letter, he's not," Doc said.

"Wonder what he's gonna do when he finds out that Bob Trevor killed his son?" Graham said.

"Yeah," Doc said, "I kinda wonder about that myself."

Chapter Two

The midget brought him the news.

There was a time, early in his run with Colonel Haversham's Wild West and Medicine Show, when Ray Coyle had felt sorry for the midget.

Nobody ever talked straight to the little guy, or went long without smirking in his presence, as if he were some kind of inferior species they couldn't quite contend with.

But Coyle'd soon enough learned the truth about the midget. It was the little fella's aim to make everybody else as miserable as he was.

Given his size and stealth, the midget could get all sorts of places nobody else could. And he did so regularly.

The midget knew which wife was getting a little screwing on the side, which husband was really responsible for the young girl's swollen belly, which roustabout had really killed that colored boy in the scrape after the dice game.

And he told the guilty people what he knew, too, so that the show was populated with people who feared the midget's secrets. Nobody loved human misery more than the midget. It dazzled his eyes and delighted his soul.

The time was right after the midday performance. Coyle had just finished up his sharpshooting exhibition, and his lecture on western gunfighters. The shooting he didn't mind at all, but the lecture had always shamed him. Colonel Haversham saw it as just one more way to peddle his various tonics and elixirs. Get a legendary gunfighter up on the wagon talking about his days as a gunny, and you had the perfect opportunity to do some major hawking. The words still embarrassed Coyle. He'd look straight and fierce at the crowd, after just reciting his wholly bullshit tale of how he'd once backed down Jesse James, and then he'd say, "And you know what the top guns always told me? Now, you fine folks can believe this or not, but it's the God's truth, I swear it is. The top guns always told me that they would never have been any good without their daily dose of Colonel Haversham's All-Purpose Tonic. They said it improved their speed, their agility, and their vision, the three things a gunfighter relies on most." At which point, the midget, who was usually painted up as an Indian — with war paint and a big headdress, which people found funny as all hell — at this point the midget would hold up a bottle of the tonic and the young men in the crowd would swoop and swoon to buy themselves some.

Never women, who were too sensible. Never old men, who'd dreamed their dreams long ago. But young men with the jingle of shiny coins in their damp hands, and fantasies of gunfights filling their heads.

Colonel Haversham's All-Purpose Tonic. The very same stuff the Dalton Brothers always drank. And Billy the Kid. And Bat Masterson. Yessir, the very same stuff. A man like Ray Coyle, he wouldn't lie to you, would he? Of course he wouldn't. Gimme three bottles of that stuff, Mr. Midget. Or, hell, make it four.

Coyle looked up and watched the midget walk over to him. Billy Ryan was the midget's name, the poor little bastard. Coyle prayed that someday he might actually hate Billy, but that was unlikely because no matter what the little prick did, Coyle knew the sorrow that pushed him to do it.

"Good thing you're not making nice with Wanda no more," Billy said in his piping little voice. "Know why?"

"No, I don't." Coyle smiled. "But I bet you're going to tell me."

"She was lettin' the Indian do it to her last

16

night down by the creek. He made her scream about every five minutes. I never heard nothing like it."

"I'm happy for her, Billy. She's a nice woman." And she was, too. They'd had some time together, but neither was the settling-down kind. They were still friends.

"How many times a night *you* make her scream, Coyle?"

Coyle smiled again. "Six, seven hundred."

Billy had the grace to smile right back. "Maybe I should ask *her* how many."

"Why don't you just do that?"

"Damn heat," Billy said, and took off his headdress, which was all fancy feathers and shiny fine beads. Billy stood three feet eight and weighed maybe seventy pounds. Coyle had never been able to figure out how Billy kept the huge headdress on.

Billy mopped his sweaty face with his naked arm. The war paint rubbed off. He'd have to make up again before the show tonight.

"The Colonel told me to find you and give you this," Billy said, and dug down the front of his buckskin leggings and pulled a letter forth with great delicacy.

"I'm not sure I want to touch that after where it's been," Coyle said.

17

"You want me to tell you what it says?"

"I figured you probably read it."

"The envelope came unsealed."

"Sure it did, Billy. And then the letter popped right out and jumped right up into your hand."

"Your son's dead, Ray."

Coyle had been so caught up in their banter that at first his mind went right past the words.

Then he said, "What did you say?"

"You know what I did after I read the letter, Ray? I went right back to the Colonel and I told him what it said and I told him I didn't want to be the one to have to tell you, and he said, 'You get your little ass over there and tell him or I'll fire you.' And he would've, too, Ray. You know how he is when you disobey a direct order. I'm sorry, Ray. I really am."

And then Ray surprised them both by putting his hands to his face and crying.

He had to do something, and he didn't know what else was appropriate right here. So he cried. In his head was a photographic album of his son's life.

Billy's respectfulness vanished quickly. Within moments, he'd gathered a good twenty carnies to stand around in a semi-circle over Ray, watching him cry.

You watch a hard-ass gunfighter like Ray Coyle bawl his eyes out, you've seen something worth remembering, something to be savored when the moon rode high and talk turned to campfire tales worth telling and retelling: One day I seen Ray Coyle — you know the gunfighter? — I seen him bawl his eyes out. And that's no lie. I honest to God did.

Then, after a while, Wanda, who always played the virginal young woman the Indians lusted after when the Wild West show turned to dramatics, knelt down next to Ray and took his head and placed it gently against her wonderful breasts that Billy Ryan so often dreamed of, and quietly shooed all the people away so Ray could at least be spared the embarrassment of having the carnies standing around and listening to him.

When he finally got done crying, he staggered down to the nearby creek that shone silver in the sun and puked his guts up.

Chapter Three

"The letter say what happened to him, Ray?" Colonel Haversham asked. Coyle had done the show that night, and made only a few mistakes, which was pretty damned good considering what he had on his mind. Now they were in the Colonel's pay wagon, which doubled as his home.

"No."

"Just that he's dead?"

"Just that he's dead."

"I sure don't want to lose you."

"I want to go get the body and take it to his mother."

"He was how old?"

"Nineteen."

"Sonofabitch," the Colonel said. "Son-of-a-bitch."

"I'll need at least a month."

"I'm not gonna hard-ass you, Ray. You take all the time you need."

The Colonel had a whiskey-red face, a billy-goat beard, and a totally fictional explanation for the "Colonel" in his name. In truth, he was an accountant from Cincinnati who'd left his wife and children for circus life. The only battles he'd ever

20

fought were with the whiskey bottle.

"I appreciate it," Coyle said. He spoke softly, and was greatly distracted. His eyes saw inward, not outward, his mind still going through the photographic album of his son.

"When you think you'll leave?"

"Tomorrow morning."

The Colonel put out a meaty hand. "Godspeed, my friend."

"Stony'll do you a good job, Colonel. I know he will."

Stony was the Czech trapeze artist who spent all his time practicing to be an American cowboy. This included learning the quick draw. He was getting good. He knew how to do at least half of Coyle's tricks now. He'd make a good substitute for Coyle.

Coyle stood up.

"You had a drink yet?"

Coyle shook his head. "The kid had to see me drunk most of his life. I'm not gonna let him down now."

"You're a good man, Ray."

"No, I'm not," Coyle said quietly. "I'm a selfish asshole just the way my wife said I was."

Around midnight, Coyle ended up in

Wanda's wagon, sprawled out on her cot while she rubbed his shoulders and back. A rubdown from Wanda was most devoutly to be wished.

"You're going to see him again someday," Wanda said as she gently applied the heels of her hands to his spine. "You know that, don't you?"

"I wish I did know that."

"You don't believe in God?"

"I believe in something. I'm just not sure what, I guess."

"Well, take it from me, you'll see him again. I talk to the departed all the time."

"You do?"

"Yesterday, I talked to my brother."

"Oh."

"He died when he was twelve."

"I'm sorry."

"Yesterday, I opened up the wagon door and there he was. Standing by this cot. Waiting for me."

"Waiting for you, huh?"

"I know you think I'm crazy, but it's the truth," she said. "The absolute truth, Ray."

They talked some more about all this af-terlife stuff and then she blew out the lantern and lay down next to him and said, "I guess you don't feel like it tonight, huh?"

She lay on her side, directly against him,

and she could feel that he wasn't in the mood.

"I'd feel guilty."

"Yeah, I guess I probably would, too."

"I'm the one who should've died."

"Oh, Ray, don't talk like that."

"It's true. He had his whole life ahead of him. Mine's all done."

"Oh, Ray."

Then he felt like it. Sudden-like, an erection filled his pants. He had to do something to take his mind off his son or he knew he'd take a drink. Feeling guilty about having sex was preferable to feeling guilty about having a drink.

She felt him. "I guess you kinda changed your mind, huh?"

"Yeah, I guess I kinda did."

"It'll feel good to have you inside me again, Ray. It's been a long time."

"Yeah, it has been."

"You're gentle, and I appreciate that."

They made love, and then he lay there for a time, and then the moon was high and he was leaving her wagon, and moving quickly through the shadows. He still had packing to do tonight.

He was about halfway there when Billy Ryan came magically out of nowhere. This time of night, he always wore his cowboy duds, including a ten-gallon Stetson that was half as tall as he was.

"I didn't hear her scream once," the midget said.

"You little bastard, you were listening, huh?"

"I tell you how many times the Injun made her scream?"

"Yeah," Coyle said, "yeah, you told me, all right."

Chapter Four

The train was running pretty much on schedule, which was to say four hours late.

But since most of the passengers were eastern tourists headed to Denver, they were just grateful the train hadn't been attacked by Indians or robbed by highwaymen.

Harry Winston was on the train, too. He was prison-pale and prison-wary, glancing suspiciously around at everything and everyone. He wore the checkered drummer's suit that was one size too small, the one the warden had given him the day before, and he wore the hard-eyed look of menace and malice he'd worn pretty much every day of his life, including the interminable days of his court trial for robbing a stagecoach. If he'd smiled more, his lawyer had told him afterward, the judge might not have gone so hard on him.

Winston took his carpetbag and walked onto the platform. Women in big picture hats and bustles and pastel-colored dresses floated past, as did dusty-faced kids who came down to the depot every time a train pulled in. Kids couldn't get enough of trains.

Winston walked away from the depot, toward the center of town. He'd been told to stay out of saloons, but what the warden didn't know wasn't going to hurt him.

Harry Winston had gone into prison weighing 230 pounds. He came out weighing 160 pounds. He'd changed in other ways, too. His hair was gone, and the little fringe left was virgin white.

There was a trolley car now, a lone black car pulled wearily by a black horse. Inside were more ladies with big picture hats in pastel-colored summer dresses.

Many years earlier, Third Street had held all the saloons and taverns. The town fathers, who ran to high-minded Lutherans and Methodists, hadn't wanted Main Street to be an "advertisement for sin," as one of the council members put it.

That particular set of town fathers must have died off, Winston thought, looking up and down the refurbished sight of Main Street. He counted three saloons and two imposing gambling halls right in plain sight, a clear advertisement for sin if he'd ever seen one. Three blocks of false fronts, two general stores, two banks, a huge livery and feed, and at least four different restaurants.

Derby dangling from his right hand, he crossed the street, the trolley bell ringing festively at the opposite corner. Winston smiled at all the stares his hardcase face attracted. He especially liked the stares of the women. Unlike most men who went to prison, he never allowed himself to have sex with a man. His desire for a woman had burned fierce and steady in the most secret part of his heart. His pride was that no man had ever touched him in any untoward way. Now he could finally do something about a woman. A few drinks, and then he'd go in search of a fancy house. With all this activity in town, there still had to be at least one such place.

The saloon was busy with townsmen on their lunch hour. They drank giant schooners of beer and lunched on free hard-boiled eggs and ham slices and wheat bread. There was a player piano trilling away and a poster that read: 65 DIFFERENT KINDS OF DRINKS — COUNT 'EM! And so there was. But what kind of white man had ever heard of such concoctions as a Rochelle Do, a Fewett's Fancy, or a Phlegm-cutter?

Winston walked over to the bar in the ancient crack-leather bluchers the warden had given him along with the suit, and ordered himself a beer. Then he proceeded to slap together a ham sandwich, three slices deep, and he plucked a couple of hard-boiled eggs from the bowl to complement the sandwich.

He wanted to break down and cry, the sandwich tasted so good. All those years of prison gruel . . . he'd had no idea that real food would taste as good to him as a woman.

His beer came. He brought it quickly to his lips but then paused. He should take his first drink with great, almost theatrical care, the way a priest sipped altar wine that had been changed into the blood of Christ. He should venerate this beer, not just throw it down.

He venerated the beer.

He venerated the sonofabitch so well that within three minutes he was ordering another one. And he venerated that one, too. And then another and another. What a venerating sonofabitch he was.

In the same time that he venerated five beers, he ate two sandwiches.

Then he burst out the back door to the dirt alley and vomited it all back up.

Fella comes out of prison after eight years, he has to be careful of how much and how fast he venerates.

He went back into the saloon and started venerating all over again, and as he stood there at the bar, feeling like a free man for the first time in the two days he'd been out of prison, he started thinking of that sonofabitch Bob Trevor, and of how Trevor was going to make him rich. Right-away rich. For-life rich.

Either Bob Trevor was going to make him rich or Harry Winston was going to make him damned sorry. Damned sorry.

He found the fancy house at two o'clock that afternoon. It was an Italianate Victorian with a slightly pitched roof and round-arched windows. The woman running the place had obviously done pretty well for herself. The September air smelled wistfully of burning leaves. You didn't get treated to smells like that in prison.

He knocked. The door was opened almost immediately by a buxom woman with red hair streaked gray that was almost white. Her velvet dress, clearly expensive, was red, too.

"Yes?"

"You Ione?"

"I am Ione, yes."

"Guess you know why I'm here."

Ione smiled. "Just in case you're one of the minister fellas who comes out here every once in a while to do some spyin', why don't you tell me who you are?"

"Name's Winston."

"All right. Where you from?"

"Territorial prison."

Her eyes narrowed. "You know somethin'?"

"What?"

"I spotted that right away."

"Ya did, huh?"

"Ya know *how* I did?"

"Huh-uh."

"Your size."

"My size?"

"Big, strappin' fella like you, he shouldn't be actin' so nervous. Look at you, way you hold your derby in your hands. Big, strappin' fella like you shouldn't hold it that timid sort of way. A bank teller, that's how he'd hold his derby. But not you."

"I guess you're right."

She squinted at him again. "How long's it been?"

"For what?"

"For what? You some kind of stupid bastard? How long's it been since you had a woman?"

"Oh."

"Three, four years?"

"Eight."

"God a'mighty, mister. I'm gonna have to give you the very best one I got."

He grinned. "That'd be all right by me."

30

"What kind you like?"

"Big tits and big asses. Especially the asses."

"Juanita's the one you want. Got an ass on her like a stud horse."

He grinned again. "Sounds like she's the one for me."

"C'mon in, mister, and meet the girls."

Which is just what he did.

Chapter Five

Though they wouldn't meet for twenty-four hours yet, Ray Coyle rode the same train that brought Harry Winston to Coopersville.

Instead of finding a saloon when he walked from the depot, Coyle looked for the office of Sheriff Jim Graham, the man who'd sent him the letter about Mike being dead.

His journey led him to a short street off Main, to a two-story redbrick building that housed the county court, the sheriff's office, and a small jail. Bars covered some of the windows on the second floor.

Inside, the floors of the sheriff's office shone with wax; the three deputies he saw were young, trim, and polite; and the two young women he saw working behind desks did so with pleasant efficiency, smiling at him as he passed their door.

"May I help you?" the brunette asked.

"I'm looking for Sheriff Graham."

"Out back," she said. "He's working with his dogs."

Coyle nodded his thanks, straightened his suit jacket, and walked to the back of the building. He owned only one suit. It had been sold to him as a year-rounder, but in Indian summer weather like this, it was a mite heavy.

Jim Graham was a tall, slender man turned brown and tough-skinned by the sun. He had skeptical but not unfriendly blue eyes and an intelligent, straightforward manner.

"My name's Coyle, Sheriff."

Coyle saw a moment of embarrassment in the lawman's eyes. This had to be the worst part of the job, facing the relatives of dead people.

"I'm sorry about your son."

"You knew him?" Coyle asked.

"No, afraid I didn't." Then: "Just a second. Be right with you."

There were three small oak trees in the grassy back. In the shade of the heavy branches, two bloodhounds sniffed their way around each one.

"I stuffed a kerchief into a knot in that third tree there," Graham said. "I'm hoping these boys'll be able to find it. We had a little girl fall into an abandoned well last year. We might've saved her if we'd found her in time. So I got me this pair of hounds. They haven't really been called on to do much, but I want them ready when I need them."

The dogs passed on tree one and then went on to tree two.

They sniffed the base, then they climbed up as high as their doggy legs would take them, which wasn't far. Then they stayed in that position and sniffed some more.

"I gave them a whiff of my little granddaughter's blouse," Graham said. "That's the scent they're looking for."

After they got done with the second tree, the hounds stopped, as if they'd been absolutely flabbergasted. Their floppy ears and sad doggy eyes were almost comic; Coyle felt sorry for them. They had to carry a hell of a burden for being just plain old dogs.

Then one of the hounds sort of sidled over to the third oak and started sniffing. Soon enough, he was making a whimpering noise low in his throat. His sniffing got almost frantic. He started barking. His buddy soon joined him. When they barked in unison, they were damn loud.

"Good boys," Graham said, patting them on their heads. He reached up to the head-tall knot and pulled the emerald-green kerchief free.

There was a run built of chicken wire off to the right. Inside the run was a large, shingled doghouse. Hard brown turds littered the dirt inside the run. Graham opened the gate for the hounds and shooed them inside. "I let them out four, five times a day. I just want to make sure they're around when I need them."

He closed the gate and spoke a few more words to them in what was essentially baby talk. Infants and animals could render the direst heart vulnerable and foolish.

"Now, Mr. Coyle," Graham said, "let's go inside and get on with your business."

"Near as I've been able to tell, Mr. Coyle, your son wasn't here more than two hours before it happened."

Graham's office was just as orderly and clean as the shiny waxed floors and the clean, pretty office women would lead a person to expect. There was a rack of Winchesters on the east wall, a number of framed commendations on the west wall, a rolltop desk, a spittoon, and three very comfortable-looking chairs for visitors.

"That's my trouble," Coyle said. "I still don't know what 'it' is. That killed him, I mean."

"You mean nobody's told you yet?"

"No, sir. Nobody's told me yet."

"Oh, hell, Mr. Coyle. I'm sorry. I just assumed you know."

Coyle shook his head.

"A gunfight."

"A gunfight?"

"I'm afraid so."

"There were witnesses?"

"Oh, yes."

"And it was a fair fight?"

"Oh, yes. Absolutely."

"He was good. From the time he was four, I taught him about gunfighting. I've had some experience with gunfighting myself."

"You're too modest, Mr. Coyle. I know who you are. The whole town does."

"I just don't see how Mike could've lost. If it was a fair fight, I mean."

"I don't know all the particulars, Mr. Coyle. He might've had too much to drink. I just don't know the circumstances. All I know for sure is that he went outside willingly, and then got himself shot in the chest."

Coyle'd told himself to remain calm when he was talking to Graham. Coyle had a bad temper, and almost always it led him to say or do something foolish.

Right now, he either wanted to cry the way he'd been crying the five days since getting the letter about Michael, or he wanted to bust up Graham's office, and then bust up Graham.

He said, "Do you know the man he fought with?"

"I know him quite well."

"Then he's a local?"

"Oh, he's very local. His father practically built this town by himself."

"What's his name?"

"The man who got into a fight with your son, his name is Bob Trevor. His father's name is Ralph Trevor."

"I'd like to speak to this Bob."

Graham looked at him for a long, long moment. "I was hoping it weren't going to run this way, Mr. Coyle."

"Run what way?"

"You wanting to talk to Bob Trevor and all."

"I said talk, Sheriff. I didn't say anything else."

"Man kills your son, fair fight or not, you want to do a lot more than talk to him."

"That's all I have in mind."

"That's bullshit, Mr. Coyle, and you know it and I know it. A man like you —"

Coyle smiled. "I figured we'd get around to that."

"To what, Mr. Coyle?"

"To 'a man like me.' "

"You're a gunfighter."

"You'd better update your files, Sheriff. I

37

haven't been a gunfighter for ten years."

"Oh?"

"I spent five years traveling around for a gun manufacturer putting on shooting displays, and then I joined up with a Wild West Show. I've been with the show the last five years. Going on six, matter of fact."

Graham sighed. "I'm sorry for your situation here, Mr. Coyle."

"I appreciate that, Sheriff. But I really don't intend any harm. I just want to see him, talk to him a little."

"For what purpose?"

Coyle shrugged. "To see how Mike was at the last, I guess."

"It's not going to do anybody any good — you, me, or Bob Trevor — if you hang around town and start asking questions, Mr. Coyle. It was a fair fight and your son lost, and I'm sorry as all hell for you but now there isn't a damn thing I can do, or a damn thing you can do."

Coyle stood up and walked over to the window.

"He should've had a wife and kid," he said, though not exactly to Graham, probably to himself more than anybody. "He should've had a nice little house and a nice little job and a nice little carriage that he took out on Sunday afternoons. He shouldn't have died at his age, or died the way he did, and maybe it was all the way you said, Sheriff, all fair and square and all that, maybe it was just exactly like that. But I'm his father, and I have a right to know how my son spent his last hours."

Neither of them spoke for a long time after that.

"Doc Tompkins has got his coffin over at his office," Graham said quietly after a time. "I can have one of my deputies take the coffin over to the depot and you can be headed back on the nine o'clock train tonight. Will you at least think about it, Mr. Coyle? Please?"

Coyle smiled sadly. "I'll think about it, Sheriff. But I won't think about it real hard."

One minute later, he left Sheriff Graham's office and went to find Bob Trevor.

Chapter Six

The smiles they gave her were genuine.

Cass was the only one of the three Trevors the townspeople cared for. She worked as a volunteer three times a week in the tiny four-bed hospital; she personally delivered food items to people in need — a husband hurt in a work accident, a young child seriously ill, an old person facing nothing but hunger and death. And if you did something that displeased her bullying brother Bob, she'd listen to your appeal and usually intercede on your behalf, calling Bob off like the angry dog he could be.

She was pretty, too, in a kid-sister sort of way, with freckles and a quick, lopsided smile, and a nice girly laugh. She sang every Sunday in the Methodist choir but never got a solo because of her tendency to go off-key every other line or so. She loved dogs, cats, raccoons, the Fourth of July canoe races (she'd taken two blue ribbons), and playing banjo with some of the hands on her father's cattle ranch. She'd been married once, but only for six months. It was a subject she never discussed with anybody, and as a consequence the topic remained a mystery to the townspeople. What the hell had happened to that husband of hers, anyway?

Eight years earlier, when she'd been sixteen, her twenty-one-year-old brother, Don, the person she'd loved above everybody but her cholera-dead mother — her brother Don had drowned in a swimming hole. Nobody had ever explained how or why. Don had been an excellent swimmer, he'd been perfectly sober the afternoon of his death, and the water at its deepest point was six feet. Don stood five-ten, so six feet of water shouldn't have been a problem.

This particular afternoon, Cass was in town shopping. She bought all the staples for the bunkhouse, she got an assortment of chewing and smoking tobacco for the ranch hands, and she bought herself a couple of books. Her favorite author was Louisa May Alcott.

Her last stop was the millinery shop, where she looked at skirts for the grange dance that night. Booming as Coopersville was, it still didn't offer much of a fashion selection. Cass always bought a lot when she accompanied her father to Denver. Otherwise, she ordered regularly from the big red Sears catalog. But buying outside the town made her feel slightly guilty. The merchants here were good, honest people, and they needed all the business she could give them.

She was just leaving the millinery store when she saw Sheriff Graham walking toward her up the board sidewalk.

"Afternoon, Cass."

"Afternoon, Sheriff."

"You happen to know where Bob is this afternoon?"

"I think he's helping some of the men round up orphans." Orphans were motherless calves that had to be raised by the hands at the ranch. Bob worked only when he had to. But right then the spread was short-handed and so her father made Bob put in a couple of days a week.

"Appreciate it if you'd give him a message for me."

"Be happy to."

Graham frowned. "You know that fracas he got into last week?"

Cass frowned too. Much as Bob assured her and her father that the other man had started the fight and forced it to its conclusion, Cass was skeptical. She loved her younger brother in a formal sort of way, but she really didn't like or respect him much, and she rarely believed his side of a story.

"I remember."

"Well, the kid Bob shot? His father came to town today."

"Oh, Lord."

"He wants to see Bob." Graham paused. "He's a gunfighter, or was — claims he quit a long time ago — name of Ray Coyle."

"I've heard of him."

"Had himself quite a reputation for a long time. Doc and me found a letter in the kid's pocket from his father. We always knew he belonged to Ray Coyle, but we didn't say anything because we didn't want to worry Bob or your father."

"I appreciate that."

"He came over to the office and we talked, and he got pretty choked up."

She couldn't help herself. Even though this Coyle represented a possible threat to her family, Cass couldn't help but be moved by the picture of a man overwrought by the death of his son. She thought of how her father had wept on and off for months after Don's drowning.

Then Graham said, "There he is now."

The lawman nodded across the street to where a tall man dressed in a dated and dusty suit was just leaving a small diner.

She was immediately struck by the melancholy sense she had of the man. Something in his slightly stooped shoulders, something

43

in his handsome face — even from a distance — spoke of a sorrow she recognized all too well. Her own sorrow, over Don, over her marriage, over the early death of her beloved mother, was not unlike this ragged man's grief.

"Maybe I'll go talk to him."

Graham looked at her oddly. "Now, why would you go and do that, Cass?"

"Maybe it'd make him feel better. About his son and everything. Besides, I've got half an hour before Dad'll be here to meet me at the courthouse. We've got to countersign some old deeds of Mother's."

Graham looked warily at Coyle. "You be careful. He says he isn't a gunfighter anymore. But that don't mean anything. People'll tell you anything they think you want to hear."

She thought of her former husband when Graham said this. Handsome, slick Lawrence had been a master of telling you what you wanted to hear. And how innocent she'd been about such men — until it was way too late.

"You just be sure and tell that father of yours that I was against this," Graham said. Like most men in this town, he was afraid of her father's considerable wrath. It was just something you accepted when you lived here — her father's ire — the same way you accepted floods and fires and blizzards.

"You be careful."

"I will."

Graham stood there watching Cass walk across wide, dusty Main Street, waiting to walk between the clinking and clanking wagons that rolled in and out of town. The Indian-summer afternoon was pungent with the scent of road apples. Traffic had been heavy all day.

Graham saw her approach Coyle, who was walking toward the east end of town, and then touch a hand to his elbow.

Coyle turned around and looked at Cass. From there, Graham couldn't read his expression.

The whole exchange was in pantomime. She spoke and then Coyle spoke, and then she spoke again.

Graham was watching all this when somebody tugged on his shoulder.

"She's doin' it again, Sheriff."

"Aw, shit, Lem," Graham said. "This ain't about that wife of yours, is it?"

"It sure is," short, squat, alcoholic Lem said. "And this time I've got proof."

Lem was a bender drinker. He could go weeks without imbibing, and then all of a

45

sudden he'd drink till the saloons closed, and then he'd be there when they opened again at dawn. Lem had one obsession when he was drinking: that his chubby, quiet, sincere, and good-natured wife was screwing half the men in town.

"What's this proof you got?" Graham said skeptically.

"This name she kept sayin' in her sleep last night."

"That don't mean shit, Lem."

"It don't, huh? She was moanin' while she said it. Moanin', and you know what that means, don't you, when they moan like that?"

Graham had been distracted just long enough for Cass and Coyle to have disappeared. He wondered where they'd gone. If only that damned Lem hadn't come up.

"And you know who's name she was moanin', Sheriff?"

Graham sighed. "No, Lem, I don't know whose name she was moanin'."

"She was moanin' *your* name, you sonofabitch! She was moanin' *your* name!"

And that's when Lem hauled off and hit Sheriff Jim Graham right in the jaw with a pretty damn good right hook.

Chapter Seven

It was more of a cottage than a real house. It sat on a corner lot. All the carefully planted summer flowers — snapdragons and marigolds and petunias — told you that the people who lived here took pride in their snug little home. The white picket fence told you the same thing.

Harry Winston stood across the street, in the shade of a sprawling oak, looking at the little girl jumping rope by herself. She was a sweet little girl, eleven years old that past July, a sweet little girl of blond curls and endearingly thin limbs.

Her name was Jane and she was Harry Winston's daughter, and the last time he saw her she was three years old and crying in her mother's arms. That particular day, in an apartment on the other side of town, Harry Winston had been headed for prison. His estranged wife Ellen had brought Jane over to say good-bye.

Every few moments, Jane looked over at Harry. She had likely been warned about strangers. In prison, Harry had known a man who'd molested and then murdered a little girl. The man went five years before somebody finally got him one late afternoon in the wagonworks the warden ran. Dug his eyes out with a pocket knife, then cut his cock off and stuck it in his mouth. The whole thing was so savage, Harry almost felt sorry for him. Almost.

Jane stopped skipping rope then and took a final long look at Harry, clearly suspicious now, then turned and ran inside the house.

A chunky man in a work shirt and denims came out almost immediately. He went down the walk till he stood where Jane had been.

"Help you with something, mister?" he called from across the street.

"Nope."

"Who are you?"

"None of your business."

"I can always call the law."

"You do that."

Then Ellen was there, on the doorstep, and then, moments later, right behind the chunky man next to the street.

"It's all right," she said to the man.

"Who is he?"

"It's Harry."

"Harry Winston? I thought he was in prison."

"You go inside and see to Jane."

"I don't want you talkin' to him."

"I'll be all right. You go on in now."

"The sonofabitch."

"You go on in now."

"Who the hell's he think he is, anyway, scaring Jane that way?"

Ellen gave him a gentle nudge. The man made a show of not wanting to go. He made the show all the way back to the door, all the way inside. He was a chickenshit, was what he was. A chickenshit who liked to put on a show that proved he *wasn't* a chickenshit. Prison was filled with guys like this.

Harry Winston walked across the street. The closer he got to Ellen, the older she looked. All her youth had been blanched out of her. She looked tired and gray and nervous.

"Surprised you showed up, Harry."

"Wanted to see her."

"Well, you saw her."

"She's pretty."

"Yes, she is," Ellen said. "She sure is that."

"Who's the guy?"

"My husband."

"He's an asshole."

"No, he isn't, Harry. He just wanted to look good for me and Jane."

"You always did go for nancies."

She smiled, some of her youth evident

again briefly. "He knows how to satisfy a woman, Harry, so I seriously doubt he's a nancy."

"We had some pretty good times, me and you."

"Yes, we did. Bed was good, but everything else was bad, Harry, and you know it."

He watched her wipe her hands on her gingham dress, a stray piece of gray hair fluttering in the slight breeze.

"You tell her about me?"

"I told her you were dead."

"That's pretty goddamned nice."

"You want me to tell her you were in prison?"

He made a face. "I suppose not."

"Sam's her dad, Harry. Not you. Being a dad is something you have to earn. You never cared much about her when she was a baby, so why should you care about her now?"

He looked at her again and made another face. "When prison got bad sometimes, when I didn't think I could goddamn take it for another minute, she was all I thought about. And you can believe that or not. She was the only thing kept me going. I wanted to live long enough to get out of there and see her. And now you tell me I *can't* see her."

50

"You saw her, Harry."

"You know what I'm saying."

"I told her you were dead. How would I explain you coming back?"

"Tell her there was a mistake. Some kind of accident, and they only *thought* I was dead."

She shook her head. "We have a nice life here, Harry, the three of us. I don't want to go and ruin it."

"I'd pay you."

She smiled. "That's pretty sad."

"What is?"

"Offering to pay me to see your own daughter."

"It'd be worth it to me."

"How'd you come into money when you were in prison?"

"I haven't come into it yet," he said. "But in a day or two I will."

She studied him a moment. "Bob Trevor, huh?"

He shrugged.

"Your old friend," she said. "Harry and Bob, Bob and Harry. Friends to the end." She said this in a mocking way, of course. She'd always hated Bob. He was a bully and Harry always put up with him, even the time a drunken Bob had tried to have sex with her one night when Harry was away. All

51

Harry had said was, "That's just how Bob is. It don't mean anything." But it had meant something to Ellen. It had meant a great deal, in fact.

"He's watching us," Harry said. "From the window, I mean."

"If I was your wife, you'd be watching me, too."

"So I can't see her?"

"You can't see her."

"Goddammit."

"I'm sorry, Harry, that's just the way it has to be."

"What's that asshole do, anyway?"

"He makes axles for buckboards."

"Sounds like a shit job."

"You always had big dreams, Harry. Too bad none of them ever came true."

"I want to see her."

"No."

"You don't have any right to stop me."

"Sure I have a right, Harry. I've been the one taking care of her all these years. You were either running around or in prison."

She raised her face, her pert, sweet nose, and sniffed the air.

"You need to clean yourself up, Harry. The woman you were with needed a bath." For the first time, bitterness was in her voice. "I still remember you comin' home late every night, Harry, smellin' of the whorehouse. I'm glad to see that nothing's changed."

Harry had noticed that, too, in fact, the girl at the fancy house smelling kind of sour.

"I want to see her, Ellen."

"Well," Ellen said, "you're not *going* to see her, Harry. And that's all there is to it."

Harry glanced over at the window again. Sam was peeking out around the curtain like a scared little kid. Goddamned nancy was what he was.

"Good-bye, Harry," Ellen said.

And then she was gone.

Chapter Eight

Coyle liked the Trevor woman a hell of a lot more than he wanted to.

She'd asked him to have a cup of coffee in the same small diner where he'd had lunch. They'd taken a table at the back, where they'd been sitting now for the past few minutes.

Part of the time, he felt as if he was betraying the memory of his son. This woman shouldn't be so nice or so decent or so pretty. He wished she'd had made it easy to hate her.

"Sheriff Graham tells me you want to see Bob," she said.

"I'd appreciate it if you could arrange it."

"Do you mind if I ask *why* you'd like to see him?"

"I guess I'd feel better if I knew what happened. The sheriff says that Mike started the fight. I guess I just want to make sure that's what happened."

"I guess I was like that when my brother Don died," she said.

She spoke quietly — everything about her was quiet, in fact — but with the precise feeling of one who has thought a great deal about her words.

"I just wanted there to be one witness," she went on, "to how Don could drown, I mean."

"He was by himself?"

She nodded. "Which was another thing. Don always went swimming with other people. Never alone."

"People break habits sometimes."

"Apparently, that's what Don did that day. Broke a habit, I mean. And then drowned."

Her eyes glistened with tears. Her voice was raspy. "I guess it's just something I'll never understand." She smiled sadly. "Until I meet up with him in the next life, anyway."

Along the counter, a couple of men laughed at some joke among themselves, their voices harsh and impolite in the silence of her sorrow.

He knew now why she'd been so dutiful to his own loss: She'd shared a similar loss, and remembered just how it felt.

She sniffed tears back, looked down at her work-roughed hands, and then looked up again at Coyle.

"I guess I should be very honest here, Mr. Coyle."

"You could call me Ray."

"Ray, then. I think you want to see my brother because you don't believe what Sheriff Graham told you. Is that right?"

"I guess you could say it that way. I'd just feel better about it all if I heard it from your brother."

"He has a bad temper."

"I kind of figured he would."

"And he's not used to answering questions. Our family — well, in the valley here, my family isn't used to answering questions. At least Dad and Bob aren't."

"People get that way sometimes. When they have power."

"That's not to say Dad and Bob are bad people."

"I understand."

"It's just that they don't feel they have to answer to other people."

"I'll bet Don wasn't that way, was he?" Coyle said softly.

Her eyes flickered with sorrow again. "No, he wasn't. He was more like — me, and my mother. That's why I had hopes for the ranch. Being the oldest, he was next in line to inherit it when Dad retired in a few years. He would have run it differently. And treated the townspeople differently, too."

"Bob inherits it now?"

She nodded. "Dad's a little worried, to be honest. Thinks Bob needs a little more time to grow up."

"I see."

Her cheeks were suddenly tinted red. "I sound like I don't care for Bob. I do. Most of the time he's a very decent young man." She paused. "He's not a killer, Ray. He really isn't. If he said your son started the fight —"

"I'd just like him to tell me that to my face, is all. Then I'll put the coffin on the next train, and take it back to his mother's to bury." He looked at her steadily. "You can't blame me for that, can you?"

She sighed. "I guess not."

"I'd be grateful if you'd ask him to talk to me."

She thought a moment. "I guess I could do that. We're both going to the grange dance tonight. I could introduce you there and stay around so things went smoothly."

"I'd really appreciate that."

She looked out the diner window at the lengthening shadows of afternoon.

"Guess I'd better be going," she said.

"It was nice talking with you. I appreciate your concern."

She stood up. "The grange hall is what you'll be looking for tonight. We'll be there after eight o'clock."

He took her hand and held it a long moment. Then he felt guilty again. He found himself drawn to a woman whose very own brother had killed his very own son. It wasn't right.

He eased his hand away.

"Thanks again," he said, only this time there was no warmth in his voice.

Chapter Nine

"You bitch!" Jimmy Clinton said as he slapped Barbara Potter. "You whore!"

The one time Jimmy had really beaten Barbara up, he'd found himself in dire trouble with Ione Moorehouse, the woman who owned and ran the whorehouse where Barbara worked.

Ione argued, reasonably enough, that men weren't likely to sleep with a girl who was sporting a couple of black eyes and a swollen lip. So Ione barred him from the house for a full week and then gave him a few pointers on how to beat up a girl without leaving any marks on her. Ione did it with her own girls all the time, and you didn't see any noticeable bruises on them, did ya?

But that afternoon, Jimmy forgot all about Ione's pointers, and just started slapping Barbara around, bouncing her off walls, hurling her into chairs, and then blinding her with hard, quick slaps to the cheeks and mouth and eyes.

The bitch. He knew she was going to do it someday, and now she had.

"Please, Jimmy! Please stop!" Barbara

sobbed. "I think you broke one of my ribs!"

"This is just the start, bitch! Just the start."

This time, he raised a Texas-style boot and kicked right on the edge of her shin.

She screamed, and folded up, and collapsed to the floor, gripping her leg and trying to curtail the pain.

Then he kicked her in the ribs again, the same area he'd been working on when she'd fallen down before.

James Avery Clinton was twenty-three. He stood five-ten, was given to the sort of fancy western duds you saw on the covers of the better yellowbacks, and was legendary locally for tasting human flesh.

Jimmy was just sixteen at the time, and his folks had just moved here from Kansas. He was wilder than hell; the law in Kansas where they'd lived had pronounced him "a public nuisance." Which meant that his first and best friend here just had to be Bob Trevor, who was the same age and liked to raise hell even more than Jimmy did.

At the time, there was a notorious lawman named John Johnson who hated Crow Indians so much (they'd killed his wife and daughter) that after he killed them, he cut them up in pieces and roasted them over an open fire. And then proceeded to eat them.

Well, you know how boys love to imitate adults. One whole summer, Jimmy and Bob Trevor discussed the exploits of John Johnson (or "Liver-eating Johnson," as the yellowbacks were apt to refer to him) and wondered if they could ever bring themselves to eat human flesh.

Then, one starry September-cool evening, they found the tramp lying along the railroad tracks.

There was no doubting he was dead. Birds had already picked his face apart.

The idea came quickly. Seemed here was the perfect opportunity to test out one's cannibalistic tendencies. Just cut off a little piece of him and swallow it down. Who needed a fire?

Jimmy said he'd do it if Bob would, and Bob said he'd do it if Jimmy would, and Jimmy said he'd do it if Bob would. And so on and on for an hour as they sat on the moon-silver railroad tracks and stared at the dead tramp.

Finally, Bob said why didn't they flip a coin, that was the fair and square way to do it, whoever lost being the first one to saw off a piece and have a bite.

Bob flipped the coin. Jimmy lost.

What Jimmy really wanted to do was run. But he knew he couldn't chicken out. Not after spending a summer boasting that he could do it if the opportunity ever presented itself.

So he did it, squatted down by the tramp and took out his Sears pocketknife and cut off a piece of the tramp's arm, about the size of the fudge his aunt Ida always gave him.

It was pretty bloody, which he hadn't counted on. Smelled sour, too.

"Go on," Bob said. "Go on, you lost, and now you gotta do it."

"Aw, shit, Bob. Maybe the guy's already poison and it'll kill me."

"Never killed Liver-eatin' Johnson, did it?"

"Yeah, but they were *fresh* when Johnson ate 'em."

"Tell you what. You cut me off a piece and we'll eat it at the same time."

"Really?"

"Really. Now cut me off a piece."

So Jimmy cut him off a piece — once again the same size as Aunt Ida's fudge — and handed it over to Bob, and Bob without hesitation put the piece right up to his mouth and said, "You ready, Jimmy? Let's just get it over with."

So Jimmy put his piece to his mouth and Bob said, "Go!" And so Jimmy flipped the flesh into his mouth and started eating immediately.

It tasted like owl shit and raccoon shit and bear shit and fish shit and pig shit combined. God, but it was awful! And Jimmy spat it out after only a few bites, but he'd already swallowed some of it and was already starting to puke.

And Bob Trevor just sat there and laughed and laughed and laughed, because he hadn't partaken of the flesh at all. He'd just tricked Jimmy into partaking, and forever after, and as far and wide distant as his tongue could be heard, Bob Trevor would tell the story of the night his friend Jimmy Clinton had partaken of human flesh. . . .

Barbara was still on the floor now. She grasped his legs, pleaded with him not to hurt her no more, no more, Jimmy, please please please . . .

"I knew you'd fuck him someday," Jimmy said, miserable and lonely and mean, really wanting to kill her being what he *really* wanted to do.

Then it was gone from him. Sudden as it had come up, now it was just as sudden gone, all his rage, and he went over and sat quietly down in the plump armchair that had come with this little room he rented — sat down in the armchair and stared at her and said, "I don't mind it when you fuck just regular guys. That's your job, and I forced myself to get used to it. But why did you have to go and fuck Bob Trevor? That's what I'd like to know."

"I was drunk, Jimmy. That's all it was, I was drunk."

She sat in the middle of the floor, still naked, her little breasts black and blue from where he'd squeezed them, but there was hope in her voice now because when she could get him talking like this it meant he wasn't going to hit her no more. Least, not for the time being.

Jimmy had found out from the landlord that one night when he was gone last week, Bob, all drunked up, had come up here and paid a late-night call on Barbara. That's just how the landlord had put it, too, "a late-night call."

Barbara was mostly Comanche, and sometimes her Indian-ness, in certain lights at certain angles, looked beautiful. Other times, as now, it looked coarse and ugly. He wanted her to put some clothes on. At odd moments, he could be as sanctimonious as a Baptist Bible-thumper.

"You know he always does that, don't you?" Jimmy said miserably.

"Does what?"

64

"Fucks my girls. Like he has to prove that he can have anything of mine anytime he wants it. He's done it to every girl I ever had since I knew him."

"That liar."

"What?"

"Oh, never mind."

Jimmy shook his head. "He sweet-talked you, huh?"

"Yeah. A little bit, anyway."

He just wished she'd put some clothes on. She was a whore — that's what Ione paid her to be — but she didn't have to look like a whore.

"What'd he say to you?"

"Oh, you don't want to hear, Jimmy. It'd just make you mad all over again."

"No, tell me. I want to hear."

She looked up at him, feeling miserable for both of them.

"Well, he just said that the only reason you had anything at all was because of him and his father."

"He did, huh?"

"He said you couldn't hold down a real job if you had to."

"That sonofabitch."

"And he said that if I was his gal, he'd buy me a lot of nice things so I'd look prettier."

Jimmy said nothing for a long time.

"Jimmy?"

"What?"

"What're you thinking about?"

"I'm thinking about you should go put on some clothes so you don't always look like such a whore."

She stood up. "All right, Jimmy," she said softly. "I'll go put some clothes on."

"And I'm thinking that I don't ever want to see you again."

"Oh, Jimmy, you don't mean that."

"The hell I don't. You think I'd want to stick my dick where Bob Trevor's been?"

"We was drunk, Jimmy. That's all. Just like you was drunk when you did it with Gwen. We was drunk."

Jimmy was about to say more when the knock came on the door.

Jimmy and Barbara looked at each other a moment, then Jimmy said, "You go in the bedroom and get some clothes on."

Barbara nodded and swiftly left the room, her nakedness flashing through the shadowy apartment that sat above a general store on Main.

Jimmy got up and went to the door. He was hoping it was Bob Trevor. Oh, how he was hoping it was Bob Trevor.

He opened the door and there stood

Harry Winston. Not the old Harry with great piles of red hair, but a bald and much more sinewy Harry. The drummer suit was so cheap and badly cut, it was almost laughable. But you never wanted to make the mistake of laughing in Harry's face. The hard, dead eyes told you that.

"I'll be damncd," Jimmy said.

Harry smiled. "I'm sure you will be."

"When'd you get out?"

Harry shrugged. "Couple days ago." He nodded to the apartment beyond Jimmy. "You gonna invite me in?"

"Oh, yeah, sorry."

Jimmy stepped back and let Harry walk in.

Harry looked around. "Nice place."

"After nine years in the jug, any place'd be nice."

"Yeah, I suppose you're right. And it was eight years."

Barbara came out of the bedroom.

"Hi," she said, looking nervous.

Jimmy watched Harry look her over. The first thing he looked at was her face, then her breasts, then the ankles below the line of her yellow summer dress. Then his gaze went back to her face and to the bruises there. Jimmy was definitely going to catch hell from Ione. No doubt about it.

"I'm going to work now," Barbara said.

Harry put out a hand. "Harry Winston."

She took his hand. "Nice to meet you."

"I'm an old friend of Jimmy's."

"Yes. He's spoken about you."

Harry smiled. "That wasn't me who went cannibal. That was Jimmy."

She laughed emptily. "Wish I had a penny for every time I heard that story." She looked desperately to the front door, wanting out. "Well, nice to meet you, Harry."

"Same here."

She nodded at Jimmy and then left.

When she closed the door, Harry said, "See you're still beating up your women, Jimmy."

"Fucking whore. You know what she did?"

But Harry didn't want to change the subject. "I always figure that a man who'll beat up a woman'll do damn near anything."

Jimmy got defensive. "Well, you don't know what she did to me."

Harry shook his head. Jimmy seemed to disgust him. "Screw it. No matter what kind of little speech I give ya, you'll go right on beatin' up your women. Always did, always will. How about a drink? You got any bourbon?"

"Not very good bourbon."

"Remember where I came from. Right

now *any* bourbon is good bourbon."

"I thought cons always made their own hootch in prison."

"Yeah, and about a third of 'em go blind or lose their minds or die. I didn't figure it was worth the risk."

Jimmy got him a drink, half a glass of pure rotgut bourbon that Barbara stole from Ione, then sat down again. Thinking of how she was always stealing stuff for him, he felt sentimental about her for a moment. And then he remembered what she and Bob Trevor had done to him.

"I hear somebody's looking for our friend Bob," Harry said.

"Oh?"

"Gunfighter name of Ray Coyle."

"Ray Coyle? No kidding? Looking for Bob?"

"Bob killed his son last week."

"Oh, shit," Jimmy said. "I was there, too. If he's looking for Bob—"

Harry finished his sentence for him. "Then he might be looking for you, too."

"Bob was the one who shot him."

"Kid was a gunfighter. Bob was never worth a damn with a gun. How'd he manage to kill the kid?"

Jimmy looked nervous, squirming in his chair.

69

"Hey," Harry said, "I just thought of something."

"What?"

"You and Bob were the only two there, besides the Coyle kid?"

"Right," Jimmy said, gulping as he spoke.

"Then I'll bet you used that old trick of yours, didn't you?"

Jimmy flushed, started staring intently down into his glass of bourbon.

"Hell, yes, that's the only way Bob could beat a gunfighter. That old trick of yours you always used to get Bob's ass out of trouble whenever he'd get in fistfights."

Jimmy said, "You know what the sonofabitch did?"

"Bob?"

"You know all the stuff I've done for him ever since we were kids?"

"Uh-huh."

"He fucked Barbara."

"The Indian who was just here?"

"Yeah."

"And you're sweet on her?"

"Damn right I'm sweet on her."

"How come he fucked her?"

"He fucks all my women."

"He does?"

"Yeah."

Harry shook his head. "Doesn't sound

like he's changed much."

"I don't want Ray Coyle after me for somethin' Bob did."

"But you were part of it," Harry said, looking right at him. "You and that sweet little trick you and Bob always pulled on people."

But Jimmy didn't seem to be listening. "Ray Coyle. Man, I sure've heard a lot of stories about *him*."

"I'll need you to get Bob a message for me."

"I'm not goin' near him. Not after what him and Barbara done."

Harry stared at him some more. "I seem to remember a night when I slapped away a gun that was pointed right at your heart."

In a saloon one night, Jimmy and Harry had been running their mouths, and a gunny had taken offense at something that they'd said. He'd drawn down on Jimmy before Jimmy was even able to touch his holster. Harry had slapped the gun from the gunny's hand and then cold-cocked him.

"Yeah, I guess that's true."

"You know what old man Trevor thinks of me. I can't go out there and visit Bob. He has to come into town and see me."

Jimmy sighed. "I'll have a hard time not killin' the sonofabitch, I'll tell you that."

"That's up to you. Just don't kill him before I see him tonight. There's a dance at the grange hall. I'll be there. I expect him to be there, too."

"You don't sound like you like him any better than I do."

"I've got a couple good reasons not to like him."

"He was with you the day you stuck up that stagecoach, wasn't he?"

Harry shrugged. "It don't matter now."

"You serve eight years and he don't serve a day. I'd be awful damned mad if I was you."

"You just tell him nine o'clock and then just tell him one more thing."

"What's that?"

"Swimming hole."

"Swimming hole? What the hell's that mean?"

"Don't matter what it means, Jimmy. Just tell him that. And tell him nine o'clock."

Of all the kids who ran with their gang, Harry had always been the scariest. You just never knew what he was going to do. Jimmy had been horrified the night Harry had kept telling his dog to shut up — they were all drinking cider on Harry's dad's back porch — and the dog wouldn't shut up, so Harry went over and kicked it to death. Just got so mad that he couldn't stop kicking, and Bob and Jimmy together couldn't pull him off. Harry just kept kicking and kicking and kicking the dog, broke the poor sonofabitch's spirit, and then broke its back. They buried him a couple of alleys away, under a big boulder, and Harry told his old man that the dog must've run off in the middle of the night or something.

Harry Winston stood up.

"Way you kicked the shit out of that Indian girl?" he said.

"Yeah?"

"Better be careful somebody don't kick the shit out of you like that sometime, Jimmy. Awful easy for a man to be brave with a woman. Not so easy to be brave around another man."

He put on his derby and left.

Chapter Ten

Coyle could hear the baby crying a good half block away. He was apparently being mistreated terribly. First he'd scream, then he'd kind of squeal, and finally, he'd kind of scream-squeal.

Coyle knew what was really going on, of course. The poor kid was having to endure the ministrations of Doc Tompkins.

The Tompkins house was a big two-story frame job, newly painted, with a screened-in porch that looked made for sipping lemonade on hot July evenings.

Coyle went up the stairs and onto the porch. "Come In," the sign read, so that's what Coyle did.

There was a small vestibule with a coatrack, two pairs of dusty winter boots on the floor, and beyond the vestibule, a parlor converted into a waiting room. The air was tart with medications. Several folding chairs lined the east wall, a couch the west. Against the north wall, and in front of long, narrow windows, was a desk with a stern-looking woman behind it. Her sharp bones and dour demeanor reminded Coyle of every teacher he'd ever had, which numbered exactly three.

"Help you?"

"I'd like to see the doc."

"A lot of people would like to see the doc."

"I need to talk to him."

She frowned. "We don't have no secrets, the doc and me. I've heard every story there is about every male orifice there is, if you catch my drift."

Coyle smiled. "Oh, I catch your drift. I just don't happen to be here for any ailment."

Her hard, birdy eyes looked him over more carefully, and her beaky nose leaned toward him sharply. "Then why're you here?"

"The doc saw to my son the other night. Mike was killed in a gunfight."

His words had no effect on her. Her eyes showed no mercy or tenderness, nor did her voice soften. "Oh, yes. You're Coyle."

"Yes."

"The gunfighter."

"Well, not anymore."

"Fine thing, bringing your son up the same way."

Coyle was going to deny her words, but then he thought: Isn't that just what I did? Didn't I bring him up to be just like his old man? Isn't that one of the things his mother and me were always fighting about?

He disliked this old bitch, but he couldn't deny the accuracy of her accusation.

She was about to say something else when the door opened and a loud voice said, "It's just a cough Wilbur's got, Mrs. Dooley. Nothing to worry about."

The infant who had done all the crying was actually a cute little bugger with big blue eyes and rosy cheeks. He rested in the arms of his mother, looking over her shoulder at the many splendid wonders of the doctor's office.

"I really appreciate this, Doctor," said Mrs. Dooley, a plain, strong-looking woman in gingham bonnet and dress.

"Well, I really appreciate the apple pie," the doc said. He patted his ample stomach. "Though Lord knows, I don't need it."

When Mrs. Dooley left the office, Doc Tompkins said to Coyle, "And what am I going to see you about, young man?"

Coyle managed a smile. "Nobody's called me a young man for a long time."

"Well, relative to me you're sure as hell a young man," the doc said.

"He's Ray Coyle," the nurse said, "the gunfighter." She pronounced the latter

76

word as if she were saying, "Ray Coyle, the feces-eater."

"Oh, yes," the doc said. "About your son."

Coyle nodded.

"C'mon into my office."

Coyle nodded again, free at least from the disapproving scrutiny of the nurse.

The doc's office was a massive mess of papers, medicine bottles, medical books, and charts of the human body. A fuzzy coating of dust had settled on much of it. Coyle was only too happy to blame the cranky nurse for the dust. Maybe if she didn't spend so much time out front castigating the patients, the doc's private office would be in better condition.

"The nurse tries to keep this place clean," the doc said. "But I won't let her in here. I know where everything is, and if she ever cleaned it, I'd never be able to find anything."

Coyle was disappointed. He had to find something to pin on the nurse. Though he didn't like to think so, he was sometimes just as petty as she obviously was.

Coyle sat in a wingback chair across the cluttered desk from Doc Tompkins. The doc sat down and fired up the stub of a cigar.

"Gunshot."

"Gunshot?"

77

"To the chest," the doc said.

"I see."

"Nothing remarkable in any way."

Coyle nodded.

"About the wound, that is."

"There was something else?"

"There was a cut on the forehead."

"A cut?"

The doc nodded his silver head. "But I don't know what from."

"How big a cut?"

"Maybe a half inch. Deeper than it looked."

"Trevor say anything about it?"

"Trevor?"

"Bob Trevor. The man who killed Mike."

The doc smiled. "You think Bob Trevor'd answer any questions anybody asked him?" He hacked a minute from the cigar smoke he'd just inhaled. "I should give these damn things up. Been coughin' like this since I was a boy, and now I'm eighty-four."

He was a fine specimen for his age. A damned fine one.

"There's something you need to understand, Mr. Coyle," the doc said. "The Trevors don't ever explain or apologize. They just do what they do, and if you don't like it, tough. Old man Trevor built this town from the first brick up, and he don't take shit from nobody, including me."

Coyle tried to fit the Trevor woman into this picture and couldn't.

"I understand there was one other man at the fight," Coyle said.

" 'Man' is a term I wouldn't necessarily apply to him. His name's Jimmy Clinton. Clinton and Trevor and Harry Winston grew up together and they terrorized this town for a long, long time. And nobody could stop them, because every time the town tried to do something against them, old man Trevor'd step in and take his son's part. All Clinton and Winston had to do was hide behind Bob. Clinton's still doing that. Winston robbed a stagecoach and got sent to prison, though I just heard he's out now."

"I'm not sure what this has to do with the cut on my son's forehead."

The doc hacked a little more. "Neither am I, exactly. It may not have *anything* to do with your son's death, Mr. Coyle. I'm just giving you the background and letting you draw your own conclusions."

"You told the sheriff this?"

"I sure did."

"And what'd he say?"

The doc smiled around his stub of a cigar.

"He said what he always said. That he'd think about it."

"You don't trust the sheriff?"

"Most of the time I do. Most of the time he's a damned good, honest, reliable lawman. Doesn't take any kind of override from the whorehouse or any of the gambling places, which is sure as hell to his credit, the way most lawmen would operate in a place like this. The goddamned Earp brothers bled every town dry they were ever in. If they hadn't been so damned foolish with their money, every one of them would've died a millionaire. But like I say, Sheriff Graham isn't like that. Even goes to church on Sunday mornings."

Another brief, violent burst of hacking. "His only blind side is the Trevor family. He knows that if he'd ever cross Ralph Trevor, his days would be over here. And he's getting too old to go looking for another job. So he does what we all do here: We just stay out of Bob's way."

"Jimmy Clinton? That's Trevor's friend?"

The doc looked at him. "Can I give you a piece of advice?"

"I'll listen, anyway."

"Take your son's coffin and put it on the train and then get the hell out of here, Mr. Coyle. No matter what you do, you're not going to bring your son back anyway. Maybe it was a fair fight. Maybe it even happened the way Bob said it did, that your son was crowding him, and that your son insisted on drawing on him. Maybe that's the gospel."

"How about the cut on his head?"

"That one I can't answer. I mean, the obvious cause would be that he struck something when he fell down. After being shot, I mean."

"That sounds logical."

"And if I had to put money on it, that's what I'd put it on."

"But you're still not sure?"

The doc shrugged. "I've seen a lot of dead men, Mr. Coyle, especially gunfight dead men. They have a certain look. Usually, a chest full of blood and a look of pain on their faces. They generally die right when the bullet hits them. They can make some pretty eerie death masks, believe me."

"Did my son have the look?"

The doc nodded. "Yeah, he did. Except for his forehead." Then: "His coffin's down in the root cellar. It's cold down there and keeps things cool. I've got a wagon and an old colored man who hauls things for me. Why don't you let him give you and your son's coffin a ride to the train station?"

81

"You sound like Sheriff Graham."

"Graham don't want to see anybody else get killed, son. That's all."

Coyle smiled. "I'm not sure your nurse would be all that sad to see me go."

"She's one of those people who left the East to come out here and start a new life. Unfortunately, she's been here fifteen years and still hasn't found anything she likes about the frontier. She doesn't think we're very civilized, I'm afraid."

"We're not."

Doc laughed, which started another hacking spell. "No, now that you mention it, I guess we're not."

He stood up and said, "You don't look like your reputation."

Coyle stood up too. "I'm afraid the dime novel boys have created me out of whole cloth. I had six gunfights, and I didn't ask for a one of them. But I won the first two against a couple of well-known hired guns, and so then I started hearing stories about myself."

"The gun your son was wearing, he was a gunfighter too."

"Yeah," Coyle said quietly. "I'm afraid he was."

The doc stuck his hand out. They shook. "You seem like a decent fella, Mr. Coyle. I don't want to have you put in a coffin too. Just take your son and be on the nine o'clock back Denver way."

The doc walked him to the outer office. "You give what I said some thought."

"I will," Coyle said.

As Coyle walked past the nurse's desk, he nodded to her and said, "Been a pleasure, ma'am."

She caught the sarcasm and frowned.

Chapter Eleven

At three o'clock in the afternoon, the Sunset Saloon was already packed with cowboys, merchants, whores, drummers, Indian agents, whores, cardsharps, bankers, army personnel, whores, horse buyers, farriers, hostlers, teamsters, ice cutters, and whores.

It was in the Sunset, right in front of everybody, that Jimmy Clinton planned to shoot and kill his lifelong friend Bob Trevor.

Before entering the saloon, Jimmy walked up and down the boardwalk, unaware of the amused looks of the men in the barbershop, who speculated aloud (never kindly) about what a chickenshit bully like Jimmy Clinton was probably contemplating.

Could he actually do it? Sure, he could actually do it.

How the hell was he ever going to screw Barbara again after Bob'd been inside her? The very idea of it made him sick.

How could he ever believe her when she said that she wanted to run away with him and learn how to be a good woman when he couldn't even trust her with his best friend?

How could he ever hold his head up when

the town was snickering behind his back? There was no bigger gossip in town than Bob Trevor (it was Jimmy's experience that women could keep secrets far better than men), and wouldn't he just delight in telling the story of how he'd screwed his best friend's woman?

He could hear Bob laughing now, the sonofabitch.

So up and down in the dusty afternoon he paced, the sun starting to slide down the cloudless blue prairie sky, the children starting to wear down from a day of hot play, the clanking street traffic of wagons and carriages starting to diminish with the dying of the day.

He paced. And told himself he had to do it. And then always wondered if he actually *could* do it.

Could he really gun down Bob?

Then he realized what was making him so nervous: He was doing all this thinking and stewing without a single solitary drop of liquor in him.

That's what he needed. A few drinks. *Then* plug the bastard.

Jimmy could sneak in without Bob seeing him, stay down at his own end of the bar. Yes, that was the idea. Stay down at his own end of the bar and then, when he'd gotten a little courage up, *then* face the sonofabitch down.

Not even give him a chance.

Not even say a single word.

Just step right up to him, draw down on him, and kill him.

That's just what the bastard had coming, and that's just what the bastard was going to get.

Jimmy turned right around on the board-walk and stalked up to the Sunset, climbed the three steps, walked across the floor, and pushed on through into the choking smoke, the tinny and overwhelming sound of the player piano, and the stench of the outhouse that was right out back in the boiling day.

There, just about where you'd expect to find him, standing right at the center of the bar as if he owned the place, stood Bob Trevor.

Bob was funning with a whore. This was one of his favorite pastimes when he was drinking. No matter how rough or nasty he got with the whores, they knew they had to be nice to him or the bosses would climb all over them. In this town, you were nice to Bob Trevor or there was hell to pay.

Bob was too busy to even notice Jimmy, so Jimmy worked his way to the opposite end of the bar and ordered himself a rye and a schooner of beer.

All the time he waited for his drink, he kept his hand on his holstered Colt, and his eyes straight down the bar on Bob Trevor.

You pushed just a little bit too far this time, Trevor, he thought. Just a little bit too far.

At the same time that Jimmy was swigging down his first drink of the day, Coyle was knocking on the door of Jimmy's apartment.

No answer. He tried again.

As he stood there, what he mostly thought about was the cut the doc had described, the one on Mike's head.

What had caused the cut? Who had put it there?

Maybe Mike had simply cut himself when he'd fallen down from the gunshot.

Or maybe he'd bumped himself earlier somehow.

There was still no answer.

Coyle knocked for a third time.

Behind him, he heard footsteps echoing down the narrow hallway.

A figure was silhouetted against the daylight at the far end of the hall. The figure seemed to be female. It moved slowly, its shoes flapping against the floor, and it heaved like a great beast that was drawing its last frantic breaths.

Then she got closer and Coyle got a look at her, and he immediately saw one of those wretched and wasted figures the frontier produced so frequently.

God only knew how old she was, maybe eighty or ninety. God only knew the kinds of trouble she'd seen. Her nose had been broken a number of times; she had a glass eye; and her knuckles looked as if they had been worked over with sledgehammers. Her clothing was a tentlike piece of shabby, dirty gingham that kept her decent but that was about all. Ratty gray hair gave her hawkish nose and jutting jaw an even more ferocious look. She carried an armload of fruit.

"He ain't home," she said.

"Happen to know where I could find him?"

"My guess'd be the Sunset."

"That a saloon?"

She smiled with stubs of black-rotted teeth. Now that he was this close to her, he found himself holding his breath. He felt genuinely sorry for her — she was definitely one of God's castaways — but he didn't want to spend a whole lot of time with her, either. It was like those missionaries who willingly went to leper colonies. He couldn't imagine how a person could do something like that.

"You ain't from around here, huh?"

"No, ma'am."

"Well, it's a saloon all right, and it's where he spends most of his time. Girl he sees is a whore, so she spends most of her time on her back." She was apparently proud of her wit. She cackled. "He's pretty mad at her right now, I can sure tell ya that."

"At his girl?"

"Uh-huh. She was with his best friend Trevor the other night. He just found out about it last night. He beat the hell out of her. They was still arguing when I left this morning."

That was a development certainly worth noting, a possible rift between Jimmy Clinton and Bob Trevor.

"You tell me where the Sunset is?"

"Over on Third Street."

"I appreciate it, ma'am."

"Gotta give him one thing, though."

"Oh, what's that?"

She cackled her crone cackle again. "He gets all he wants from that girl of his and he don't have to pay her a cent." She winked at him. "Now his best friend's gettin' it free, too."

"Yes, ma'am," he said. He'd started out feeling sorry for her. But now he only wanted to get away from her. She rejoiced too much in the grief of others.

Then he was gone.

He wanted to be outside again, in the sunlight and fresh air.

He headed for the Sunset Saloon.

He wondered if the crone's smell was on him.

He had two more ryes, Jimmy did, and then he started feeling pretty good about himself, pretty confident that he could actually do it, pretty certain that within the next ten minutes, Bob Trevor was going to be lying dead right out there on the floor.

The Sunset was starting to get packed now, quitting time and all, and so sometimes Bob disappeared from sight, lost behind groups of heads ducking and bobbing in laughter as one thigh-slapper after another peppered the air.

He really loved the bitch.

That was the thing. As somebody who'd been raised a Christian, and who still more or less believed in Christian precepts, especially heaven and hell, Jimmy knew that it wasn't right to love a whore the way he did Barbara.

But he couldn't help it.

When she smiled, it goddamn near broke his heart.

And when she talked about leaving town even if he wouldn't go with her, it filled him with a terror he'd never known before.

How could she leave him?

Didn't she love him as much as he loved her?

The answer to that was no.

If she did, she would never have slept with Bob, even if she was just paying Jimmy back for drunkenly sleeping with one of the other whores in the house where she worked.

No, no; a man cheating on his woman, that was a venial sin. Bless me, Father, and so on and so forth. But a *girl* cheating on a *man* — well, that was mortal sin territory. That was fires of hell territory.

So she hadn't left him any choice.

He had to defend his honor.

He had to finally deal with Bob Trevor, a pig bastard who had been pushing Jimmy Clinton around all his life.

But who had gone too far this time.

Oh, yes, too far.

As he started to set his empty shot glass down, he realized that he was already sort of feeling the effects of the alcohol.

Facing somebody else, that might have

worried him a little. Facing that gunfighter, that Ray Coyle who was looking for Bob, that was when you had to be stone cold sober.

But facing Bob Trevor? Hell, Jimmy knew Bob's terrible little secret. Bob wasn't worth a damn with a gun. Not a damn. Got so scared sometimes that he couldn't even get his gun to clear his holster.

So a few drinks wouldn't slow ole Jimmy down. No, sir. Not ole Jimmy, who was actually pretty damned good with a gun (just ask him), especially after a few belts.

He put the shot glass down.

He hitched up his holster and his Colt.

He put a nice, lady-pleasing slant to his black flat-crowned Stetson.

And then he pushed away from the bar and started his spur-jingling way down the saloon floor to Bob Trevor.

Coyle had gone a block when he saw Sheriff Graham coming out of the general store. Graham carried a new pair of rolled-up denims and a pair of socks.

"Afternoon, Mr. Coyle."

"Afternoon, Sheriff."

"I was by the depot earlier," Graham said, "and I told the ticket clerk to be expecting you."

"That was nice of you. I appreciate that."

"So you're planning to leave tonight, Mr. Coyle?"

"If I get my business all wrapped up."

"You mind if I ask what business that might be, Mr. Coyle?"

Coyle looked straight at him. "I was talking to the doc, and he told me that my boy had a cut on his forehead."

Graham shook his head angrily. "That damn doc and his forehead cut."

"You didn't mention anything about that to me, Sheriff."

"Mention it? Why the hell should I?"

"The doc thought it might mean something."

"Yeah, and you know *why* he thought it might mean something? Because he figured it might be a good way to get back at Ralph Trevor."

"What's he got against Trevor?"

Graham frowned. "I hate to go back through all this again. Ancient history, far as I'm concerned." He spit tobacco into the dirt street. "Ralph blames the doc for the death of his wife. He was so mad when his wife died, he tried to run the doc out of town. Said the doc didn't know what he was doing. Said a good doctor could've saved his wife. Well, for once, the townspeople stood up to Ralph. The doc had been good to most of them. Doc stayed. But he never forgave and he never forgot. So now every chance he gets, he tries to get back at Ralph. I probably don't blame him, given what Ralph tried to do to him, but I get damn sick and tired of havin' to stand between those two."

He paused. Then: "What the hell would it be, Coyle? Your son fell down and hit his head. That's all."

"You really believe that?"

"Hell, yes, I really believe that."

"But you wouldn't mind if I ask a few questions on my own?"

"What kind of questions? And to who?"

Coyle smiled tightly. "Nothing illegal, Sheriff. Just a few questions, is all."

"I take it you're not gonna be on that train tonight?"

Coyle stared at him hard. "If I get my questions answered, I will."

"I guess that's up to you, Coyle. But let me tell you something. I'm not going to put up with any bull of yours. I'm sorry about your son, but from everything I've been able to learn about that night, he was the one looking for the fight. Not Bob Trevor."

"Then I guess Bob Trevor doesn't have anything to worry about, does he?" Coyle said. "And I guess you don't, either."

And with that, he walked on past the lawman, headed for the saloon, where he had been told he'd find Jimmy Clinton.

Bob Trevor was just hoisting a fresh schooner of beer when Jimmy Clinton reached him.

Trevor, seeming to sense the presence of his friend, looked at the mirror behind the bar and saw Jimmy standing behind him.

"Hey, you old hell-raiser, where you been all afternoon?"

You never knew what face Bob Trevor would show you. When circumstances dictated that he be happy, he was frequently dour. And vice versa.

This afternoon he was in a festive mood, his cheeks flushed with alcohol, his blue eyes burning with his high opinion of himself. There were times when he wanted to share himself with others like a great, grand gift, and this was one of them.

"What the hell you doin' with an empty hand?" Bob said. Then he turned his head at an angle and shouted for the bartender to fetch his friend a schooner.

"Hey, get over here," Bob said, reaching out for Jimmy's sleeve and tugging him closer.

The men Bob had been talking to soon saw that he was far more interested in his friend than he was in them, so they started talking among themselves.

Jimmy accepted the beer. His hand was trembling as he brought the schooner to his mouth. The beer tasted sour.

"You see that new gal they got in here from Mexico? Tits on her like a young heifer, I swear."

And so on. Bob was running at the mouth and making it difficult for Jimmy. The way he'd planned it, it would've been so simple. He'd just walk up and do it.

But he *had* walked up, and he wasn't doing anything more than drinking beer.

He decided to at least rattle Bob a little. He kept thinking of Harry Winston, and what Harry had told him to tell Bob. Jimmy didn't know what the phrase "swimming hole" meant, but he sensed that it was something that would trouble Bob.

"Guess who I saw?" Jimmy said, starting slow.

"Who?"

"Harry."

"Harry Winston?"

"Uh-huh."

"He's out?"

"Oh, he's out, all right. He was at my

place about an hour ago."

"I'll be damned." Bob's jocularity had vanished with the mention of Harry Winston. "Where's he at now?"

"Now, I'm not sure. But I know where he'll be tonight at nine."

"Oh?"

"The dance at the grange hall."

Bob watched him carefully. "He say anything else?"

"Just to mention the 'swimming hole' to you."

It wasn't any big thing, no dramatic jolt of the head or shocked sigh. But in the blue eyes of Bob Trevor, Jimmy could see a shadow of fear. Just as Jimmy had suspected, the meaning of the "swimming hole" was not a pleasant one.

"You all right, Bob?" Jimmy said, enjoying the obvious effect his words had on Bob.

"He say anything else?" Bob said, his tone getting progressively grimmer.

"Just mentioned the gunfighter looking for you."

"What the hell are you talking about? What gunfighter?"

"Guess Sheriff Graham didn't get around to telling you yet. That fight last week, the guy who died? Guess who his old man turned out to be?"

"Who?"

"Ray Coyle."

"You're kiddin' me."

Jimmy smiled. "Now, I would never do anything like that to my best friend, would I, Bob?"

"You think this is funny, Jimmy?"

"Nope."

"Then what the hell you smilin' about?" This was the more familiar face and voice of the drinking Bob Trevor, angry and accusatory. Then he said, "Ah, hell, sorry I jumped on you like that, Jimmy. This just ain't been a very good day." He looked down at his empty whiskey glass. "The old man's all over my ass about workin' more regular hours. And my sister's trying to talk me out of goin' to the dance tonight. She's afraid I'll end up 'embarrassing her,' as she puts it."

"Harry thinks you're goin'."

"Harry," Trevor said, shaking his head, as if he were in physical pain. "That sonofabitch."

And it was wonderful, just great, the way Bob looked just then. Absolutely miserable.

It was just plain wonderful to behold.

"He's which one?" Ray Coyle asked.

"Tall one with the leather vest on."

"Appreciate it."

The old-timer nodded and went back to looking at his checkerboard. He was too tired and too poor for the kind of sex they offered here, so he had to content himself with checkers.

So Coyle got his first look at Jimmy Clinton, and his first look at Bob Trevor, and he couldn't say he was all that impressed.

These two were like a lot of lawless men in the West. When you heard about some of the things they'd done, the men took on the aspect of gods, at least in your mind. But then, when you saw them, you were inevitably disappointed. Because human monsters rarely look like monsters. These two, for instance, looked like the kind of rube would-be gunfighters you could find in any small western town. They wore the leather and the sneer and the swagger of the gunfighter, but they looked too callow to be taken seriously.

Bob Trevor was a good example: Beer and laziness had put twenty extra pounds on a frame that couldn't support it. His blond hair was thinning and his shoulders were stooped. Not exactly a fine specimen of either a man or a gunfighter.

Yet this was the man who'd killed his son.

A fair fight seemed even more out of the question as Coyle stood there sipping his beer and watching Trevor and Jimmy Clinton talk.

All he could think about was what the crone had told him about Trevor moving in on Jimmy's girl.

A man moves in on your girl that way, you're probably not favorably disposed to that man.

Coyle was going to wait here and then follow Jimmy Clinton out when he went.

He was sure he could have a real interesting conversation with Jimmy. Real interesting.

Harry Winston bought himself a decent cigar and once again walked down Main. He enjoyed seeing the little explosions of recognition of the faces of the townspeople. Ever since he'd been a boy, these people had prayed devoutly that the Good Lord would take him away — fire, flood, bear, snake, they didn't much care. As long as Harry finally got his due.

Now he was back, bold as ever, that sneer on his face and that strut in his walk.

Harry Winston. Didn't God answer prayers at least some of the time?

Harry had a particularly good time with the women. It was widely believed — and in fact was true — that Harry had one night forcibly soiled the chastity of a schoolmarm new to the town. He'd hidden his face behind a mask. Nobody could ever prove it — though a number of people sure tried hard — and Harry, of course, denied everything.

When he reached Third Street, he turned left and walked slowly toward the Sunset, which had long been his favorite saloon — it was Bob Trevor's favorite, too.

He didn't plan on going inside. He didn't want to see Bob yet. He knew that, by now, Jimmy would have given him the "swimming hole" message. Ole Bob had probably peed his pants when he'd heard that one. That was the one and only way to ensure Bob's presence at the grange dance tonight, that sweet little mention of "swimming hole." Sometimes the power of words — especially two seemingly innocuous ones like those — absolutely amazed Harry.

Inhaling the smoke of his cigar, tipping his derby to a bustled lady sporting a pink parasol, Harry reached the Sunset and stood a ways down from its bat-wing doors.

He was thinking about the money again. Bob's first line tonight would be that there'd be no way he could ever get his hands on money like that.

Then Harry would use two more words, words just as powerful as "swimming hole."

"Ralph's safe," he'd say.

And then he'd watch a look of utter terror work itself across Bob's face. Ever since they'd been little boys, they'd speculated on what was to be found in Ralph Trevor's safe in his office at the ranch. Bob had seen stacks of greenbacks there many times when his father had opened the safe in front of them. Payday, Harry knew, was the day after tomorrow. Ralph Trevor was not a man who liked to change his routine. Even all these years later, Harry knew he could count on payday being right when he remembered it. Ralph employed more than fifty men, which meant that tomorrow there was going to be one hell of a lot of cash in that safe, enough to ensure Harry Winston a good life for a long time to come.

He was thinking about how he'd spend the money — San Francisco and New Orleans always played prominently in his fantasies — when he saw the two men push their way through the bat-wing doors and stand on the front porch of the Sunset.

Jimmy Clinton. And the man he recognized as Ray Coyle, Coyle having been pointed out to him earlier in the day.

What the hell were they doing together? Did Bob know about this? But if so, why would Bob let Jimmy and Coyle spend time together?

Then Harry thought of what Jimmy had told him, about his girl sleeping with Bob (ole Bob had to sleep with everybody's girl, just to prove that a Trevor could do what he damn well wanted to).

Jimmy and Coyle went left, and Harry went right. In prison, he'd promised himself that when he was a free man he was going to treat himself to at least one steak dinner a day.

It was a promise he intended to start keeping right now.

Chapter Twelve

In every town, there was one saloon where the drifters and deadbeats drank. The Mad Dog seemed to be the one in Coopersville. The owners were content to serve their beers on a bar of unvarnished pine. The floor was sawdust, mixed with dog droppings from the mutts that wandered through. The bartender wore an eye patch and enough tattoos to start an art gallery. In a shadowy corner, a whore sat atop the lap of a bald-headed man who was obviously screwing her sitting down. At a nearby table, beneath the lone Rochester lamp, sat five gruff men playing stud. "You goddamned cheat!" "You bastard!" "You piece of shit!" These were the pleasantries the men exchanged as they played. In general, the Mad Dog was one of those taverns where you could puke on the floor as long as you didn't get it on anybody's shoes.

"Nice place," Coyle said.

"I just picked the closest one," Jimmy Clinton said defensively.

They went over to the bar and bought their beers. They got as far away from the cardplayers as they could.

"So how'd you find out about Trevor and Barbara?"

"The woman who lives down the hall from you," Coyle said. "She told me."

"Nosy bitch."

Jimmy worked on his beer. The two-block walk seemed to have sobered him up.

"The old bitch tell you why Barbara did it?"

"Uh-uh."

"I porked one of Barbara's friends."

"Porked?"

"Screwed."

"Oh. Guess I haven't heard that one before."

"I seen her downtown, this little gal, and I had me a load on, and the next thing I knew I was over in the park with her, and we were doin' it like rabbits."

"And Barbara saw you?"

Jimmy shook his head. "Hell, no. Bitch told her."

"The girl you were with, you mean?"

"Right. I didn't know that her and Barbara hated each other. Seems this girl had this real good customer, this state senator, and all of a sudden he took a liking to Barbara, and this girl never forgave her. So what do I do? I go and screw this girl that hates Barbara. Well, she couldn't wait to get

105

back to tell the other girls, so they'd be sure and tell Barbara."

"So she was paying you back?"

"Yeah."

"Sounds like you should be madder at her than you are at Trevor."

"You don't know Bob. If it hadn't been this time, it woulda been some other. He's like that with all his friends. He's got to screw their women, prove what a big man he is."

Coyle sipped some beer and said, "You and Trevor had it out yet?"

Jimmy frowned. "That's why I went to the Sunset. I was gonna shoot him. Had it all planned out and everything. Walk right up to him — the way they say Hickock always done — just walk right up to him and shoot him while he was still tryin' to draw."

"What stopped you?"

Jimmy seemed embarrassed. "Oh, you know how you get. All these notions in your head. But you never actually do anything about them. Guess I needed to be drunker than I was or something. I saw him standin' at the bar and I walked right up, but when I got . . ."

Coyle watched Jimmy closely. "You've hated him a long time, haven't you?"

Jimmy shrugged. "Yeah. A long time."

"There's an easy way to get back at him."

"Yeah?"

"Yeah."

"And how would that be?"

"I think you know already, Jimmy. You just want me to say it out loud."

"Maybe."

Coyle fortified himself with some more beer. He was about to speak again when the poker players erupted with another volley of obscenities.

"Somebody's going to get shot over there," Coyle said.

"Nah," Jimmy said, "those bastards've been playin' like that since I was a little kid."

They fell into silence again for a time, and then Coyle said, "My son was killed."

"I'm sorry about that, Mr. Coyle."

Coyle noticed that Jimmy couldn't meet his eye suddenly.

"I don't think it was a fair fight."

Jimmy suddenly got very interested in taking another drink of beer. He gave the whole thing a real theatricality, picking it up real slow, then holding the beer in his mouth, savoring it.

"One thing I have to say for this place," he said. "They got the best beer in town."

Coyle went back to silently watching Jimmy. Jimmy did a little more playacting

107

with his beer — even giving Coyle a damn-this-is-good-stuff kind of expression at one point — but then all that was left of the beer was suds, and unless he wanted to start lapping it up with his tongue, there wasn't a whole lot left he could do to his schooner.

Coyle said, "It wasn't a fair fight."

Jimmy's face pinched into a scowl. "You know that for a fact, Mr. Coyle?"

"I don't. But I think you do."

"That's supposed to mean what, exactly?"

"You were there that night, Jimmy, with Bob Trevor. You know what happened." Because the poker boys were warming up to another good swearing festival — only a scattering of dirty words now but building back up to symphony level — Coyle leaned forward and said, "You want to get back at your friend Trevor, the easiest way is to tell me what really happened that night."

"Bob's good with a gun."

"No, he isn't."

Jimmy got defensive. "I didn't say he was great. I just said he was good."

"He isn't even good, Jimmy, and you know that, and so do I."

Jimmy leaned back in his chair and said, "Just what the hell you getting at here?"

"Did you help Bob out? Was that how it worked?"

"I want another beer."

"I'll go get us one. You stay right there."

"I don't have to stay here unless I want to." Jimmy sounded eight years old.

Coyle got up. He walked over to the bar, and as soon as he got there, he turned around to look at the table and make sure that Jimmy hadn't tried to sneak off.

Jimmy just sat there, scowling at him. Then, suddenly, he started to push back in his chair, as if he might be thinking of getting up and running out.

Coyle stopped him very simply. He let his right hand drop to his gun, as if he was getting ready to draw down on Jimmy.

Jimmy scowled some more, then drew his chair back closer to the table.

Coyle ordered two more schooners. His eyes never left Jimmy for more than a few seconds.

When he brought the glasses back to the table and sat them down, Jimmy said, "You can't make me stay here."

"Sure I can, Jimmy." Coyle smiled. "You've heard all about me. About how tough and mean I am. And you know that at least fifty percent of it's bull. But you don't know *which* fifty percent. So instead of pushing me, and finding out, you're going to sit here like a good little boy."

"You sonofabitch."

"Sounds like you should go over there and join that poker table." Then: "How'd you do it, Jimmy?"

"Do what?"

"Distract Mike."

"I don't know what you're talkin' about."

"That's how these things work. The gunfighter has an accomplice. The accomplice always distracts the opponent right before he's supposed to draw. The doc tells me that Mike had a cut on his forehead." He looked at Jimmy and said quietly, "You used the old rock trick, didn't you?"

"Bob Trevor don't need no help."

"Sure he does, Jimmy, and I bet you've been helping him all his life, taking the blame for things he did, letting him push you around." Coyle smiled nastily. "You're even going to let him get away with sleeping with your girl, aren't you? Because at the last minute, you couldn't go through with it. You walked right up to him and could've shot him right on the spot, before he even had a chance to draw, but you couldn't. Because you're afraid of him. Because deep down you think he's superior to you and if you ever went against him, he'd make you pay somehow."

"Like hell I'm afraid of him." Jimmy had been visibly upset ever since Coyle had mentioned Barbara again.

Coyle thought of the midget back at the Wild West Show, and how Billy might harass Jimmy Clinton. He owed the midget one. "What if she liked sex with Trevor more than she likes it with you? You ever thought of that? What if she keeps sneaking around and seeing him on the sly?" The midget knew just how to play on the sexual insecurities of most men. "What if you can't satisfy her again? You think you'd be able to stand up to Trevor then?"

"You sonofabitch!" Jimmy said, and leaped to his feet, the whole saloon turning to see what was going on.

Jimmy's left hand dipped down to his holster, but before he could tug his gun free, Coyle's Colt was pointed right at his chest.

"Don't be stupid, Jimmy," Coyle said. "You helped murder my son, and there's nothing more I'd like than killing you right now. But I want the triggerman — I want Trevor — and you're going to help me get him. You understand me, Jimmy?"

And then he couldn't help himself anymore. Coyle jerked to his feet and slashed the barrel of the gun across Jimmy's face, opening up an ugly red wound that made the younger man cry out and sink back down in his chair.

"I'm not up for any more of your bullshit, Jimmy," Coyle said. "Now we're going to have a serious discussion here. A real serious discussion."

Jimmy didn't say anything, just held his hand to his face and glared across the table at Coyle.

Sometimes it was fun to be God, to ride into town from the north and look at what he'd accomplished in less than a quarter century. Indians, floods, drought, thieves, assassins, carpetbaggers, and doomsayers had all tried to waylay Ralph Trevor from building not only his sprawling ranch but the town of Coopersville, a name he took from one of his favorite uncles.

Not too long before, the land here had been nothing but forest and prairie. Not too long before, not even the railroad had been interested in stopping here. But Ralph knew how to snare citizens and railroads alike to this town he had envisioned. And by God, they came. And by God, they prospered, just as Ralph had prospered.

Now the town expanded every six months or so. Back east they were talking about telephones and electric lights; and now, even out here, you heard the same talk. Wouldn't be long, no sir, wouldn't be long at all.

And the man who'd done all this — well, when he rode into town in his carriage with his daughter, as he was doing this late afternoon, people stared at him. They didn't see him that often, and when they did see him, it was never for long.

So they looked at him. Or gaped at him, more accurately. Because he was a special kind of man and they knew that they didn't themselves possess those very special qualities it took to build a town like this. Even when they hated him, as most of them did, they paid him the supreme compliment of deference.

This kind of attention always pleased him — and made his daughter Cass uncomfortable.

Ralph watched the people watching him, nodding hello to most of them. Cass, however, stared straight ahead, wishing they'd soon draw up to the county jail.

The temperature had dropped four degrees over the past hour. That was the thing with Indian summer, hot as July at three p.m. then cool as October at nine p.m. Good sleeping weather.

"Hope he's still there," Ralph said.

"He's a hard worker, Dad. He puts in a full day."

"I never could figure out why you like Graham so much."

She smiled at him. "Because he's one of the few people around here who'll stand up to you. Not as often as I'd like him to, but every once in a while. Which is more than you can say for most people."

His grin dimpled his cheeks and made him look ten years younger. "Sometimes I think you secretly hate me."

"Not hate you, Dad. But I do think you get your way too much." She reached over and touched her hand to his. "It's good to be skeptical about powerful men. Otherwise they start believing that everything they do is right."

"Don was like that." Melancholy colored Ralph's voice when he mentioned his dead son.

"He sure was."

"That's why he would've made such a great foreman for the ranch."

"That's something he really looked forward to," Cass said quietly.

They were in the middle of town now, Ralph tightening the reins on the prancing black horse pulling the fringed carriage.

"I'll just never understand how he

could've have drowned like that."

"Me either, Dad. Me either."

Seeing her father's sudden gloom, she leaned over and kissed him on the cheek.

"Maybe Bob'll just all of a sudden grow up."

"Maybe," Ralph said. But there wasn't much belief in his voice.

The carriage had reached the county jail.

Ralph pulled up in front, near a hitching post. He tied up the reins and then followed his daughter into the outer office.

"Sheriff Graham here?" Ralph said to the young police officer who was standing just inside the door.

"Yessir, Mr. Trevor. I'll tell him you're here."

The officer was clearly intimidated in the presence of Ralph Trevor. In fact, his last few words had been stammered.

When the young man had left, Ralph leaned over to his daughter and whispered, "Now, there's a young man who'd never question anything I told him."

She poked him in the ribs and grinned. "That's what you want, too, isn't it? Total obedience. Like a potentate or something."

This had been the nature of their relationship ever since Cass was a little girl. Why *couldn't* girls be cowhands? Why *couldn't* girls play baseball? Why *couldn't* little girls question what their fathers told them to do?

And Ralph — far from resenting the questioning nature of Cass's mind — had always enjoyed their verbal combat. Not even the eldest, Don, who'd been very smart and very independent, had dared challenge his father the way Cass did.

"Afternoon, Cass. Ralph."

Jim Graham had an easy, authoritative manner that Ralph appreciated. Too many lawmen were little more than thugs with badges, as crude and uncivilized as the men they pursued. But Graham was the new style of western lawman: bright, poised, polished.

"Why don't we go back to my office?" Graham said.

They followed him back and took chairs.

After seating himself behind the desk and firing up his pipe, Graham sat back in his chair and said, "I'll bet I can tell you why you're here."

"I figured you might be able to guess," Ralph said.

"Ray Coyle."

Ralph Trevor nodded.

"That fight Bob had with his son," Ralph said. "You know and I know it was a fair fight."

116

Graham surprised him by not agreeing.

"You have some doubts about the fight?" Ralph said.

Graham looked momentarily at Cass. "Well, Cass and I spoke about it yesterday. I'm taking the word of your son and Jimmy Clinton that it was a fair fight." He looked back at Ralph. "Since there was nobody else present, Ralph, I guess I'll have to take their word for it."

Not exactly a ringing endorsement of Bob and Jimmy.

"But to put your mind at rest," Graham said, "I've spoken to Mr. Coyle at length, and I've told him my opinion — that the fight was fair, and that nothing would be served by him staying around here and making trouble."

"What'd he say to that?"

Graham shrugged. "He said he wanted to talk to Bob."

"That's the part that bothers me," Ralph said. "Cass has arranged for Bob and Coyle to meet at the grange dance tonight. I'm afraid what that might lead to for Bob. There's no way he could go up against a gunny like Coyle."

"He says he's not a gunny anymore, Ralph. And you know what? I think I believe him. Gunnies always come across a certain way. This Coyle is real quiet and real respectful. He hasn't been a gunny for a long, long time."

"The reason I came to town, Jim, is to ask you a favor."

"Of course."

"I'd like you to be at the grange dance tonight. To make sure nothing goes wrong when they meet. I'd be happy to send a few of the men from my ranch, but I figured you'd probably want to handle this officially."

Graham exhaled blue pipe smoke. "Be happy to, Ralph. That's a good idea, in fact."

"I appreciate that, Jim. Then one more thing."

Ralph Trevor glanced at his daughter before he spoke. "I'd like you to make sure that this Coyle fellow is on the noon train tomorrow." Then: "Cass doesn't think I have any right to order anybody around like that."

"He lost his son," Cass said. "I think we should try to be as nice to him as we can. Ordering him out of town doesn't strike me as very hospitable."

"I'm worried about your brother," Ralph said. Anger tensed his voice as he glared at her. "Even if you're not."

Obviously, Graham didn't want to sit here and get caught between two arguing family members, so he said, "Why don't we do this? I'll go to the dance tonight. And I'll get between Bob and Coyle so nothing happens. And we'll let Coyle have his say. And then maybe he'll feel more like getting back on the train and going home. Let's just take it real easy, not push him at all for a while."

"That sounds better to me," Cass said.

Ralph looked angrily from Cass to Graham. "You two sound like you don't believe Bob and Jimmy at all."

Neither Cass nor the Sheriff said anything.

Ralph stood up, still angry. "In my day, girls stuck up for their brothers — and sheriffs always remembered who got them their jobs in the first place."

He put his white Stetson on his head, turned sharply and faced the door, then marched out of the office without another word or even a glance backward. He was gone.

"I'm sorry I couldn't make him happier," Graham said.

"You told him the truth, Sheriff. That's all you *can* do."

"Whether he wants to hear it or not?"

"Yes," she said, "whether he wants to hear it or not."

She nodded good-bye and went to catch up with her father.

Chapter Thirteen

An hour before the dance was to begin, Ray Coyle left a restaurant named Ma's Place. He'd eaten only a slice of apple pie. Coffee was what he most wanted. He needed a little edge if he was to meet Bob Trevor. He not only expected trouble; he welcomed the prospect of it. By now, he was pretty much convinced that Jimmy had pulled the rock trick on Mike. Hit a man in the forehead right before he's to draw, and you've distracted him right into his death.

With lamplight shadows soft against the front of the buildings, and a fat round harvest moon riding the sky, Coyle enjoyed his walk around the town. He ended up down by the river and the dam watching a handful of fishermen sitting on the bank. The water smelled of fish and the day's heat. He remembered when he'd come back into Mike's young life. Coyle and his wife had agreed to split up when Mike was only four. Coyle came back three or four times over the next few years. Two or three times, he'd taken his son fishing. Memories of those days almost choked him now. He felt sentimental for Mike, and brutally unsympathetic to himself. Why should he be sympathetic? He'd been about the worst father you could be. Then, when he'd finally taken the boy for a few years when his former wife came down with scarlet fever, he'd turned the eleven-year-old into a gunfighter — something the boy had never wanted to be.

As he walked back toward the center of town, he heard the fiddle music starting up for the night, and then the voice of the caller. Out here, people used just about any excuse — weddings, barn raisings, husking bees, apple-parings, sleighing frolics — to assemble a couple of fiddles and a caller. Not that anybody could blame them. For all the seeming civilization the people of the plains enjoyed these days, life was still hard, and very much subject to the caprice of the fates. Dancing was one way to forget the hard winter ahead, and the dead young children (cholera being the predominant killer) left behind.

All the time he walked in the flickering flames and shuddering shadows of the lamplights, he thought of Mike going to dances like this one, good-looking, gentle-natured Mike. A few times he'd almost married and settled down. Letter after letter came about one of the girls, and Coyle, cold

122

sober and traveling with Colonel Haversham by then, had images of himself as a granddad and sitting down to a big Sunday meal made especially for him by his daughter-in-law. But it had never happened, and he never quite knew why. "My engagement to Lavina has been called off," Mike's last letter had said. "I'll tell you about it next time I see you." But all there was to see now was a corpse inside a pine box.

The fiddle was heartbreaking on nights like this, a nightsong that put romance in the heart and lust in the groin and memories of past ladies and past times in the head.

Ten minutes later, he stood on the edge of the grange hall grounds.

Buggies, carriages, carts, horses, and even a mule or two filled up the dirt area on the west side of the hall.

In the double-wide front doors were silhouetted a few dozen people in fancy bonnets and fancy hats, and behind them the fiddlers and the callers and the dancers in the bright brusque lantern light of the hall itself. The scent of cider meant that children had not been brought along tonight.

Coyle pulled out his pocket watch.

Eight-twenty.

He wondered what time Bob Trevor would get here.

And then, suddenly, he didn't have to wonder at all.

Because there in front of the doors stood the man he'd seen Jimmy Clinton talking to in the Sunset late this afternoon: the one and only Bob Trevor himself.

The very same man who'd shot his son Mike to death.

"She isn't here, Jimmy."

"Bull."

"You're drunk, Jimmy."

"Where the hell is she?"

"You get out of here, Jimmy."

"You want me to tear this place apart for you?"

All this was in the vestibule of the whorehouse where Barbara worked.

Jimmy had spent the past three hours working his way up and down the two streets packed with saloons.

The more he drank, the angrier and more hurt he felt about what had happened with Barbara and Bob Trevor.

So his first visit after finishing up with the saloons was here, the whorehouse.

The girl he was pestering was Ione, a stout redhead who held him at bay with a six-shooter she'd produced from some-where within the folds of her organdy dress.

"You blind, Jimmy?"

"Blind?"

"You see this gun I'm holding on you?"

Jimmy rocked back on his heels, his eyes trying to swim into focus. "Yeah, I see it. So what?"

In the soft lantern light of the vestibule, Ione took two steps closer to him, her gun leading the way.

"We got an agreement with the sheriff," she said.

"So?"

"So he said we have a right to defend ourselves. And that means you can't come here and bother us this way."

Jimmy's rage seized him again. "She's my goddamned girlfriend, and you can't stop me from seein' her!"

He started to lunge toward her, but she now put the gun directly in his face.

"You can see her anytime you want — as long as it's not during working hours. Now, you get your ass out of here."

Jimmy smiled bitterly. "See, I knew she was here. She's upstairs, isn't she?"

"Never mind where she is. You just haul your ass out of here — you understand me?"

Jimmy tried to see beyond the red-blue-green-gold of the beaded curtain. There was a parlor set up in there where the customers sat until it was time for them to go up. The place was provisioned like a bar — whiskey, cheese, ham, bread, even a slice or two of very sweet cake. This was a place that took care of your every need, including the culinary one.

"Get out, Jimmy."

Jimmy thought of grabbing her hand, slapping the gun away, but her size made her seem a lot more competent and formidable than most women. Even in his drunkenness, Jimmy sensed that she wasn't lying to him. She'd kill him without even thinking about it. Hell, she'd probably even take pleasure in it.

"You bitch, I'll be back."

"Just remember what I said, Jimmy. We have an agreement with the sheriff. We have the right to defend ourselves. And that means that I'll kill you if I have to."

The door opened behind him and Jimmy turned to see who was coming in.

Tried to turn, anyway, the suddenness of the movement making him stumble into the west wall of the vestibule.

A couple of sober cowhands looked at him with amusement and contempt, then took note of the gun in Ione's hand.

One of the cowhands snorted. "I was gonna ask the young lady here if she needed any help." He nodded to Jimmy. "But it looks like he's the one who needs help."

And with that, the cowboys each took one of Jimmy's arms, pulled him away from the wall, and escorted him out the door.

When they reached the edge of the porch, they winked at each other and then gave their sagging new friend a vast great heave clear of the porch. For a very comic moment, Jimmy was suspended in midair, but awkwardly so, like a bird who was having trouble with its wings.

Then the bird, with no grace at all, came crashing to the ground, smothering on its own curses as its jaw slammed against the hard-packed dirt, and its nose was smashed nearly flat.

"Hell," Ione said, joshing them the way men josh each other, "you two boys went and spoiled my fun. I was just about ready to shoot the dirty bastard."

They all had a good laugh over that one, and then she led them inside where she fixed them up with whiskey and good, long looks at her ample breasts.

Ever since she was a little girl, Cass had wished that she were a better dancer.

She just wasn't graceful, and there didn't seem to be a darned thing she could do about it. Now, out on the dance floor with one of her many eager but uninteresting would-be suitors, she glanced around at some of the other ladies. They glided across the floor with perfect ease, flattering the music with their poise and grace.

Then she chastised herself for her vanity.

There was a lot more to be concerned about tonight than her dancing skills, or lack thereof.

Her gaze darted around the packed dance floor and then over to the area where the cider was being served. She saw Sheriff Graham talking to one group of men, and her father another.

Where was her brother?

She would never be close to Bob, but she wanted to see that he survived his various misadventures. If something happened to Bob, her father would probably end his own life. Bob wasn't his favorite, to be sure, but a man as proud as he was wanted a son to leave his holdings to. All these long years, she and her father had been waiting for Bob to grow up. They were still waiting.

Where was he?

As much as she'd been taken with Ray Coyle — and she had to admit she was, despite the threat he obviously meant to her brother — she had no doubt as to why he'd come here. He said he just wanted to talk to her brother. But Cass knew better. Some man kills your son, you want to do a lot more than talk to him.

As the music ended and she gently declined her partner's request for the next dance, she felt panic flutter in her chest.

Where was Bob at the moment, and what was he doing?

Harry Winston stood in the shadows of the oak trees next to the well, watching as Bob Trevor left the front of the grange hall and started walking toward him.

The funny thing was, Bob didn't recognize the man who stood less than three feet away from him as he reached the grass: Ray Coyle.

Harry watched Coyle watching Bob.

Harry's first thought was that Coyle was going to suddenly lurch out and grab Bob.

But Coyle let him walk on by.

Then Coyle faded back with the other people silhouetted in the open double-doors of the hall, the fiddle music almost as sweet as the laughter. It had been a long time since Harry had heard anything like this, and the festive human sounds filled him with loneliness and self-pity. At this very moment, he felt like the most isolated man on the entire planet.

"Hey," he said, "over here."

Bob apparently hadn't seen him and was about to pass him by.

Harry stepped from the shadows and smiled. "How they hangin', friend?"

Bob smiled, but it was an icy, nervous smile. "Hey, good to see you, Harry." Bob hadn't changed much, little less hair maybe, the beginnings of a tidy little paunch.

"Good to be back."

Bob kept on smiling. "Bet the first thing you did was get laid, right?"

"One of the first."

"So," Bob said, sounding more nervous than ever, sounding as if he had just run out of his small-talk allotment, "I heard you wanted to see me."

"Why wouldn't I want to see you, Bob? We're old friends, remember?"

"Remember? Hell, man, you're the best friend I ever had."

Harry smirked, couldn't help it. "Yeah, I noticed that the day we robbed that stage and you left me there when I was wounded."

That's how Harry had been caught that day. Bob had run up some bad gambling losses, losses his old man wouldn't pay off. For several years, Harry and Bob had been pulling off quick stage robberies whenever money ran short. Nobody suspected them.

But then came the frosty November morning when the two men swept down on the midafternoon stage. They disarmed the guards with no problem, they even got the leather satchel of greenbacks intended for the bank. What they didn't do was disarm the passengers. No passenger had ever given them trouble, so why would one give them trouble now?

But one had indeed given them trouble, whipped out a pistol just as Harry and Bob were riding away, and shot Harry in the back.

Bob had kept on riding.

Harry was taken into town, patched up, put in jail, then tried and convicted of the robbery charge. Ten years he was given. Because he'd been no trouble in prison, he'd served only eight.

Jim Graham had stayed on his back for three months about who his accomplice was. It was clear that Graham knew who'd been with Harry that day. But he needed Harry's confession to confirm it.

But Harry's confession was never forthcoming.

He spent all those years in prison and didn't say a word.

"I figure you probably spent all the money by now," Harry said, looking Bob over in the moonshadow of the evening.

"Yeah, 'fraid I did."

Bob had not only ridden away, leaving Harry alone, he'd ridden away with the money.

"I need some money, Bob."

"God, Harry, you know I'd help you if I could. I'm up to my ass already."

Harry smirked again. "Seems I remember something about you havin' the richest daddy in this part of the Territory."

Bob's head jerked back in irritation. "What the hell you think, Harry, I'm gonna go up to him and tell him I owe you some robbery money I spent?"

"I didn't say anything about you asking him for money, Bob."

"What the hell's that supposed to mean?"

"You know what it means, Bob."

"No, I don't know what it means. Why don't you tell me?"

"Remember how we used to lie out at night in the barn and smoke all that corn silk and wonder how much money your old man had in his safe?"

"Oh, no."

"There'll be a bank shipment go out there tomorrow, to the ranch I mean. Greenbacks to pay his hands. There'd be plenty in there to pay me my split of the robbery money."

Bob shook his head. "Prison musta addled your brain, Harry. Steal from my old man's safe? I want to inherit the ranch. He ever caught me doing anything like that —"

Harry held up a silencing hand.

"You didn't let me finish, Bob."

"Oh?"

"You won't have any choice."

"I won't, huh?" The familiar edge of Bob's voice was back now.

"No, you won't. Because the kind of money I want, there wouldn't be any other place to get it from *except* your old man's safe."

"There wouldn't, huh?"

Harry smiled his icy smile. "I figure you owe me maybe two thousand dollars for my share of the robbery. But I want fifteen thousand."

"Harry, what the hell're you talking about? That'd probably be everything in the safe."

Harry turned toward the grange hall and the lovely melancholy fiddle music.

"Eight years I dreamed of that," he said softly. "Civilized things. But you know what

I had instead, Bob? I had eight years of listening to men shit and puke and bleed and cry. Eight years of that, Bob, and you didn't pay a single day. Not a single day. Well, now I figure it's my turn to collect."

Bob started to say something, but again Harry held up a halting hand.

"It ain't the robbery, Bob, or the fact that you never even visited me in prison. You know what I'm talkin' about here — why I want fifteen thousand dollars. You know what I'm talkin' about, Bob."

Almost under his breath, Bob said, "You sonofabitch."

"I want fifteen thousand dollars, Bob," Harry Winston said, "because I helped you drown your brother Don out at the swimming hole that day."

Coyle was standing by the cider bowl, watching the dancers, when he felt fingers tug on his sleeve.

He turned to see Cass Trevor standing there.

"Mr. Coyle, I'd like you to meet my father, Ralph," Cass said, nodding to the older man next to her.

Coyle had seen the man with Cass several times tonight, and just assumed that he was her father. They had the same good looks,

134

the same slightly imposing bearing.

"I'm sorry about your son, Mr. Coyle," Ralph Trevor said.

"Thank you."

"I know why you're in town, and I've told my son to be as helpful to you as he can."

"I appreciate that, Mr. Trevor."

"In fact, I was looking for him a little earlier," Ralph said. "He must've stepped out for a few minutes."

"I'm sure we'll find each other," Coyle said, as blandly as possible.

The situation made him uncomfortable. He had come to this town to question and possibly kill this man's son. He had nothing against this man, just as Ralph Trevor had had nothing against Mike.

"Are you a dancer, Mr. Coyle?" Cass said.

"Afraid not."

"Good," she said, "because neither am I." She extended her arms.

"You're not as bad as you say," Cass said after they'd been dancing for a time.

"I guess I could take that as a compliment."

She laughed. "I guess it is sort of damning with faint praise."

They danced some more. The caller had an easy way with square dancing, a way that

135

made things relatively simple even for stumble-footed men like Coyle.

"You're not planning to fight him, are you?"

He looked directly at her.

He could lie. But he sensed that this was a strong woman who appreciated the truth even when it wasn't what she wanted to hear.

"I hope not. I hope your brother can convince me that everything happened just the way he said it did."

"You really have doubts?"

"I'm afraid I do."

They danced some more.

"I told you about my brother, Don."

Coyle nodded.

"If anything happened to Bob —"

Coyle said, "Let's hope for the best."

Just as the dance ended, she said, "You know the thing I don't understand?"

"What's that?"

Her cheeks were flushed suddenly. "That you may kill my brother but I like you very much anyway."

And with that, she spun on her heels and walked back to where her father was standing talking to a group of men.

The time had come at last.

As Bob Trevor listened to Harry Winston talk, he realized how long Harry had been shaping and planning this very moment. The moment Bob had been dreading ever since that day at the swimming hole.

A man in prison like that, he'd had a lot of long nights to lie on his bunk and plan how things were going to be when he got out.

Harry had obviously spent a lot of his time thinking about Ralph Trevor's safe.

Ralph was a believer in knowing his ranch hands as well as possible. From the very first, years and years earlier, he'd insisted on paying his men himself. There was another reason for this, too. Ralph let it be known that any man who had any complaints about the way the spread was run, this was the time to speak up. Ralph would give you a serious listen, and if he saw merit in your complaint, he'd act on it. Over the years, Ralph turned many of his men's complaints into useful ideas.

But it wasn't ideas that had seduced Harry Winston. It was money. Stacks and stacks of greenbacks in the safe.

"Do you have any idea how much fifteen thousand dollars is, Harry?"

"I sure do, Bob." Harry laughed. "And that's why I want it."

"I can't get into his safe."

"Sure you can."

"I don't know the combination."

"Sure you do."

"Sure I do? What makes you think I do?"

"I know you, Bob. You've been dreamin' of that safe as long as I have. I figure by now you've managed to learn the combination."

Bob took out the makings of a cigarette and started rolling himself one.

"Then what?" he said.

Harry shrugged. "All depends on how you want to handle it. Either you tell your old man I forced you to open the safe, or you get out of this town along with me."

"This is dangerous, Harry."

"I know it is. But it could also be very profitable."

"He'd kill you if he could."

"He's gettin' old, Bob. He'd have to catch me first."

Bob finished rolling his cigarette. His face looked leathery in the burnished flame of the stick match.

"And he'd be a hell of a lot madder about the swimming hole than he'd be the safe." Harry spit on the ground, then looked back at Bob. "He ever found out what you did to Don, he'd kill *you*."

"He'd kill both of us. You helped me kill

him, Harry. Don't forget that."

There was a sudden hoot from the grange hall. Party favors and prizes were always given out at fandangos such as this one. Apparently somebody had just won something.

"Tomorrow night, Bob. I happen to know that your old man's going to be in town here at some dinner for the Governor. That'd be a perfect time."

Bob rubbed the back of his head in frantic frustration. "Robbing my dad's safe — God, Harry, nobody'd ever think of doin' something like that."

"That's why we can get away with it. Because nobody'd be expecting it. And again, Bob, you want me to take the blame for it, fine. Tell him I forced you to do it. I'll never tell anybody you helped me." The smirk again. "Just the way I never told anybody you helped me rob that stagecoach — or kill your brother."

"You bastard."

"C'mon, Bob. We just got through tellin' each other what good friends we were."

"I won't do it."

"Sure you will, Bob. Or I tell your old man what we did at the swimming hole that day."

Harry reached out and grabbed Bob by his hair, giving it a vicious twist. Bob flailed like a small boy being picked on by his older brother. Bob flicked his cigarette into the grass, where it exploded like a Fourth of July firecracker. He kept on flailing, trying to get free of the man who had seized him with great strength by the hair.

"You bastard," Bob said.

Harry laughed. "I think you already said that, my friend."

Bob flailed some more. Uselessly.

And then Harry pushed him to the ground, where he fell on his ass in an unceremonious way no Trevor was used to.

Darkness. Pain. Confusion. Groping. His hand was reaching out and . . . feeling . . . dirt.

He tried to sit up. Pain sliced directly down the center of his forehead. It traveled so deep, it reached his sinuses.

What the hell had happened to him, anyway?

Two possibilities came to mind: One, somebody had jumped him when he was leaving a saloon just around dusk. Two, he had been riding a horse and had been thrown off and landed here on this dark road.

This time he managed to sit up straight, and there in front of him, shimmering in the darkness as if it were a magical fancy rather than a reality, was the whorehouse.

And then, moment by moment, his last few hours came back to him. Incredible bitterness about Barbara. Drinking, drinking, drinking. A few shoving matches in a couple of saloons. And then going to find Barbara.

The whorehouse. Yes, the whorehouse. A gun in his face. Ione.

Then the two cowboys. Hassling him. Kicking him out —

His first response to the memory was to pat his holster. His gun was still there. Nobody had taken it away from him, at least.

What he ought to do was go right back in the whorehouse and kill those two cowboys, kill Ione while he was at it, and then go upstairs and find Barbara. And beat her until she begged him for forgiveness. Till she promised she'd never again have anything to do with Bob Trevor.

Then the thought of Bob Trevor sent him reeling down other corridors of his memory.

All the ways Bob had abused him and taken advantage of him ever since they'd been boys.

The sonofabitch. The stinking sonofabitch. And now he'd gone and screwed the only girl Jimmy Clinton had

141

ever loved. So what if she was a whore? Who said you couldn't fall in love with a whore?

And lying there in the dust of the road, the tinkle of laughter of the whorehouse making him sick and angry — right there, right then Jimmy Clinton decided that Coyle had been right, after all.

Jimmy really had been a chickenshit.

He never should have walked away from Bob this afternoon. He should've stood right there and killed the bastard.

Chapter Fourteen

Cass ended up making the introductions.

After her dance with Coyle — and her rash admission that she was attracted to him — she stayed near the open doors for sight of her brother Bob. He'd promised her he would come inside and meet Ray Coyle.

She'd seen him earlier outside, talking to some of the townspeople. But the next time she checked, he was gone, and now she wondered if he might have decided against meeting Coyle.

As much as she didn't like to think so, Bob was probably lying about the circumstances of the gunfight. Bob had never been gifted with a gun. In fact, one of the things he'd envied so much about his brother, Don, was the easy, natural way Don took to firearms of all sorts. Over and over they'd had quick-draw contests with toy guns, and Don had always won.

She also suspected, as did Coyle, that Jimmy Clinton had had something to do with Mike Coyle's death. Jimmy, Harry Winston, and Bob had been inseparable as boys. Jimmy and Bob were still inseparable — which was mysterious to her, because

Bob treated Jimmy pretty badly, ordering him around like a servant, always belittling anything Jimmy tried to do on his own. She'd always wondered how Jimmy took it.

She tried outside again, searching among the men smoking their pipes and discussing cattle prices and still arguing over last year's massacre at Little Big Horn. Some of the men felt that Custer had fought bravely and wisely; others deemed him a showboat who had sacrificed his men in a final moment of ego and vainglory.

She didn't find Bob.

Then, just as she was turning back to the grange hall, she saw two silhouettes standing directly beneath the bloodred harvest moon on the other side of the road. To her, the figures were instantly familiar: her brother Bob and Harry Winston. She'd heard Harry was back. She'd also heard that Harry had changed a lot, lost his hair and lost weight, too. But he was still unmistakably Harry.

The two figures separated. Bob walked across the road to her.

"I was beginning to wonder if you were going to meet Ray Coyle," she said.

"Well, I'm not looking forward to it, believe me."

She noted how tightly wound he seemed.

She wondered what he and Harry had talked about. She frequently saw her brother angry, but she rarely saw him anxious this way.

"Well," she said, "let's go get it over with, Bob. Then you can go see Harry some more."

Bob smiled bitterly. "Still don't care much for my friends, do you?"

"No," she said, "I don't."

"Anybody can get into a little trouble."

"Robbing a stagecoach isn't a 'little trouble,' Bob. It's big trouble."

"Maybe he's changed."

She realized then that Bob wasn't defending Harry. He was defending Bob. Sometime around age ten, she'd stopped liking Bob. She'd always felt guilty about this and wanted to change her feelings toward him. But he'd given her no opportunity. Bob was always in trouble with somebody, and the worst thing was he was usually able to get somebody else to take the blame for him. They wanted to stay in the good graces of the Trevor family.

"For right now, let's just worry about Ray."

Bob laughed harshly. " 'Ray,' huh? Sounds like you're getting real friendly."

"His son died. I feel sorry for him."

Bob walked into the grange hall with a smirk on his face. He'd always enjoyed putting his sister on the spot.

Cass looked around and saw Ray near the back, sitting at a table with her father. For some reason, the sight of the two men together made her very happy. They were both lonely men, and maybe this would be bond enough to become friends.

"That's Coyle," she said, not calling him "Ray" this time because she didn't want to see Bob's smirk again.

"I'll be damned."

"What?"

"He doesn't look like much. Hell, his son looked like a lot more."

"He isn't a young man anymore."

"Yeah?" Bob laughed. "Well, I am."

On that obnoxious note, Cass led him to the table where Ray and their father sat.

Both men stood up when they saw Cass and Bob approach.

"This is my son Bob, Ray," Ralph Trevor said.

Coyle knew that he was expected to shake hands. He did so with great difficulty. The right hand, the one that had held the gun, the one that had the finger that pulled the trigger that fired the gun and killed his son.

He forced himself to shake hands.

They sat down.

"We could waste a lot of time on small talk here," Ralph said. "But there's no sense to that." He looked at his son. "Bob, I want you to tell Ray everything that happened inside the saloon, and then at the gunfight."

Bob glanced at Cass. Then at Ray. "Well, I'm going to be real honest here, Mr. Coyle. We both kind of started the fight. Inside, I mean. I had a snootful and so did your son."

"I thought he'd only been in town a few hours," Coyle said.

"A man can get a bag on in a couple of hours, believe me," Bob said, his nervous grin saying that he'd managed to do just that many times.

"All right," Coyle said. "Then what happened?"

Bob shrugged. "We just didn't take to each other."

"Oh?"

"You know how it is. Some people you take to, some you don't. We'd look over at each other every once in a while, and the more we looked, the less we liked."

"But you didn't exchange words or anything?"

"Not right away."

"So how'd the fight start?"

"Well, he went outside to take a leak or something, and when he came back in, he bumped me."

"You sure *he* bumped *you?*"

"The place was real crowded, Mr. Coyle. I guess he might have been nudged into me, or something like that. But I don't think so. He bumped into me hard enough to spill my beer all over me. So I got mad."

"And that's how it started?"

"That sure enough *is* how it started, Mr. Coyle."

The mask Bob wore now was a familiar one to Cass. All his life, Bob had been able to take off the familiar rough-hewn face he wore most of the time and become this aw-shucks innocent. He was playing the innocent now. She found the performance vaguely disgusting. It also made her increasingly suspicious about Bob's version of the gunfight story.

"I've asked around myself," Ralph Trevor said, "and everybody I've spoken to — who was there that night, I mean — they all give the same version of the story."

Coyle nodded to Ralph, then went back to questioning Bob.

"Most gunfights I've seen," Coyle said, "there's usually a crowd. How'd it end up with just the three of you in the alley that night?"

Bob shrugged. "We didn't even know it was going to be a gunfight, Mr. Coyle. Jimmy and I — Jimmy Clinton — we just went outside to get our horses and there was Mike — your son — at the head of the alley. I figured he'd ridden off about half an hour earlier."

"So he was just waiting for you?"

"Yessir, that's what he was doing. Just waiting for us."

Bob glanced at his father as if for approval. Ralph looked grim. And noncommittal.

"What did Mike say to you?"

Bob shook his head. "Not much, really. He just told me to stay wide of my horse and to go for my gun. I didn't really want to fight him, Mr. Coyle. No offense, but he looked like a gunny. I've never been in a real gunfight before."

"So then the fight started?"

"That's right. He started to draw —"

"He was faster than you, then?"

"At first, he was. But somehow I was the one to actually get out my gun first. And fire. And then he just fell over."

"He didn't get a shot off?"

"Well, I think he did. I mean, I couldn't

really say for sure. Maybe Jimmy'd remember."

Jimmy, Coyle thought. Everything that Bob Trevor was telling him was a lie. He was sure of it. So that left him only one person he could get the true story from: Jimmy Clinton. He'd have to work on him for a while, but he was sure that with enough booze, and enough reminders of what Bob Trevor had done with Jimmy's girlfriend, Jimmy would eventually break down and tell him.

"So he just died right there?"

"I'm sorry, Mr. Coyle. I really am."

"The doc told me there was a cut on his forehead."

"A cut?"

Bob Trevor was a good actor. He could trod the boards anytime, Coyle thought. According to this wide-eyed innocent, he didn't know anything at all about a cut on Mike's forehead.

"Yes. I guess about an inch long or so."

Bob shrugged. "Sorry, Mr. Coyle, I wouldn't know anything about a cut at all."

Then he looked at his father again. This time, the older man didn't look so grim. He looked as if he was happy with his son's version of the story, and believed every word of it.

Coyle had just lost himself an ally.

Puking sobered Jimmy up.

He'd always been afraid of puking; had an uncle who had strangled on his own puke while drunk.

So all the time he was throwing up, fear coursed through Jimmy. Was he going to start strangling?

No, as things turned out, it wasn't choking that was going to kill him, but embarrassment.

He'd almost made it to the grange hall before he started puking.

He did his deed right there in the street. Just in time for two of the town's most prim and proper old maids to be happening by on their way home from a brief visit to the dance.

The women clucked their disapproval and passed on quickly.

"Bitches," Jimmy said, loud enough for them to hear him.

The closer he got to the grange hall after splattering vomit all over some burned-out grass, the better he felt.

Things were coming into perspective again. Sober perspective.

Barbara-and-Bob perspective.

He could forgive Barbara because she was

a sixteen-year-old farm girl who'd never had schooling of any kind, and who was not exactly a genius. Girl like that gets mad at a fella, there's really only one thing she can do: find somebody else is what she can do, and that's just what she'd done.

Bob, on the other hand, there was no forgiving.

A tumble of images filled his mind again, all sorts of unforgivable things Bob had done to him over the years.

And now this.

This.

The closer he got to the grange hall, the oftener he touched the Colt riding his right hip.

Too bad I don't have somebody to throw a rock at Bob just when I'm ready to draw, Jimmy Clinton thought bitterly.

Instead of anger now, there was a cool resolve. He had chickened out this afternoon. But not tonight.

No sir. Not tonight.

Harry Winston watched as Jimmy Clinton came into the lamplight outside the grange hall. Most of the men had gone back inside.

Jimmy's walk was labored, as if he was trying very hard to look sober.

Harry crossed from the darkness across the road and placed himself directly in front of where Jimmy would be in a few moments.

"You look like you need to sit down for a while, Jimmy."

At first, Jimmy clearly didn't recognize who was speaking to him.

But when he was within three feet of Harry, his eyes narrowed and recognition shone in his eyes.

"I suppose you're out here with Trevor."

"We had us a nice little talk."

Jimmy spat. "Well, I'm gonna do more than *talk* to him, you can bet yer ass on that."

"What're you talking about?" Harry said, feeling a sudden sense of alarm without quite knowing why.

"This is what I'm talking about," Jimmy said, and whipped his Colt free of its holster. "This is what I'm talking about. I'm gonna kill the sonofabitch, just the way I should've this afternoon."

"Kill him?" Harry said, alarm overwhelming him now. Tomorrow he was going to have all the money he'd ever dreamed of. And Bob Trevor was going to get it for him. But not if Jimmy killed Bob.

"Hey, listen," Harry said soothingly. "Why don't we walk back to town and get us some coffee?"

"Get out of my way, Harry."

"Aw, Jimmy. This is crazy. It really is. I been in prison, my friend, and you're not gonna like it there. Let me tell you that. You're not gonna like it there at all."

"You heard what I said, Harry. You're blocking my way."

Jimmy tried to get around him on the left, but Harry was there. Jimmy tried to get around him on the right, but Harry was there.

"Jimmy, you got to sit down and think about this thing," Harry said, sensing that the windfall he'd been planning on was slipping away from him.

"Jimmy, listen, please —"

But he didn't get to finish, because that's when Jimmy brought the gun up fast and then brought it back down just as fast against the right side of Harry's head. Harry might be one tough hombre most of the time, but this was an exceptionally strong blow, and within moments his knees were giving out and a cold rushing darkness was filling his eyes and ears and nose.

Jimmy stepped over him and started for the grange hall.

"I don't know about you, Mr. Coyle," Ralph Trevor said, "but I think Bob's done a good job of making his case. It was all a terrible, unfortunate incident." He touched his coat. "I'd like to pay the train and the funeral expenses, if you'd let me."

"That'd be nice of you, Ralph. But I'd just as soon pay for those things myself."

His eyes met Cass's. She could clearly see that he hadn't believed her brother's story at all.

"Well," Bob said, "I told a couple of the boys I'd be meeting them about now." He extended his hand again. "It's been nice meeting you, Mr. Coyle. I hope I got all your questions answered."

For the second time, circumstances forced Coyle to shake Bob Trevor's hand. He could have declined, but that would have told them that he was still planning to find out what really happened.

"Sis, I'll see you and Dad back at the ranch tonight."

He was just about to stand up when his name — "Bob Trevor!" — was barked out like a gunshot.

All the people at the table, Coyle included, turned to see who had called the younger Trevor out this way.

Jimmy Clinton didn't look any more sober to Coyle than he had late this afternoon. If anything, given the way he weaved, he was drunker.

He'd also worked himself up into a fevered anger, his eyes wild, spittle foaming on the sides of his mouth as he shouted.

"You ain't gettin' by with it this time, Bob! You're gonna go for your gun, and then I'm gonna kill you! Now, stand up!"

The entire grange hall was silent, of course. Everybody watched Jimmy Clinton.

"Stand up, Bob!"

"It just happened, Jimmy, is all," Bob said, whining like a child. "It was all her idea. Honest, Jimmy."

"I said stand up!"

"You really gonna waste your life over somebody like her?"

But it was the wrong thing to say.

"Barbara and me's fixin' to get married — and gettin' out of this town. But first I gotta take care of you. This's been comin' for a real long time, Bob. A real long time."

Coyle's thoughts were selfish: He didn't really give a damn if Jimmy died. But he needed Jimmy to prove that Mike had been murdered. If Bob drew down on him and killed him —

But he didn't have to worry about Bob. The younger Trevor clung to his chair and the table. The notion of him as a gunfighter was laughable. He was so scared, he couldn't move. There was no way he could

156

have beaten Mike in a fair fight.

"Bob, if you don't go for your gun, I'm gonna shoot you anyway. And I think you know I ain't bluffin'."

Bob Trevor looked frantically at his father for help. But in this situation, nobody could help him. Theoretically, somebody could sneak up behind Jimmy and knock him down. But he'd risk his life doing it.

"Jimmy," Coyle said. "There's a better way to handle this, and you know what it is. What we talked about this afternoon."

"It's too late for words now, Coyle," Jimmy said. "So you might as well shut up."

His hand dropped to his gun. He had just whipped his Colt free of its holster when the two shots boomed from behind the table where Coyle and the others sat.

Jimmy Clinton's gun fell to the floor, and he soon pitched over after it. Nobody in the entire grange hall moved for at least thirty seconds. There was the smell of gunsmoke, and the echoing boom of the gunshots.

Coyle turned around and saw Harry Winston standing there, a Peacemaker in his big right hand.

"Goddamn, Harry," Bob Trevor said. "I sure owe you one for that."

"You didn't have to kill him," Coyle said. But again, his thought wasn't of the dead man. It was of what the dead man could have done for him.

Then everybody was moving, and a hundred people at a time were speaking.

Coyle went over and knelt down next to Jimmy Clinton.

Clinton was on his face, arms spread out. He smelled of sweat and beer and blood. Soon enough, he'd also smell of urine.

"He dead?" somebody said.

Coyle checked the pasty neck and the dry wrist. "He's dead."

As Coyle stood up, he saw Ralph Trevor shaking hands with Harry Winston.

"We haven't always gotten along in the past, Harry," Ralph was saying, "but I expect those days are behind us now. My whole family thanks you for what you did."

Coyle looked coldly at Harry Winston. He was suddenly the man of the moment. People who, minutes before, wouldn't have had any time at all for an ex-convict were now crowding around him as if he were a bona fide celebrity.

The fresh air felt good. Coyle stood outside the grange hall, alone, staring up at the harvest moon. The scent of autumn was in the cool air. Few smells were as rich and pleasant.

Then, suddenly, he wasn't alone anymore.

"I just wanted to see how you were doing," Cass said.

Coyle smiled emptily. "Oh, about as well as you can expect, I guess."

"You didn't look happy that Jimmy got himself killed."

"I had some unfinished business with Jimmy."

"Unfinished business that involved my brother?"

"I'm not sure I should answer that, Cass."

She walked a few feet ahead of him, pretty and feminine in her blue dancing dress. She looked up at the moon. "When I was young, I used to believe that I heard these voices calling me from the moon. Sometimes when I'd wake up in the morning, I felt as though I'd *been* on the moon the night before, that somebody had summoned me up there somehow. And whenever I was sad, I always knew I could count on my moon dreams. They'd always make me feel better." She turned back to him. "That's the trouble with being an adult, I guess. You don't have dreams like that to escape into. You just have to keep facing reality."

Yeah, Coyle thought. And reality was that, because of the way I helped raise him, a young man is dead. He walked and talked like a gunfighter and it had ultimately cost him his life, thanks to a couple of prairie rubes who knew how to distract somebody at the last moment.

"Your father's probably going to buy Harry Winston a very nice present," Coyle said.

She made a face. "Harry Winston. Even if he did save my brother's life, he's still Harry Winston. I never did like him or trust him. One day at school, he poured some oil on an Indian boy's hair and then set it on fire. He thought it was really funny. The Indian boy was never the same afterward."

"Sounds like a real good man, Harry."

"All three of them were like that — Harry and Jimmy and — and my brother. Nothing made them feel better than causing other people pain. When my brother Don was alive, he pretty much rode herd on Bob. Kept him in line. But after he died . . ."

From inside, they heard the caller speaking very loudly.

"Ralph Trevor wants me to ask everybody to toast the man of the hour, Harry Winston. But heck, let's let Ralph lead the toast himself."

"I'd better get back in there," Cass said. "You coming?"

160

Coyle smiled sourly. "Guess I just don't feel up to drinking a toast to anybody like Harry Winston."

"Or my brother?"

Her tone dared him to speak. He took the dare: "Or your brother."

She looked at him sadly a moment, and then, in a rustle of dress, said, "I guess I'd better get back in there."

After she left, Coyle felt completely isolated. He liked her a lot more than he wanted to admit. But he didn't think about Cass very long.

Soon enough, he was back to the death of Jimmy Clinton.

How was he going to prove that Mike had been distracted right at the moment of drawing and firing?

Who else knew what Jimmy Clinton had done that night in the alley?

Only one other person, that being Bob Trevor. And he wasn't likely to admit anything.

Nothing at all.

Part 2

Chapter One

In small towns like this, you didn't see a whole lot of white girls becoming prostitutes. White girls meant trouble. It was fine if you wanted to run a whorehouse with Indians, blacks, Chinese, or other ethnic minorities, but put a lot of white girls in your house, and you had problems with the local authorities. As everybody knew, Indians, blacks, and Chinese didn't have any morals to begin with, so you weren't corrupting anybody when you used them as prostitutes. But white girls had been born to be virtuous, and so when you corrupted them you were defiling the community ethic. And were likely to get your ass thrown in jail.

The girls Coyle saw that night at Ione's bore this out.

While red-haired Ione looked white at first, closer inspection showed a good deal of Spanish around her eyes, nose, and mouth. There was even a little Negro blood there, too.

"Just wondered if it was too late," Coyle said as he was escorted into the parlor.

"Too late?" Ione said, clapping him thunderously on the back. "Too late? Hell, son, we're here till dawn after most nights. What's your poison?"

"I wouldn't mind a glass of plain cider."

"Cider it is. And then I'll bring out some of the girls for you to see."

"I know who I'd like, ma'am."

"Oh?"

"Girl named Barbara?"

Ione smiled. "Like 'em small and delicate, do you?"

Coyle couldn't think of anything appropriate to say, so he just nodded.

"Not too much in the tits department but has a lovely, lovely ass, that little girl."

"Yes, ma'am."

"You just have yourself a couple of drinks and she'll be finished up and ready for you in no time."

"Thank you, ma'am."

She looked at him a little longer. "Don't know why, but you don't look like a Barbara kind of fella. Sure you wouldn't like a nice, big, pillowy pair of tits?"

"Barbara'll be fine."

She shrugged and smiled. "You're the boss, son. You're the boss."

She exited stage right, to a darkness beyond a doorway filled with hanging beads that clacked and clicked as she pushed them aside.

A few moments later, she brought him a fancy cut-glass tumbler that was filled halfway up with cider.

"Thank you, ma'am," Coyle said, knowing he'd never drink this much. He just wanted a couple of swallows, just enough to give him an edge when he went upstairs.

A knock on the front door. Drunken voices, laughing, giggling. Three cowhands not old enough to vote, yet stumbling and swaggering into the parlor. Reeking of the range, reeking of the saloon.

"Guess I don't have t' tell ya what *we* want, do I?" the freckled one giggled to Ione.

She winked at Coyle. "No, you sure don't. Now, you boys sit over there on the couch and I'll get you some coffee."

"Coffee? What the hell you talkin' about, lady?" said the one with the fancy red kerchief and dried beer stains on the front of his fancy white shirt that was all done up in fancy green piping.

"You're too drunk to enjoy my girls right now," Ione said. "So you just have yourselves a little coffee and a little rest, and then I'll send you upstairs and you'll have the sweetest night of your life."

As she spoke her last words, the cowboys

started grinning and poking each other with their elbows.

Ione led them to the overstuffed parlor set that looked as if it had come right from the Sears and Roebuck catalog. She got them seated and then went to get them their coffee.

For a few minutes, they actually sat there without saying anything or even moving. They looked like little boys who were being disciplined by a particularly scary teacher.

Then the one with the long blond, Hickock-style hair looked over at Coyle's glass and said, "Hey."

Coyle smiled pleasantly at him.

"I said, 'Hey.' "

"Hey, what?"

"How'd you get that?"

"Get what?"

"Goddamn glass of whiskey." To his friends he said, "Goddamn glass of whiskey." Then, turning back to Coyle, he said, "Goddamn glass of whiskey."

"I guess I just say my prayers at night," Coyle said, "and God takes care of me."

"That ain't funny, mister."

Coyle held his glass up. "It's cider."

"Bull it's cider," Hickock said.

The West was filled with overeager young drunks like this. The only reason Coyle

168

didn't get up and hit him in the face was that he'd been pretty much like this himself when he was young.

Ione came back bearing a tray with three cups of coffee.

"How come he gets a glass of whiskey," Hickock said, "and we only get coffee?"

Ione winked at him again. "Because he's my husband."

The cowboys looked flabbergasted. "He is?" Freckles said.

"Really and truly?" Red Kerchief said.

"I think she's lying to us," Hickock said.

"C'mon, dear, time for you to get some sleep," Ione said, coming over and taking Coyle's arm, tugging him toward the staircase on the north wall.

"I bet he ain't really her husband," Coyle heard Freckles say as he followed Ione up the stairs.

"Hey," Hickcock said, "he left his glass. I got first dibs on it."

There was a silence from below just as Ione and Coyle reached the top of the stairs, and then they heard Hickock say, "Damn! It really *is* cider!"

"That sumbitch," Freckles said. "That dirty sumbitch."

"Takes all kinds," Ione said, laughing as she led him down a narrow, lantern-lit hall.

There were eight doors altogether, four on a side. Every few feet or so, Coyle could hear somebody groaning or gasping or gibbering. Ione must put on a mighty fine spread here, Coyle thought.

At the rear of the hall was a staircase leading down to a back door. A lot of whorehouses were set up this way. There were certain men who just couldn't afford to be seen around a whorehouse — politicians, business leaders, clergy — and so they had to come and leave by the back way.

They stopped at the final door on the right. Ione knocked discreetly.

"You set up for the next one?" she whispered.

The door opened a peek and one of Barbara's eyes and part of her nose could be seen.

"Yes."

"He looks right nice," Ione said. Then: "How'd it go with Melvin tonight?"

"He didn't even try to hit me. I guess last time did the trick, when I got him in the groin."

"No rough stuff," Ione whispered over her shoulder to Coyle. "That's our only rule. No rough stuff. Got a guy in town here who can't get pleasure unless he beats up the girl first. We're teachin' him different."

Then Ione stepped back with a certain grand and festive air, and beckoned for Coyle to step inside.

"Enjoy yourselves," Ione said grandly.

And then Coyle was in the room, alone with Barbara.

The room was bed, bureau, guttering lamp. It was a room of ghosts and secrets, a room of whispers and confessions, a room of pleasure and shame. Shadows played like children on the walls. Barbara, naked except for a pair of frilly bloomers, was smiling her best professional smile. She had sweet little civilized breasts and nicely curving hips and perfect coltish legs and cute little feet. She was the kind of girl men just naturally wanted to protect: lover-daughter-mate all in one. And she was spending her youth in whorehouses.

"I'd like to wash you first, if you don't mind," Barbara said.

"That won't be necessary."

"Those are Ione's rules, mister. Not mine."

"How much for a half an hour up here?"

"Ten dollars. Why?"

He dug the proper amount out of his pocket and laid it on the bureau. "There you go."

"There I go? Mister, we haven't done anything yet."

"Not yet, we haven't. You go over there and sit down on the bed and then we'll do something."

"On the bed? Alone?"

"Uh-huh. On the bed alone."

Reluctantly, suspiciously, she did what she was told.

"Now what do we do?" she said, watching him as he stood on the opposite side of the room.

"Now," he said, "we talk."

Just then, a man in the next room let out a Texas yelp that made the walls tremble.

"Mr. Banister." Barbara smiled. "He's seventy-one and he has a real good time when he comes here."

Coyle smiled. "I'll bet he does." Then: "I need to tell you something, Barbara."

"You law or something?"

"I'm not law. I'm just a friend."

She scowled. "Yeah, sure you are. Every man who walks through that door claims to be a friend of mine."

Coyle said, "Jimmy Clinton got killed a little while ago."

She just stared at him. "You're not kidding me, are you?"

"No, I'm not."

"He's really dead?"

"He's really dead."

Her reaction to this news fascinated him. There were no tears at all. He saw how hard she was, how hard she had to be to survive an environment like this. She just held her stomach, as if she was suddenly feeling great pain, and said, very softly, "It was because of me, wasn't it?"

"I guess you played your part."

"You know the funny thing?"

"What?"

"I only did it to hurt Jimmy. He kept promisin' he'd take me out of this town, and we'd start a good life for ourselves in Colorado or Wyoming."

"He thought it was because he'd slept with another girl."

She shrugged. "That didn't bother me." Then she smiled bitterly. "You know another funny thing? Trevor just *thinks* we did somethin' that night. He was so drunk, he couldn't do nothin' at all."

"Why does he think he did?"

She shrugged again. "In the morning, when I was finally able to wake him up, I saw a way to really hurt Jimmy. Figured maybe if he saw I was going to start sleeping around with his friends, he'd take me out of this town. Never bothered him when I was with paying customers. But his friends — that was somethin' he couldn't stand."

"Harry Winston shot him."

"Harry Winston?" she said. "I'm surprised it wasn't one of Bob's gunny friends."

"I think Harry shot him as a favor to Bob."

"What kind of favor?"

Then he told her who he was, what he was doing here in Coopersville.

"I think he shot Jimmy so Jimmy wouldn't tell me what really happened the night my son was killed." He paused and used his next words carefully. "Jimmy happen to say anything to you about that night?"

But she was no longer listening.

She lay back on the bed and stared at the ceiling and said, "I as good as killed him myself. He wouldn't have gone after Bob if it wasn't for me."

"You didn't know this was going to happen."

"I killed him, mister. I killed him."

And then the tears came. She began sobbing with a violence that was almost frightening to see. Madwomen sobbed this way.

And they weren't quiet sobs, either. They were so loud, so aggrieved, you wanted to cover your ears. All up and down the corridor, you could hear people talking about the weeping. This wasn't real conducive to sex.

He sat on the bed next to her, trying to get her to stop, holding her and then not holding her, speaking softly to her and then not speaking at all, rocking her gently and then not rocking her, but none of it made any difference. She continued to sob and sob and sob.

And then there were thunderous fists on the door. And the door was flung inward.

And there, filling the door frame, was Ione, with not one but two six-shooters in her fists.

"I don't know what you done to her, mister," Ione said, "but I want you to get the hell out of here right now and never come back."

Coyle started to protest, but just then Barbara's sobbing became even more fulsome, and he saw there was no point in staying.

He had been holding her as the door burst in. Now he laid her down on the bed and stood up.

"Maybe you should give her some whiskey," he said.

"Maybe you should get your ass out of here," Ione said, waving the six-guns at him.

He left by the back way.

Chapter Two

He had a deputy, Sheriff Graham did, Abner Tralby by name, and there was nothing the sonofabitch liked more than you turning him loose on somebody you were interrogating. You leave Abner alone in a room with a prisoner, and five minutes later you'd have your confession. It might be a coerced confession — the poor bastard might be as innocent as a five-year-old — but you'd have your confession.

Unfortunately, Abner had broken his arm playing baseball the other night, and had taken two weeks off the sheriff's staff to start healing up.

And equally unfortunately, Graham didn't go for that sort of thing himself. He didn't mind shooting people — it was sort of impersonal and all when you thought about it — but beating them was another matter. You saw how vulnerable not only the prisoner was — the crack of bone, the stench of blood, the cry of pain — but how vulnerable you and your children and your wife and your friends were. The difference between life and death was slim sometimes, so slim it was scary. Took a special kind of person to

enjoy beating people, and much as he sometimes wished he was that kind of person, Jim
Graham just wasn't.

So now Jim Graham sat in one of the back
rooms in the lockup. Across the table from
him was Harry Winston.

"So the warden didn't tell you not to fre-
quent saloons?"

"No, sir, he didn't."

"Or not to attend public functions where
liquor of any kind is served?"

"No, sir, he didn't."

"Or not to buy or possess firearms?"

"No, sir, he didn't."

"The warden seems to tell every other
prisoner these things. Wonder why he
didn't tell you."

"I wouldn't know, sir."

"Maybe he was having an off day."

"Maybe, sir."

"I want to go over this again."

"That's fine with me, sir."

"So there you are at the dance tonight."

"There I am, sir."

"And you see Jimmy Clinton out front
and he tells you he's going to kill Bob
Trevor because of this Indian whore. Am I
right so far?"

"Yes, you are, sir."

Like most cons in Graham's experience,

Harry Winston had learned how to be extremely polite yet at the same time mock you and your authority. The "sir" was the thing. They could put the mocking "sir" into you deep as a dagger.

"So you're unconscious for a minute or so 'cause Jimmy cracked you over the head."

"Yes, sir."

"And you get up."

"Yes, sir."

"And you run into the dance?"

"Yes, sir."

"And you see Jimmy over at the Trevors' table?"

"Yes, sir."

"But you want to talk him out of killing Trevor."

"Yes, sir."

"You don't want to shoot him."

"No, sir, I don't."

"So you run around to the back door."

"Yes, sir."

"And there're a couple've men standing there watching Jimmy and the Trevors."

"Yes, sir."

"And one of them's holding a Colt Peacemaker."

"Yes, sir."

"And you grab it out of his hand and run inside."

"Yes, sir, that's just what I do."

"But it wasn't your gun."

"No, sir, it wasn't."

"It belonged to one of the men standing there."

"Yes, sir, it did."

"But you don't know his name."

"No, sir, I don't."

"Or what he looked like."

"No, sir."

"And you weren't able to find him and give his gun back."

"No, sir, I wasn't."

"But the gun doesn't belong to you?"

"No, sir, it doesn't."

"And you're not in violation of your parole."

"Not that I know of, sir." Then: "Sir?"

"What?"

"How come, sir, if Ralph Trevor thinks I'm a hero and that I saved the life of his son and all — how come you've got me over here asking me all these questions?"

"Because I believe you were breaking parole and that the gun was really yours. And I also believe you came back to town here to cause some trouble. All I've heard about since the day I took office seven years ago is you. And how when you finally got out of prison there was going to be hell to pay."

179

"I can't help what people say about me, sir. I'm just trying to be a plain, honest citizen."

"Sure you are, Harry. Sure you are."

"I'd really like to go now, sir. I need to get up bright and early and start looking for a job."

"Jimmy Clinton didn't tell you anything about Bob's gunfight last week, did he?"

This was one of the chief reasons Graham had brought Harry over for questioning. He wanted to know about tonight, true, and what a just-released parolee was doing with a gun, but he also wanted to know about the gunfight. He had a natural curiosity to know how Bob Trevor had managed to beat Mike Coyle to the draw.

"I wouldn't know anything like that, sir. I sure wouldn't."

The mock innocence made Graham want to throw up.

He was one of the bad ones, was Harry. Graham had seen so many of them in his time. Oh, there were some ex-cons who really did go straight, really did try to deal honestly with living within the framework of law. But there were too many, with their little smirks and mocking "sirs," who saw the law as something only fools adhered to. Graham had a brother like that back in Arkansas. Kid was in and out of jail half a dozen times a year, working his way slowly but surely toward a long stretch in a hard-time prison.

"You can go, Harry. I can't prove that that gun belonged to you. Not this time. But next time —"

There was a knock.

"Jim Trout is in the drunk cell, sir," a male voice said, "and he's throwing up pretty bad. I wonder if you'd come look."

"One thing I can't stand," Harry Winston said, "is people who don't obey the law. I'm not going to be like that at all, sir. I'm going to be a model citizen. I really am. Sir."

All the time smirking.

Graham made a face, then walked to the door. He looked back contemptuously at Harry Winston and then went out into the corridor. Jim Trout, the drunk, was a good family man who went on benders every once in a while. Other than that he was sober all the time. But there was one problem when Jim got drunk. He was epileptic, and his drinking scared the hell out of everybody.

Graham hurried to the cells on the second floor.

Chapter Three

He supposed it looked kind of funny, leaving so suddenly the way he had. Especially since *he* was the one who should be celebrating.

But Bob Trevor knew this would be his last chance to try his father's safe.

After Harry had killed Jimmy, Ralph Trevor had invited a lot of family friends over to the Longbranch for a night of wine and celebration. His son had survived. That was something to thank the gods for.

Bob had spent the first hour drinking along with everybody else, and accepting all the toadying pats on the back the townspeople put on him in full view of his father. Never hurts to butter up the son of a powerful man.

But all he could think of was Harry, whom Sheriff Graham had mysteriously dragged away right at the start of the celebration.

Bob wondered if he really could get the safe open. Over the years he'd written down the combination numbers, but he'd never really tried them out.

And maybe he was wrong about the numbers anyway. He'd never been closer than three feet to his father when Ralph was opening the safe. Maybe he was wrong about one of the numbers.

So it was tonight that he had to give it a try. He could have stayed at the celebration and come home drunk along with everybody else, and then when his father was sleeping gone to the safe.

But with Ralph, you never knew. Some nights, even when he'd been drinking a lot, he couldn't sleep and he was up all night roaming the house.

No, better to check the safe while Ralph was gone.

As he approached the ranch now, he saw lights in the bunkhouse and the barn. There was always calving to do, or checking out a horse with mysterious complaints. The barn was generally busy twenty-four hours a day. As he rode in, he was struck by how magnificent the spread was. Throughout the Territory, the Trevor spread was spoken of enviously and somewhat wistfully. Everybody wanted a spread like this one, with its Spanish-style main house and the dozens of elegant refinements inside.

He got his horse bedded down and then went into the house, all without seeing any of the hands. Which was just as well. By now, at least one or two of them would have heard about Jimmy trying to shoot him. A number of the hands had been at the dance earlier. They'd ask him questions he didn't feel like answering.

Inside the house, he poured himself a stiff jolt of bourbon and then stared up at his mother's portrait above the wide stone fireplace. She'd been a pretty woman, freckled but somehow delicate and feminine the way Cass was. He'd been six when she died. Like his father, his mother had always preferred Don and Cass to him. His brother and sister were decent people who usually spent their time well, playing safe and sane games, or reading their schoolbooks, or helping their folks around the ranch. From his youngest years, Bob had been in trouble, leaving behind him a trail of grief and woe that started small — smashed windows, lighting matches that set rooms on fire — but that soon enough became big: breaking into a store and looting it, having Harry and Jimmy hold a man while Bob beat him half to death.

He knew that secretly his brother and sister envied him. They wanted to be just like him but they didn't have the nerve. Nobody *really* wanted to be good. They just pretended they did. Then his mother died, and it became increasingly clear that his older brother Don was the heir apparent. By the time Don was twelve, Dad treated him like an adult. Don became a full-fledged cowhand, learning the ranching business from every aspect. By the time he was fifteen, Don was as much the boss as the hands.

And that was the other queer thing: The hands respected Don, even though he was still only a boy, and even though his Dad had simply ceded him the job. No resentment. No squabbling. No bickering. Don told you to do something, you did it. Same as if old man Trevor himself had asked you. Then Bob couldn't deal with it anymore, all the praise and attention the old man lavished on Don and Cass. He started getting in serious trouble. Only Ralph's influence kept him from going to reform school, and then on to prison.

But what Bob especially couldn't deal with anymore was the fact that he was now fated to be his own brother's employee. Don would never share ranch power with Bob. Not going to happen. But if there was no Don . . .

The day it had happened, at the swimming hole, it was really spontaneous. Bob and Harry had come back from a trip down to a settlement of nigger shacks where they took turns screwing a girl named Maizie, and there was Don in the swimming hole. They jumped in with him, innocent enough. But then Bob remembered having to take an order from Don a few days earlier — Bob always forgot and left the west barn door open, and a couple of horses had gotten loose — and then when he saw Don submerge to do a little swimming, he grabbed the back of Don's neck and held him down. "Help me, Harry!" he'd yelled. And Harry, always up for fun, especially if there was violence involved, grabbed on to Don too.

It hadn't been easy. Don fought like a sonofabitch. He kicked, clawed, bit, gouged, rended, tore. But in the end, they got him, they got him good. And they were lucky. Though he'd put many marks on them, they'd left very few on him. So they left him there, floating facedown, and hurried back to the ranch. Later in the afternoon a hand found Don, floating there. The old man and Cass were both inconsolable. Even all these years later, they couldn't talk about Don without tears in their voices.

But Don's death didn't mean Bob's rebirth in his father's eyes.

The house was dark, quiet, unfamiliar in a curious way. He walked through the living room and down a long corridor without turning on a single lantern. He was a stranger here, suddenly, embarked upon a stranger's business. If his father ever caught him opening the safe, that's just how Bob would be treated, too — as a stranger, without mercy or remorse when the punishment was meted out.

Distantly, as he reached the den, he could hear the neigh of horses and the bunkhouse laughter of the cowhands. He felt alone. Not even the perfume of whores or the headiness of liquor could pull him back from this particular brink. This feeling had always come upon him suddenly, ever since he was a boy, and made him feel weak and female. A real man never felt like this, not a real one, his father or Don. But he felt like this now, and for a moment a garish, lurid fantasy filled his head: He'd take the money himself and flee to Mexico and there he could start life anew. He would live by the sea — a sailor had told him with almost religious fervor of life by the sea — and he would no longer be Bob, he would be somebody else, somebody more like his father or Don, and no longer would he have this sudden feeling, this isolated feeling that unmanned him and made him feel like a girl.

But no, he knew better.

There would be no Mexico, no sea, no rebirth. Two or three times he'd left home over the past ten years, but always, and quickly, he came back because he learned the terrible truth about himself. Without his father's influence, nobody paid him the slightest attention. Or deference. And so he always ran back here, where he stood now, here, his father's here, his sister's here, but not his own here. Not yet anyway, but given the plan he'd shaped riding out here tonight, he knew that his father would soon start regarding him with real respect.

Bob was going to open the safe for Harry, all right. But right after he handed Harry the money, he was going to give his old friend a surprise. He was going to start yelling, "Stop! Stop!" and then he was going to kill Harry.

By the time his father ran to the den, Bob would be standing over Harry's body. He would explain to his father that Harry had forced him to open the safe and give him the money. "But I got my gun out just as he was leaving, Dad. And I killed him."

For once in his life, he would see real admiration in his father's eyes. He would even see respect in Cass's eyes. He had defended his family. At long last he was one of them.

The den smelled of his father's pipe smoke and the peppermint candies his father liked to suck on. Yard light cast everything in deep shadow, giving the heavy, hardwood furnishings a dark and looming beauty.

To the safe. Quickly, quickly. Worried now about Dad and Cass getting back early, too. What if they'd decided to leave right after he did? What if they walked in on him?

The safe was a formidable one, made of steel and heavy enough to resist fire. It sat like a Buddha on the floor behind his father's desk.

As he knelt down next to the combination lock, he thought of bringing a lantern down here. But the light would make any onlookers suspicious, a lone, low light coming from his father's office. One of the hands would come in and check it out for sure.

The first three times, he failed. Turned the bastard left 38, right 49, left 67. And failed. Now what? These were the numbers he recalled seeing his father use to open the safe. But he was obviously wrong.

Unless his father had recently changed the combination. And then just what the hell was he supposed to do? Harry would still be all over him about the money, and he'd never get a chance to impress his father.

Sighing deeply, trying consciously to

calm himself — didn't exactly help to be overwrought when you were working something as delicate as a combination lock — he set again to business.

If those numbers hadn't worked, what about numbers very close to them?

If not 38-49-67, then how about 39-50-66?

He tried that. No luck.

Just then he felt a chill and realized that his entire body was bathed in sickly sweat.

Sonofabitch. Nothing he did ever turned out right. He always needed his daddy and his dad's power and his daddy's money to get him out of his "situations," as Cass called them.

But it was real unlikely that his daddy was going to help him burgle his own safe.

Well, if not 39-40-66, how about 40-41-67?

No luck there, either.

Sonofabitch. Sonofabitch. Sonofabitch. He wanted to jump to his feet, he was so frustrated, and just start smashing up everything in this office. Every last damned thing in this office.

Now, in addition to the sweat, now there was also a lancing headache. And his left leg was going to sleep. Great.

Had to get control of himself once again.

Took some more deep breaths, shifted on his left leg so it'd stop feeling prickly, and then leaned forward and studied the combination in the yard light.

What if he was going the wrong direction with the numbers?

He was going *up*. What if he needed to go *down?*

The first combination he'd tried was 38-49-67.

What if that should have been 37-48-66?

Another deep breath. Wiping a sweaty hand on his trousers. Applying stubby fingers to the delicate mechanism of the combination lock.

C'mon, you whore. Be there for me. Be there for me.

He didn't think the combination worked, didn't hear the kind of deep interior clicking sounds he'd expected, but it did work.

He put a trembling hand on the short silver handle on the face of the safe, brought it down, and the door opened. A woman opening herself to him had never given him as much pleasure as this. Mostly because he paid most of the women he was with, and they willingly parted their legs. That was easy. But this was hard. Very hard.

He reached inside. Groping in the darkness, he felt the stacks of bills, and the paper wrappers that kept them sorted and neat. He sneezed. The safe was dusty. Stacks ran the length of the safe, and maybe four high. Which left a hell of a lot of room. Tomorrow, after the bank guards made their delivery, the stacks would pack the safe, the night before the noon payoff the next day.

He tried to imagine Harry's face if Harry ever got to feel around in a safe like this. Like having your most vivid dream come true.

Then he thought of what Harry's face would look like tomorrow night when Bob took the money away from him at gunpoint. Harry, as always, thought of himself as a lot smarter than Bob. All those years planning how he was going to get money from Bob because of what happened that day at the swimming hole. Well, tough, Harry. Because things just ain't gonna turn out the way you want them to. No sir. Not at all.

A sound somewhere in the house.

His arms coarse with goose bumps.

His mind wild with possibilities — one of the hands somehow sensing somebody in here, and sneaking in here to see what was going on. Or his father hearing him, and now his father sneaking up on him.

He felt very vulnerable kneeling here now in front of the safe, like having a father catch you with your hand up his daughter's dress.

Had to get out of here. Fast.

Goddamn Harry. Just wait till tomorrow night.

Goddamn Cass. Just wait till she saw how his father started treating him after tomorrow night. His father would see that Bob could run the ranch every bit as good as Don could have.

Every single bit as good.

He closed up the safe and got the hell out of there.

Chapter Four

Doc Winston was having the damndest dream.

Here he was a full-grown man, yet he was somehow trapped in this womb, slimy with birth fluids, suffocating because there was no air. And screaming. Screaming so loud his throat was raw. How the hell did a grown man get trapped inside a pregnant woman's belly?

And then there was pounding.

Was that the sound of his own fists slamming into the walls of the womb?

Somehow, he didn't think so, mostly because the sound he was hearing was knuckle bone applied to wood.

And then he was awake.

On his own bed, not in any womb, and he'd been right about the sound, knuckle on wood.

Somebody pounding hard on his back door on the ground floor.

What the hell time was it, anyway?

He rolled off the bed, turned up the lantern on the nightstand, buttery yellow light covering the open book he'd been reading. This was a very serious medical treatise concerning the methods used to deal with the "continual practice of masturbation among teenage boys." E. M. Hartley, M.D., the author, suggesting that "castration is the only civilized practice, both for the sake of the youth and his family." Hartley boasted that he had personally castrated over fifty youths, and that his community was the better for it. Much as the book was lauded by *The New York Times*, Doc Winston secretly felt that E. M. Hartley, M.D., was full of shit. Castrating boys because they chased the chipmunk? Barbarous is what it was; barbarous. And if masturbation truly drove you insane, a widower like Doc himself would have been committed to the bughouse long, long ago.

He got into his trousers, his slippers, picked up his Colt, and went downstairs.

She was so short and so slight, he didn't see her at first as he peered out of the back door's spy hole into backyard shadows.

Then he saw her, and recognized her. She'd been here a couple of times needing treatment for venereal disease.

Barbara Thomas, her name was. Indian, and cuter than hell.

Ordinarily, anyway. But at this particular time she wasn't cuter than hell. Not at all.

She looked unkempt, and slightly dazed and crazed.

Doc swung the door backward and stuck his head out into the night.

"Can I help you, Barbara?"

"I need to see Jimmy Clinton."

"He's dead, Barbara. There's nothing to see."

"I don't care if he's dead, Doc. I got to see him anyway."

"It's pretty damned late."

"I know it's pretty damned late, but I loved him, Doc, and I made a terrible mistake and I just got to tell him I did."

"God, girl, he won't hear you."

"Don't matter if *he* can't hear me, Doc. *I* can hear me, and that's all that matters."

Maybe she's been drinking or smoking opium or something (some whorehouses offered their customers drugs of various kinds), Doc thought.

He sighed. "Oh, all right. You go down to that door on the end there, and I'll let you in."

"I really appreciate this, Doc."

Doc just grumbled something, closed the door on her, and then walked through the shadowy house to the back porch where he kept the corpses so he could clean them and dress them for burial.

He bumped into a chair on his way to the porch. He swore mightily when he did so, all his frustrations from the weird dream, and the inconvenience of Barbara pounding on his door so late, coming out in the curse words.

In the pale moonlight through the back porch window, Doc saw the outlines of Jimmy Clinton's body. Doc hadn't dressed him yet. Jimmy still wore the same blood-soaked shirt he'd had on when the wagon had dropped him off here.

He went to the door. Barbara came in.

When she saw Jimmy lying there on the table, a sob filled her lungs, and she looked frantically at Doc, as if he could somehow do something about bringing Jimmy back to life.

"I reckon you want to be alone," he said.

She stood a few feet from the corpse, all body-tight, as if she was afraid to go any closer, as if the corpse might sit up and grab her.

"He's really dead?"

"He's really dead."

Then she started crying. Nothing big or dramatic — no sobs, no teeth gnashing, no fall-to-the-floor weeping — just soft girlish tears, and then she abruptly stepped up to the corpse.

"He's already in heaven, Doc," she said. "I can just feel it."

"Well, like I said, I'll leave you alone with him," Doc said, fighting a smile. If there was truly a heaven and hell, Doc would put his money on the latter being Jimmy's permanent new address. "You go on and do what you want to now. I'll be back in a little bit."

But she was no longer paying attention. She was looking at the sticky blood covering Jimmy's shirt.

Doc backed out of the room and then turned toward his kitchen. This moment clearly warranted a good, stiff shot of sour mash.

Barbara had never kissed a dead man before.

Oh, men at Ione's had passed out inside her before, and she'd kissed them trying to wake them up. But they hadn't been dead. Just drunk.

Jimmy's lips were cool and tasted of blood.

She bent down closer so that she could move her little hand over the contours of his face. Such a handsome face. How she loved that face.

"Jimmy," she said, "I didn't screw Bob

that night. I just let him think I did. And let you think I did. I loved you too much to ever do a thing like that. But you didn't take me away like you promised. And then you cheated on me on top of it. Oh, Jimmy, I know you're up there lookin' down on me, darlin', and I know that you know now that I never done what you thought I done. Not with Bob Trevor, I didn't."

More tears. Another tender kiss on the cool, unresponsive lips.

Then: "Oh, Jimmy."

Then she really did begin to sob and weep.

Doc could hear her all the way out in the kitchen.

He sat in a chair at the table and thought again of his strange dream. Trapped inside a woman's womb. What the hell was that all about? He was one of those men who couldn't escape the mood of his dreams for many hours after.

He was just about to pour himself another drink when he heard the sobbing.

He lifted his head, cocking it toward the back room, and listened intently.

Now that he was curious, he decided to have only *half* a drink, and then hurry back to the back room.

He walked softly. He didn't want to startle her. He wanted to see what could inspire such sounds.

Through the house. Toward the back door. Walking on tiptoes. Careful not to bump or scrape anything. Wishing he'd taken a *full* drink just now.

The sobs louder, louder.

And, as he drew closer, a rustling, a thumping, and a bumping, and a *rustling*.

What the hell was going on, anyway?

Then he stood just this side of the back-porch doorway and saw for himself what was going on.

There, outlined in golden moonlight, lay Barbara atop the corpse of Jimmy Clinton, her hands holding his head up tenderly as she kissed him.

"Oh, Jimmy, I'm so sorry for lyin' to you the way I did," she said after letting the back of his head touch the table again.

Doc stepped into the room and coughed to announce his presence, in case his heavy stepping hadn't done the job.

He had to give her one thing. She didn't look the least embarrassed or intimidated by his presence, as if it was the most natural thing in all the world to be talking to a corpse.

"I love you, Jimmy," she said softly,

giving him a final kiss upon the lips.

And then she slid off him.

But she wasn't done. She took his hand and held it a long moment, then kissed it a final time.

"Is it true worms eat you when you're dead?" she said.

"Well, whether they do or don't," Doc said, somehow wanting to spare her feelings, "it don't matter, because you're not conscious anyway."

She gazed down fondly on Jimmy again. "He really is in heaven, Doc. While I was kissing him and things, he spoke to me from up above."

Celestial telegraph, Doc thought.

And then thought: What a grumpy old fart I am. I'm just jealous because no sweet-faced little Indian girl is going to kiss me when I'm stretched out on this very same table.

And then he no longer felt disgust over what he'd seen, he felt a real loneliness and envy. Even dead guys get more girls than I do, he thought.

"I appreciate you lettin' me in, Doc," she said.

"Oh, that's fine."

"There was just somethin' I had to tell him."

"I understand."

He wanted her. He wanted her to be on top of him the way she'd been on top of Jimmy. Doc hadn't gotten laid in three, four years. But he knew he was up to the task. All he'd need to do was brush away a few cobwebs and he'd give Barbara here the shock of her young life.

"I better go now."

He wanted to say something, offer her a drink, or ask her if she'd like to sit in the kitchen for a time. He just didn't want to let her go, because then he'd be this old fart again, dust to dust, facing his own soon-enough and lonely doom, the eternal clock tock-tock-tocking his life away. She could make him young again for ten or fifteen minutes. And it would be sufficient for an old fart like himself, ten or fifteen minutes, dick hard as a twenty-year-old's, and mind racing for ways to capture not just her body but her heart.

But it wasn't to be, and he knew it. She slid through the shadows to the back door, seeming to sense his sudden need of her. In the whorehouse she would've known exactly what to do (he was imagining her thoughts now), but here was different. Here he wanted something she could never, ever give him, his youth back, his loneliness vanquished.

"Thanks again, Doc."

"You bet," he said, sounding like "Doc" again, all fusty-voiced and weary.

Doc had been acting very strangely, Barbara thought as she closed the back door behind her.

He'd come into the back room just as she was finishing with Jimmy. And he probably thought it was profane somehow, what she was doing, or just "some Indian thing" — whenever people couldn't explain her behavior, that's what they always said, that she was just doing "some Indian thing" — but it wasn't. She'd just been overwhelmed by the lie she'd told Jimmy to make him jealous and make him mad, and at the moment it just seemed the right and natural thing to do, getting up on top of him and loving him that way.

She moved through the shadows and silence of the sleeping town.

She needed sleep herself now. She needed to be spry of mind and limb tomorrow so she could figure out how she was going to kill Bob Trevor and Harry Winston.

Chapter Five

Coyle woke up just before dawn.

He had always wondered why he didn't ever remember the good things in his life when he lay awake like this. But it never happened that way. Over and over again, the bad things that he had done, and that had been done to him, paraded across the stage of his mind. His drinking days provided dozens of bad memories, times when he'd been abusive or violent or ugly.

He saved the best for last, his years as a married man and father. Oh, had he screwed those two roles up. He kept hearing his wife scream at him the night he'd staggered in at 3:00 a.m. and bumped into the small crib, knocking it to the floor. Infant Mike had wailed and wailed in the flickering lantern light as his mother rocked him and soothed him with whispered words, while all Coyle could do was swallow steaming black coffee and shake his head in sorrow and shame.

Then came images of Mike at different ages with guns, Coyle always nearby to show him how to use various weapons.

He hadn't been there every day to push Mike toward being a gunfighter, but he'd planted the seed. And helped grow it.

His first years at the Wild West Show, there'd been almost no contact with Mike or his ex-wife. The first sober years, the first moments and days and weeks and years Coyle had been proud of since being a young man.

Then one day, his train passing through, Coyle surprised them by stopping by. Mike had just turned sixteen. Coyle would never forget the shock he'd felt seeing his boy grown man-big. And seeing the hard dead eyes and the icy smile and the Colt slung low across his right hip. His boy was no longer his boy somehow. He looked at his father and smiled icily and then reached down and performed one of the fastest draws Coyle had ever seen, far faster than he'd ever been able to draw. Mike had smiled icily, clearly aware that he had just rattled his father. "I turned out just like you, Dad. Just like you."

Just like you.

He lay in the rooster-loud, moon-faded, hotel-room morning — so many, many lonely mornings like this made up his life — and thought of Mike and of all the ways his life might have turned out good if only Coyle hadn't pushed the gunny thing so early and so hard.

Then Coyle swung his legs off the bed and sat there rubbing his beard-roughened face, and whispering the words of a prayer, though to whom it was sent, and for what exact reason it was being said, he wasn't sure. Hell, he wasn't even sure of the words, just some dimly remembered prayer of his young years, when he'd knelt next to his Ohio bed every night till his knees hurt, saying goodnight prayers to a dark and inscrutable god.

Maybe for himself. Maybe that's who he was praying for this morning. Himself. That he have some luck doing what he now knew he must do: kill Bob Trevor.

An hour later, shaved, washed up, a breakfast of eggs, bacon, and wheat bread filling him, he leaned on a corner of the hotel veranda, a toothpick in his teeth, and watched the town coming to noisy life for the day: the chinking of heavy wagons, the high pure glee of children bursting out of doors for the day, the yip of dogs and yap of townspeople gossiping, the clank of the blacksmith's hammer, and the chugging charge of a freight train as it hurried toward the depot.

He gazed on all this idly, not watching anything with any exceptional interest, until he sighted a lone rider coming into town from the north.

Is. Isn't. Is. Isn't.

He couldn't decide if this was really who he thought it was or not. One minute it would look like him, next moment not.

Then the rider was closer and there was no mistaking him.

Bob Trevor.

What the hell was Bob Trevor doing in town so early? Where the hell was he going?

Coyle pushed away from the hotel veranda, a lot more curious now about the goings-on in this town.

Barbara was dreaming of her Paiute people again. She was eight years old and had just been given the responsibility of making rabbitskin robes for herself and her mother. Forty skins would be needed for her robe, more than a hundred for her mother's. The boys skinned the animals and then turned the pelts over to her. She would cut the pelts into long strips and then weave them together to make the robe. She was very frightened. What if she did not make the robes properly? Wouldn't her mother be very angry? All her life, Barbara (or New Moon, as she was known to her tribe) had had but one purpose in her life — to please.

But the robes did not turn out well. And even now, all these years later, she could see the disappointment in her mother's eyes when Barbara proudly held up the robes. New Moon's little sister was then given the robes, which she stripped down into pelts again, and then turned into coats as warm and beautiful as New Moon had hoped to make them.

All these years later, the moment still vivid with her, Barbara awoke just at dawn and lay in the shadow of her bitter memory. There was no joy in waking now, especially not as last night returned to her, Jimmy dead, Bob Trevor strutting around town. And the disappointment in her mother's eyes.

She took her basin down the hall and returned with fresh water and let her sleeping garment slip silkily away and stood in the high clear morning light and touched a soapy cloth to various parts of her body, not wanting to reward herself in any way with sensuous pleasures, not with memory of Jimmy and her mother still so much upon her, and cleaned herself with catlike fastidiousness.

She went down the back stairs to the café half a block from her room.

She had just reached the alley when she

looked toward the street and saw Bob Trevor riding into town.

She had never heard of Bob Trevor getting up this early for any reason.

What would he be doing in town so early? Whom would he be here to see?

She forgot all about her morning coffee.

She had to find out who Trevor was here to see. Had to.

She approached the alley, saw that Trevor was now about a quarter of a block ahead of her.

She began following him, keeping at a safe distance.

Harry Winston was there right at seven o'clock, which was when most self-respecting children charged past their parents out into the world of sunlight and secret hiding places and fishing holes and fat red apples just begging to be picked. School was still a week away, thanks to the fact that farm kids still had autumn chores to do before they could begin their schooling, which meant there were still a whole lot of neat ways to get into trouble before the schoolmarm opened her rulebook and ruined every kid's life.

She was there then, too cute — as she'd been when he'd seen her yesterday — sweet as she'd been in all his prison dreams when he thought about her and how tall she'd be getting, and how warm and sweet and clean she'd smell, and how good she'd feel when she gave her ole dad Harry a hug.

He just watched her.

She came exploding from the house, following her tail-wagging, jumping-up-and-down, brown-and-white mutt.

The dog had to do his business. She waited patiently while he peed in the grass, then a little while later while he pooped in the grass.

Then she slipped a bright blue ball from her gingham dress and started bouncing it up and down, which put the mutt into a delighted frenzy.

He vaulted up when the ball went up. He shot after it when it veered away.

But all Harry took real note of was the little girl, and how shabby her clothes were, and how shabby the cottage was. She wasn't having much of a life. True, it was preferable to living a life with an ex-convict, there wasn't any doubt about that. But still and all, it wasn't much of a life at all.

Then she became aware of him, and stopped bouncing the ball, and looked over at him.

They stared at each other for a long time,

he on this side of the street and she on the other, and Harry was almost crushed by the tenderness he felt for her, and her eyes seemed to communicate the same feeling, as if she secretly knew who he really was, and how much — despite all the bad things he'd been and would be again — how much he loved her and cherished her and dreamed of her and wanted only the absolute best for her.

Then Ellen must have seen him, too, because she was suddenly outdoors, on her doorstep, hands on her hips, glaring across the way at him.

Harry Winston took a final look at the girl, then went away.

Chapter Six

There was an old-timer standing next to Coyle on the street, an old-timer who was all scratches and burps and farts and tobacco-spitting and suspender-snapping.

Coyle angled himself so he wouldn't be directly downwind of the old guy.

"What's that?" Coyle said.

The old-timer, who had some kind of rash on the left side of his face, squinted across the street and down about half a block.

"What's what?"

"That armed wagon."

The old-timer squinted some more, then passed some gas.

"You mean down by the bank there?"

"Uh-huh."

"That's Trevor's wagon."

"Why's he got six armed men in it?"

"They protect the money."

"What money?"

"His payroll." The old-timer was starting to get irritated.

"Oh, that's right," Coyle said. He'd been told about Trevor and his payroll yesterday. Liked to personally hand each of his men their pay, and see if the hand had any particular complaint about how the ranch was being run. Each man had permission to speak up any way he wanted to. This kept Trevor popular with his men. Of course, it didn't hurt any that he also paid the best wages in the Territory.

This time, the old-timer belched.

"Well," he said, taking a pocket watch out from the ratty jacket he wore over his ratty shirt. He took the opportunity to snap his suspenders again. "Looks like it's about time for the first one."

"First one?"

"Drink, son. Drink. I never drink before nine a.m." He said this with a great deal of pride.

"Well," Coyle smiled. "I can see why you're so proud of yourself."

"Yessir," the old-timer said, "that's a rule I never break."

Then he nodded, and set his eyes on the saloon across the street. "Good luck to you, son."

Then he was gone.

At forty-three, Coyle liked being called son. Too bad the old-timer smelled so bad. Otherwise he'd be worth hanging around with, just to hear that "son" stuff.

Gloved hands gripped Winchesters. Hard

eyes scanned the street. Cigarettes hung from taut lips.

The guards all looked professional. Anybody who tried to heist the Trevor payroll would be a fool.

Coyle stood closer now, watching the efficient way two men carried three large money sacks from the bank to the wagon that waited just outside. When the money appeared in the door, two of the men in the wagon stepped to the ground. One pointed his Winchester west, the other one east. One man remained in the wagon bed, his own Winchester at the ready. The driver held a Navy Colt.

The money transfer went quickly. The wagon was soon pulling away from the bank.

Ten minutes later, Coyle stood at the top of some dusty outside stairs that ran up along the side of a building down by the river.

He knocked twice, heard nothing, then put his ear to the door.

Barbara could likely see him from inside. And she certainly wouldn't be inclined to open the door to him.

He tried the doorknob. Locked.

He walked to the back of the platform and

peeked in through a dusty window.

Golden sunlight gave dusty old furnishings a kind of faded glory. You could imagine that the stuff had probably looked pretty good when it was new.

Coyle shook his head, started down the stairs.

Barbara was his last hope for ever finding out the truth about the gunfight that had killed Mike. Coyle sensed from his conversation with her that Jimmy Clinton had probably told her the truth. Somehow, Coyle had to get her to share that truth.

Cass had never known her brother to wake so early. Usually, his rousing good time the night before kept him in bed till late in the morning.

He'd made a good deal of noise when he'd left so early, waking up Cass, as well.

She got to the kitchen an hour and a half earlier than she usually did. The time was just 6:30.

Her father was already at the table, the house woman, Esmerelda, filling his coffee after a breakfast of what appeared to be flapjacks.

"Would you like some coffee, miss?"

"Thank you. I'd love some."

She had just seated herself when Ralph

215

said, "You know anything about where that brother of yours was going this morning?"

"No. I thought maybe you did."

Ralph shook his head. "I tried to talk to him a couple of times this morning, but you know how he is when he doesn't want to tell you something. He just mumbles."

"You think he's in trouble?"

Ralph's jaw muscles worked hard. "That's the first assumption you make with somebody like Bob, isn't it?" He shook his head. "I keep trying to remember when he ever got up this early before — except when I forced him to work, I mean."

She was about to say something else slightly derogatory about her brother, but then she stopped herself. "We shouldn't assume the worst."

"Oh?" Ralph said. "Why not?" His sarcasm seemed extremely harsh this early in the day.

"Because maybe he's got some legitimate business in town."

"Like what?"

"Oh, maybe he's looking for a job or something."

Ralph obviously couldn't resist a cold smile. "You don't really believe that, do you?"

She paused, choosing her words, not

216

wanting to hurt her father. "He isn't Don."

"And that's supposed to mean what, exactly?"

"That's supposed to mean that I think we both expect too much of him. Dons don't come along very often. Maybe Bob's turned out the way he has because he's always had to live in the shadow of Don."

He shook his head again. He seemed more aggrieved than angry now. All the sarcasm was gone. He just looked weary. "He's damned near thirty years old, Cass."

"I know that."

"He has to take over his own life and do something with it."

"I know that, too."

Ralph sipped his coffee, then set his cup down and settled back in his chair. "I suppose you could be right. About Don, I mean. You and I, we're always talking about Don, and I don't suppose that's good for him."

"He gets up early in the morning, and we immediately get suspicious."

"You, too."

"That's why I said 'we,' Dad."

He looked at her closely again. "What brought all this on? I haven't heard you so concerned in a long time about Bob."

"It was last night, I guess."

"Last night?"

"When Jimmy almost killed him."

"Oh."

"I saw how frightened he looked, and how young, and it made me realize that he's really a stranger to us now. We have to help him get his life straightened out before it's too late."

"That's something he has to do for himself."

"I know that. But we can help him by not talking about Don so much, and by being nicer to him."

"I'm nice to him when he's nice to me. When he's drinking, he's —"

"I know how he is, Dad. He lights into me just about as often as he lights into you. But when I saw him facing Jimmy last night, he just looked so lost and scared. He's still our flesh and blood, Dad. Remember that."

Her father wasn't much for tears, his own or anybody else's. But she couldn't help herself. As she sat here this morning, her brother was an ache inside her. They'd drifted so far apart, spent whole weeks without exchanging a civil word, said such angry and hateful things to each other over the past five years or so —

"No use for tears, honey," Ralph said. He was embarrassed. That was the thing. Ralph liked the idea of always being in control of a situation. But tears denied him that control. And that embarrassed him. He reached over and patted her hand. "You're right, honey. We should try harder to get along with Bob. I'll remind him about the offer Glen Denning made him."

She nodded, sniffling tears. Glen was a family friend who'd offered to put Bob on as a railroad telegrapher. In this day and age, most folks considered a railroad job like that a really fancy position.

"It's not too late for him, Dad," Cass said, wiping away her tears now. "We both have to believe that, and act on that assumption."

"Then that's what we'll do," Ralph said, in a much better mood now that she wasn't crying. "We'll just assume the best, and maybe that's just what we'll get."

She smiled at his forced heartiness. For all his bluster sometimes, he really was a sweet man.

Maybe even Bob's sweet, deep down, she thought.

Maybe.

Chapter Seven

Harry Winston was on the front porch of his hotel when he saw the money wagon pull past him, headed out for Ralph Trevor's spread.

A proprietary gleam shone in his eyes as he watched the wagon.

Tonight, all this money was going to be his. And it was going to change his life forever.

His prison dreams were going to come true. Finally; finally.

He was going to drink, smoke, eat, and fuck every single prison day out of his memory, out of his soul. He'd head to San Francisco — prison was filled with men who told dire but fascinating tales of the Barbary Coast — and start life fresh.

When the money wagon was out of sight, he turned away from the street and went back upstairs to his room.

Barbara followed Bob Trevor all over town. First he went to a diner for coffee, then he went to the general store for some cigarette tobacco, then he went to the livery to tell the blacksmith something about the horse he'd left there.

Then and only then did Trevor get on with the real business of his day: He walked over to the hotel where Harry Winston was staying.

Barbara waited until Trevor had been inside for at least two minutes before she went in after him.

She had just reached the bottom of the stairs that swept grandly up to the second floor when a voice said, "How dare you?"

She turned, recognizing at once the prissy hotel clerk, Potiphar O'Brian.

He wore his usual stiff Edwardian suit, which came complete with his too-fancy handlebar mustache and dapper gray gloves. One might think that Potiphar was not disposed to women. But one would be wrong. Potiphar was at Ione's at least three times a week and was known to be a real and relentless hellion in bed.

"What's wrong, Potiphar?" she said.

He looked excruciatingly embarrassed when she spoke his name out loud. "My God!" he stage-whispered, spitting all over her face. "Don't let on you know me! I have my reputation to consider!"

Then he took her, with sudden and surprising strength, to a hallway to the right of the staircase.

"What're you doing here?" he said.

"Just came to see somebody I know."

"My God!" Potiphar said. "Don't you know anything about decency?"

She was genuinely confused by his words, and his bad temper.

"Potiphar, I see you all the time at Ione's."

"But this, my dear, isn't Ione's. This is the nicest and most respectable hotel in this part of the Territory. And you —" He looked her up and down with pure disgust. "You're not only an Indian, you're also a whore!"

So there they were, the words she heard most often whenever she ventured far from her sleeping room, or far from Ione's. Indian. Whore.

There was a time when those words had had the power to hurt her. No more. Now they just made her feel dead inside. The words had hurt her one too many times, and now there was nothing left to hurt.

"I'm going to tell Ione what you were doing," Potiphar said. "She's not going to like it that you're trying to do some business on the sly."

So that was it. Potiphar thought she was peddling herself within these hallowed walls. It was almost funny.

"Now, you get out of here before we both

get in trouble!" he said.

And just then, somebody was banging impatiently on the front desk bell.

"See! You've gotten both of us in trouble already!" Potiphar said desperately. "I'm not supposed to leave my post under any circumstances!"

With that, he latched on to her wrist again and pushed her angrily toward the front door of the hotel.

She could feel the amused and judgmental eyes of the white men on her. They probably know what I am, she thought.

Then she felt bitter about Jimmy again. Jimmy had been going to save her from this life. She'd had his sacred word on that.

Jimmy; Jimmy.

She was still going to get to Bob Trevor and Harry Winston somehow. Somehow.

Coyle was just leaving the diner when he saw Cass and Ralph Trevor ride into town in a buggy. They rode over to the railroad business offices and Ralph went inside. Cass walked in the opposite direction.

Coyle headed back toward Barbara's sleeping room again.

He had to talk to her. Had to.

"I just wanted to make sure that the offer

was still good," Ralph Trevor said to his old friend Denning. The two had been among the first people to settle out here. Denning, who was about Ralph's age, had lost his wife and children to cholera. He had remarried a few years ago, and was now the proud father of a pair of new twins.

"Bob finally thinking of settling down, is he?" Denning said.

His office in the railroad building was impressive, with a large oak desk, three matching cabinets, a genuine Persian rug, and four deep leather armchairs.

"I think he's getting there," Ralph said, "slowly but surely."

"I heard about last night. He's lucky."

"Very lucky. And I think he knows that."

Denning, who had a large head encased in a full flower of woolly white hair, said, "But I can't bullshit you, Ralph."

"I understand."

"I'm his godfather, and I want to see him make something of himself. But like everybody else who works here —"

"I know. We talked about that the first time I asked you about a job for him. A probationary period."

"About fifty percent of the people wash out."

"I understand."

"Telegraphy sounds easy, but it's not."

"I realize that. But he's always been so fascinated by trains —" And that was true. Nothing claimed Bob's attention like trains. As a boy he'd sat for hours on a clay ledge above the railroad tracks, watching the trains hurtle by. The first time Ralph had mentioned this job with Glen Denning, Bob had even seemed moderately interested.

"I'd like to talk to him about the job, Glen. Last night was a close call. Maybe enough of a close call to make him think twice about how he's been living. If I could go to him with a firm job offer from you . . ."

Glen smiled. "He's my godson, Ralph. And you're one of the best friends I've ever had. He's got a firm job offer. Very firm."

Long ago, Ralph had decided that Bob needed to try some other kind of work before he appreciated all the good things that waited for him at the ranch. Six, seven months of telegraphy would likely send him running back to the ranch, where he would give his father's spread a real chance.

Ralph couldn't wait to talk to Bob. Maybe he really would take Glen up on his offer this time and start the growing-up process on its way.

"Thanks, Glen."

Glen nodded. "My pleasure, Ralph."

★ ★ ★

Barbara waited until the cooks were done dumping the morning's garbage in the cans behind the hotel.

With Potiphar on duty, there was no way she was going to get in the front way.

But Potiphar wouldn't be expecting her the back way.

The alley, baking in the hot sun, stank of rotting meat and vegetables. Dozens of buzzing blackflies circled and circled the garbage cans. A bony dog crouched nearby. Like Barbara, he was waiting until he was sure the cooks were gone for good. Then he'd go into action.

Barbara, glancing behind her, making certain that nobody was watching, started walking quickly toward the hotel's back door.

Getting inside was simple. The smell of food cooking filled her nostrils pleasantly. Off to her right pots banged and bonged as they were moved from stove to serving tables. The angle of a corner kept her from actually seeing the cooks, but she could certainly hear them. They rushed about, swearing theatrically as they moved. This sauce wasn't being prepared properly; and just who the hell was watching the bread; and goddammit, just look at that pork, it was so underdone somebody might die eating it.

There were dusty stairs angling upward. She hesitated a moment, then fled up them.

She had to find Harry Winston's room.

"An hour later, huh?" Harry said after pouring a drink for Bob and himself.

The room was a nice one. In order to pay for it, Harry had had to remind a cousin of his of an illegal favor Harry had done him a long time ago. The cousin had discovered that his wife was sleeping with a local merchant. Unlike Harry, the cousin was a timid man. Harry thought for days how to best serve the merchant the message. Then, one night in a saloon, he heard of an old Apache trick and decided to use it on the merchant. He waited until the man was walking home from a meeting one night, then he knocked him out and dragged him into a storage barn, where he stripped his pants down to the knees and slashed the man's buttocks with a Bowie knife. This was a man who wouldn't be able to sit down comfortably for at least six months. The message was not only delivered but understood. The merchant never came sniffing around again.

"Yeah," Bob Trevor said. "He was supposed to leave at seven. Now he's leaving at eight. Rancher who's giving the party had to ride fence looking for some problems today, and he's running behind schedule."

Harry said, "You look pretty calm, Bob."

Bob smiled. "Must be because I'm still asleep. Not used to getting up this early."

It was the right thing to say, Harry noted, but somehow he didn't believe it.

Bob was the nervous type. Even when they were drunk, Bob had always shown a certain anxiety. That's how he'd been yesterday, extremely tense about finally tapping his old man's safe.

But this morning, he didn't seem nervous at all. If anything, he seemed almost happy about the whole thing.

Harry wondered what good old Bob was hiding from him.

"How about another drink?" Harry said.

Bob held up his still-full glass. "I'm fine."

Definitely not his usual self, Harry thought. What the hell's he planning behind my back, anyway?

"Trevor, you say?"

"Yes, ma'am."

"Ralph Trevor?"

"No. His son. Bob Trevor."

"Oh, *Bob* Trevor."

"Yes, ma'am."

"The son."

"Yes, ma'am."

"Ralph, him I ain't seen."

"Yes, ma'am."

"But Bob, the son?"

"Yes, ma'am?"

"Him, I *did* see."

"When?"

"Oh, couldn'ta been longer than ten minutes ago."

The old woman was stooped of shoulder, glassy of eye, leathery of skin, and vague of mind. She carried a bucket of soapy water in her right hand and a dirty, dripping mop in the other. Barbara felt sorry for her, spending her last years cleaning up after inconsiderate white men. At least whores had a little bit of control over these men. This poor old white woman had none.

"Do you remember what floor he was on, ma'am?" Barbara had searched the first four floors but found no hint of Harry or Bob Trevor.

"Floor?"

"Yes, ma'am."

"What floor is this?"

"The fifth floor, ma'am."

"Then it was on the one I was just on."

"The fourth?"

The old woman thought. "No, today I'm working my way *down*, so I musta been on the sixth floor."

"Thank you very much, ma'am. Very much."

Then Barbara was overcome by pity for the old woman. Her own mother, who was now about the same age, was dying of cancer on an Oklahoma reservation.

She took the old woman in her arms and held her tenderly, reverently, and then she hurried down to the end of the hall to the stairs that would take her to the sixth floor.

"Mind if I sit down?" Ralph Trevor said.

"Not at all."

Coyle was sitting at the counter of the diner where he'd been taking his meals since coming to Coopersville.

"Saw your son," Coyle said. "He must be a pretty early riser."

Something in Trevor's expression said that he didn't want to talk about his son. He changed the subject. "You probably think we're pretty wild people, the way the dance ended up last night and everything."

Trevor ordered coffee for himself.

"Every place gets wild every once in a while," Coyle said.

"You getting things wrapped up here?" Trevor said, coughing a little. The smokers in the place had laid down a heavy cloud of blue smoke.

"Pretty much."

"I take it you've decided that my son is telling the truth."

"I haven't heard anything to contradict his story yet, I'll say that much."

Trevor shook his head. "That isn't exactly what I wanted you to say, I guess."

"That's all I can say right now."

"You planning on leaving soon?"

"Soon as possible."

Trevor sipped his coffee, stared at his big hand wrapped around the cup. "He's not a bad boy."

"As I said before, I'll take your word for that."

"He's wild. But not bad. There's a difference, you know."

"Yes, there is."

Trevor gripped his coffee cup tighter. "I'm hoping that last night changed him."

"Oh?"

Trevor raised his eyes, settled them on Coyle. "A thing like that — coming so close to death and all — a thing like that can change people. How they look at things, I mean."

"And you think it changed Bob?"

"I think it damned well could have,"

Trevor said. But he didn't sound sure of himself. He sounded as if he was just *hoping* that his son would change. Hoping against hope.

"It damned well could have," Trevor repeated softly, almost prayerfully.

Barbara found the room she wanted with little difficulty.

This time of morning, most of the rooms were empty.

All she had to do was walk slowly down the sixth-floor hallway and listen for voices. From several feet away, she heard the deep rumble of male voices in Room 617.

She put her ear to the door, listened.

At first, she couldn't figure out what they were talking about.

But slowly, what they said began to make sense. Terrible sense.

"I want you to hit me on the side of the head."

"Why the hell would I do that, Bob?"

"Well, if I'm supposed to tell my dad that you forced me to open the safe, I'd better look like you did some real forcing."

"Yeah, I guess that makes sense."

"The same when you're riding away."

"Oh?"

"I'm gonna fire in the air when I run out

of the house after you."

"Then I fire into the air, too?" Harry said.

"Exactly."

Harry walked over to the bureau, poured himself another drink. He sipped deeply and appreciatively. "This was one of the things I thought about all those years in prison. Good sippin' whiskey." His eyes turned hard as they looked at Bob again. " 'Course, you didn't have to worry about liquor or women, did you, Bob? You were free and clear outside. You could do anything you wanted, couldn't you, Bob?"

Harry could feel the old rage slowly filling his chest and mind.

"You'll have so much money tonight, Harry," Bob said, "you'll forget all about me not bein' with you in prison."

"As I remember it, you were the one who had the idea about robbin' the stage in the first place."

"Harry, you really want to go back through all this?"

"That's the only thing I had to do in prison. At nights, anyway. Lay there and think about all the fun you were havin'."

"I'm sorry it worked out that way."

"Didn't come to see me once in prison, did you?"

"Harry."

"Made Jimmy come up and see me. But you didn't come."

"I was busy."

"Sure you were. All the ladies, all the parties. Kept you pretty busy, I bet."

As she listened, Barbara was fascinated by the hatred in Harry's voice. What kept him from killing Bob Trevor? He must want the money very bad, she sensed, otherwise he'd simply destroy Bob Trevor right here and now.

"Tonight, I'm gonna make it up to you, Harry. I really am."

Another pause. "I'll be there, Bob." Pause. "I better get on about my other business."

"Everything's set," Bob Trevor said.

"I just wish I could figure out why you look so happy, Bob." His suspicion now thickened his tongue as much as his anger did. Whatever was going on in Harry's mind, it all seemed to be leading to the same conclusion: that Bob couldn't be trusted, that Bob had to be killed.

What Barbara couldn't figure out, as she listened to all this, was why Trevor seemed so nonchalant about everything. As Harry had said, they had a lot facing them. The robbery didn't sound as if it was going to be all that simple, but here was Bob Trevor, happy and easygoing.

There were a few more words exchanged, but then she heard Bob Trevor start walking toward the door, his spurs chinking.

She had to get out of there before she was found. She hurried down the hall to the stairs, which she took two at a time.

She had just reached the ground floor, in the back of the hotel, when she saw Potiphar talking to a workman, pointing out to the man some damage that had been done to the wall just inside the back door.

"You! There! Stop!" he called to her.

But she didn't slow down. Just kept walking. Hard. Fast. To the alley.

When she got outside, she turned right and started running. And that was when she reached the sidewalk and saw Ralph Trevor coming out of the diner.

Ralph Trevor, she thought, out of breath from the run she'd just had. Ralph Trevor was just the man she wanted to see.

Chapter Eight

Maybe things would turn out all right after all, Ralph Trevor was thinking as he left the diner and walked down the street.

Bob had to grow up at some point. And maybe, after last night, they'd reached the point where Bob would look around and start counting his blessings.

He stood on the boardwalk, thumbs hooked in the pockets of his leather vest, looking at the town he'd helped create. Seemed like every time he visited here he saw something new. Today it was the tall, elegant set of lanterns that sat on the edge of the city park. A man would have to go all the way to Kansas City to see something this nice.

As he stood there, many of the people passing by nodded good day to him. He knew he was not a popular man. A man as successful as he was bound to be resented, even hated. But there were some, a few anyway, who were wise enough to understand that without the Ralph Trevors of the world, without their dreams and ambition, very little would ever be accomplished. Pioneers and visionaries and innovators might not be the nicest people on the planet, but progress would be impossible without them. And so they good day'd him, and thanked him, and paid him at least a perfunctory homage, even though they might not like him exactly.

Then he saw the Indian girl and was startled. He watched her move steadily toward him. He recognized her as one of Ione's whores. Many times in the lonely days since his wife's death, Trevor had been tempted to go pay Ione a visit. But he could not bring himself to engage in loveless sex. His wife had spoiled him. Their sex life had been good because of their devout love for each other. He wouldn't find that at Ione's.

As he stood there, he kept waiting for the Indian to veer left or right. Surely she wasn't coming up to see him, was she? He had nothing against Indians — indeed, he felt that many of his white friends treated Indians badly — but still and all, what could she possibly want with him?

She was bold, he had to give her that.

She came straight toward him, a slight girl in dusty gingham, black hair gleaming a lovely blue-black in the hot sunlight, a pretty enough girl except for the hardness around the mouth and the hint of quickly riled bitterness in the lustrous obsidian eyes.

And then she stood directly in front of him, with no sense of fear or deference, only a few inches away, and said, "There's something you should know about your son, Mr. Trevor."

"My son? You know him?"

She smiled, but it was a smile of contempt. "Don't worry, Mr. Trevor. He hasn't soiled himself on the likes of me."

"I didn't mean —"

"Of course you did. But there's no time for that now. You need to know what your son's planning for tonight."

He tried to get a sense of the girl, of what might motivate her to walk up to him and say something like this. Maybe this was a joke of some kind. Maybe Bob had treated her badly one night at Ione's. He had no illusions about how Bob got when he was drinking. He wasn't pleasant to be around.

"I don't know what the hell you're talking about, young lady," he said, retreating into his angry-patriarch tone, a tone that few ever challenged.

But the Indian girl wasn't impressed.

"You don't know what I'm talking about, but I do," she said. "And I suggest you listen to me, Mr. Trevor. I suggest you listen to me real good."

Part 3

Chapter One

Cass always felt comfortable in the small Catholic church, even though she wasn't a Catholic and, in fact, found certain precepts of the faith impossible to accept, notably papal infallibility.

But she liked the solitude and shadows of the church in the late morning, the scent of incense lingering from the morning mass, the votive candles flickering their beautiful jet blues and Christmas reds and forest greens and golden yellows.

She'd first visited this church when she was a little girl, with a school friend of hers. Her parents, while tolerant of Catholicism, were strong Protestants and didn't like the idea of their daughter being under the sway of papists. But for her the experience was good, and so she returned again and again, whenever she felt the need to think about her problems in peace and quiet.

An old Mexican woman knelt at the communion rail, whispering the rosary so loudly that her words, echoing off the arched ceiling above the altar, hissed like snakes.

Cass was here today because of Bob.

She wondered how many times she'd

been here because of her brother. If it wasn't trouble with his ladies (two pregnancies that she knew about), then it was trouble with his temper (any number of smashed-up saloons), or trouble with his gambling (his father had "loaned" him thousands to pay back his losses).

And always, always Cass the Protestant came to the Catholic church to kneel in the exquisite solitude and pray.

She knew that her father, at his age, couldn't take many more disappointments with Bob.

She'd felt bad for her father this morning, his frail hope that last night's scene with Jimmy would change Bob forever.

She'd been caught up in her father's desperate optimism. She hadn't defended Bob in a long time, yet this morning she'd chastised both herself and her father for having so little faith in Bob.

But now that the spell of this morning's optimism had worn off, Cass was back to worrying that Bob might do something that would utterly crush their father.

She bowed her head and prayed.

She knew that a perfect prayer could happen only when one had pushed from the mind all other considerations and distractions but the prayer itself. But that was almost impossible to do. So she, an imperfect person, prayed an imperfect prayer for her imperfect brother.

And just as the prayer was ending, and utterly without warning, she thought of Ray Coyle.

The prayer finished, she sat in the booth and stared at the altar. Ray would probably like it here. He seemed troubled, and yet oddly serene, too, as if he was not afraid to look inside himself and learn what he was really all about. In school, the teacher had quoted a philosopher who said, "The unexamined life is not worth living." She thought about that quote frequently. Ray's would be an examined life. Much like her own.

The Mexican woman at the altar stood up, kissed her rosary, and then hurried out the side door, leaving Cass to her silence.

She shouldn't be so interested in Coyle. She knew that he didn't believe Bob's story, and that he would kill Bob if the opportunity presented itself. But she couldn't help feeling sorry for him — and being attracted to him.

She stayed fifteen minutes, then walked to the back, looking at each Station of the Cross on her way. It was the rituals, she decided, that was what she liked so much about the Catholic tradition. The rituals had a soothing effect on you. You could slip into the words, or the ceremony, and find immediate comfort.

St. Mallory's was on a downtown corner that gave her a look straight down Main Street.

A block down, a very long block, she thought she saw her father talking to a young woman. She had to smile to herself. Had her father finally found somebody to be interested in romantically?

Unlikely. No matter how often she urged him to find a woman and remarry, he always resisted her suggestions.

She started walking, enjoying the warm autumn day. Most of the people along the boardwalk recognized her with a nod, a smile, or a polite hello. The family stigma hadn't attached itself to her.

As she passed the various shops and stores, she got glimpses of dresses, saddles, shovels, stoves, candy canes, meats, shoes, and awnings.

She liked to idle along and look in shop windows.

The times she'd been to Denver and Kansas City, her father had had to practically drag her back to the hotel. He still liked to laugh about her window-shopping sprees.

When she looked for her father the next time, she saw him turn in the opposite direction and lead the young woman toward the Grower's Bank, where he kept a small office on the second floor.

Cass wondered who the woman was, and why she was with her father.

The sunlight was hot and dusty as Coyle came out of the post office. He'd wired his former wife about the death of their son and said that he'd soon be bringing the body to her. He felt sorry that this was the only way he had of informing her. But he felt he had to prepare her. He couldn't just show up at her door.

He was headed back to his room when he saw, across the street, Barbara talking to Ralph Trevor.

What the hell was that all about?

He'd just spotted them when they turned and started walking away from him.

Blackmail was the thought that filled his head.

Jimmy had told Barbara something, and now Barbara was using that information to get money from Ralph.

That was the only thing that made sense.

He walked out into the street and watched the duo as they made their way toward the east end of town, following the boardwalk, shooing away pesky children, yipping dogs, buzzing flies.

Just what the hell was going on, anyway?

"I don't know, either."

The voice was warm, familiar.

When he turned around, Cass was there, comely and friendly as always.

"You don't know what?"

"What my father's doing with that girl."

"How did you know I was looking at them?"

She laughed. "You mean, other than the fact that you've been staring at them for at least four minutes?"

"That obvious, huh?"

"That obvious."

"I know who she is."

"Oh?"

"A prostitute named Barbara."

"A prostitute?"

"You sound shocked."

"Well, I just couldn't even imagine my father —"

He was amused by her sense of propriety. Why her very own father —

"I'd say there's something else going on there."

"Oh?" she said. "Like what?"

"Jimmy Clinton was her boyfriend."

"Oh," she said. "I see." She sounded as if she understood his implication, but then she said, "So if she's not conducting her business . . ."

"Something to do with Jimmy Clinton," Coyle said. "Something she knows that your father doesn't. Not yet, anyway. She may be blackmailing him."

"Blackmailing him? Are you serious?"

"Think about it," he said. "She's Jimmy Clinton's girlfriend. Maybe she's threatened to go to the law because she knows something about your brother Bob."

Then, finally, she did see what he was getting at.

"You think she knows how your son was *really* killed. Is that it?"

"Something like that."

"But instead of going to the law, she goes to my father. And he pays her money to be quiet."

"I'm only saying that that's a possibility."

Her cheeks burned suddenly. "You're not going to give up, are you?"

"I didn't mean to make you mad."

"Well, you may not have meant to, Mr. Coyle. But you certainly succeeded anyway."

She started to walk past him but then stopped abruptly, glared up at him, and said, "My brother isn't an angel. But your son wasn't either. And there's a very good chance that your son got exactly what was coming to him."

And with that, she pushed on past him.

Chapter Two

Sheriff Graham was at his desk doing paper-work on the budget for the next town council meeting (these days, a lawman was expected to be peacemaker, gunslinger, and accountant) when his deputy, Voss, came to the door and knocked.

"You want to see a sight, Sheriff?" Voss said.

"What kind of sight?" Graham said, irritated that he'd been interrupted. He just wanted to get the damned budget over with. They'd cut it by twenty-five percent, as they usually did, and thinking about that irritated him, too.

"Ralph Trevor walking down the board-walk with a whore."

"Ralph Trevor? You must be seein' things, Voss."

"Come have a look-see for yourself, Sheriff."

Graham hated coyness, especially in men. And Voss was very good at coyness. Graham put his pen down, stood up, shoved his hands against the small of his back, stretched, considered farting and then decided he didn't need to, and proceeded to follow Voss to the front window for a "look-see," as Voss liked to call it.

And was instantly amazed.

"Now, what the hell is that all about, I wonder?" Graham said, gawking out the window.

"See. I tole ya."

"What the hell's he doin' with Barbara?"

Voss had a big, country-boy grin for Graham. "What he's doin' with her? What the hell you *think* he's doin' with her, Sheriff?"

Graham shook his head. "Not Ralph Trevor. Huh-uh. Not with any whore."

"You seen it with your very own eyes, Sheriff."

"That doesn't mean what you think it means."

The shit-eating grin was back on Voss's leering face. "It don't? Then what *does* it mean, Sheriff?"

Graham didn't have a good answer for that one. In fact, he didn't even have a bad answer for it.

Just what the hell *was* Ralph doing walking down the street with a known prostitute like Barbara Thomas?

The question weighed on his mind so much, he wasn't able to do his budget math very well. Once he added 20 and 30 so it came out 60, and once he took away 10 from 40 and came up with 20.

Damn Voss, anyway.

Why'd he have to go and tell him about Ralph Trevor, anyway?

When there was something this fascinating to speculate about, making out a budget *really* got to be a pain in the ass.

Twenty plus 40 — 60. At least he got this one right.

Then he got back to his budget and temporarily put the subject of Ralph Trevor and whores out of his mind.

When Bob Trevor got back to the ranch, he went looking for his father and sister. Today, he had to be around them a lot, so they'd see him nice and normal. So tonight they wouldn't suspect that he'd helped set the whole robbery up.

But father and sister had gone to town. Bob was restless. He almost went down to the corral to watch them break broncs, but then thought better of it. Shorty, who was the best hand with animals, always had work for Bob to do. It was clear that Shorty relished giving orders to the boss's son. Well, this was one order he just wouldn't be able to give, 'cuz Bob wasn't going to give the little sawed-off sonofabitch the opportunity.

He wandered through the house, wanting a drink badly but knowing that today of all days he needed to be absolutely sober.

Then he wandered into his father's office and stood staring down at the bulky black shape of the safe. After all these years, Harry Winston was finally going to get what was coming to him. Harry had always felt superior to Bob. Whether it was with fast women or fast horses, fistfighting, cardplaying, or even footracing, Harry had always managed to win somehow. He'd never been stupid enough to taunt Bob outright. Bob would've dropped him as a friend if he had, and in this valley, who *didn't* want to hang out with Bob Trevor? But you could see the superiority in Harry's eyes, and in his smile, and in the slightly patronizing tone of his voice whenever he explained something to Bob.

Well, tonight was going to be different.

There wouldn't be any superiority in Harry's eyes tonight.

No, sir.

He crouched, wheeled rightward, dug out his gun from his holster, all in just a matter of moments.

"Caught you, Harry," he said aloud in the silence of his father's room. "Now, put down that gun before I kill ya."

But, of course, he was going to kill Harry anyway.

He probably should do it while Harry was still crouched over the safe digging the money out. But he wanted to see Harry's face when he realized that dumb ole Bob was actually smart ole Bob. And that smart ole Bob was pulling a surprise on him. A real big surprise.

Then there was silence again, the echoes of his words still in his ears. He felt embarrassed now by his little fantasy of surprising Harry. That was the only way he'd ever achieved anything in his life — by dreaming about it.

Then he realized he was staring at his father's chair. When he was nine or ten, he'd snuck into his father's office to look around. Don could go in the office, and that was just fine with Dad, but not Bob. A year earlier, Bob had snuck into the office and accidentally knocked a very precious Swiss clock off the fireplace mantel. The clock had broken into a hundred pieces. Usually, his father spanked him with just his hand. For this, he used the hickory switch. Ten times. Both Don and Cass, feeling sorry for their little brother, had tried to stop him, but Dad was insistent. Then, a year later — well, he'd not only snuck back into his father's office, he'd had the gall, the arrogance to sit in his father's chair. And that's just how his father had caught him, too, siting behind the desk, playing lord and master of the entire Trevor ranch. No hickory switch this time. His father had merely walked over to him and slapped him across the face. The hickory switch might have hurt Bob more physically, but somehow the simple slap hurt more emotionally. Dad had slapped him the way he would slap a woman. A punch would have been preferable, the kind of punch you use with a man.

Now, all these years later, he did it again, went over and sat in his father's chair.

It was a tall, cordovan-leather chair with fancy polished-gold buttons along the stitch lines.

He tried to imagine this being his own chair someday. Maybe it would happen, after all. Maybe his father would finally see him as worthy. Harry would be dead. There'd be no chance of blackmailing Bob anymore about Don's drowning. Maybe things would finally come around Bob's way.

He sat there for nearly half an hour, boy-man, man-boy, and felt a real optimism for the first time in his life. He would finally please his father, finally be accepted into the inner circles of the family. Finally.

Chapter Three

Ralph Trevor had one of those faces you couldn't read. He listened attentively, but Barbara could see no hint of what he was feeling. The blue eyes remained stony, the full mouth tight.

His town office was one big room with file cabinets, bookcases, a small desk, and two straight-back chairs. Ralph smoked a pipe. The smell of the tobacco reminded her of her favorite uncle on the reservation. He'd liked a pipe, too.

She didn't try to be dramatic. Ralph Trevor didn't look like the kind of man who'd appreciate theatrics. And, besides, what she had to say was plenty dramatic enough.

"And this is going to happen tonight?" Ralph said when she was finished. She couldn't read the tone of his voice, either. Flat. Without any hint of what was going on inside him.

"Yes."

"And you know this for sure?"

"Yes."

"May I ask who you heard this from, about robbing my safe tonight?"

"Them."

"Bob and Winston?"

"Yes."

"They told you this, then?"

"No, sir. I overheard it."

He stared at her. For the first time, a shadow of feeling could be seen deep in his eyes. He looked angry. "You overheard it?"

"Yes, sir."

"How did you come to overhear it?"

"I guess I don't understand your question, Mr. Trevor." Her voice had begun to tremble.

"You said you 'overheard' it. Were you in the same room with them?"

"No, sir."

"I see." He glared at her. "You were spying on them?"

Her cheeks felt touched by fire. "I suppose you could say that, sir."

"And just *why* were you spying on them?"

"Because they killed Jimmy."

His mouth stretched downward in a frown. "Harry Winston killed Jimmy; my son didn't. And Harry killed Jimmy because Jimmy was about to kill Bob."

"That may've been the way it looked to you, sir."

"Oh?"

Her cheeks were still hot, her voice still shaky. Talking to Ralph Trevor was like talking to God. "Bob was afraid Jimmy would tell somebody."

"Tell somebody what?"

"You know. About the gunfight."

"What *about* the gunfight?"

"You know. How Jimmy threw the rock and all."

"Jimmy threw a rock?"

"Yes, sir. Jimmy and Bob, they had it all planned out and everything. Just when this Coyle fella was going to draw his gun —"

"— Jimmy threw a rock and hit him in the head and distracted him."

"Yes, sir."

"I see." He leaned back, his elbows on the arms of his office chair, his fingers steepled. "Now I know why you came here."

"Sir?"

"You want me to take care of them for you, of Bob and Harry, I mean."

"No, sir, I just told you all this because I thought you should know."

He smiled coldly. "And you wouldn't take any pleasure in seeing me take care of them?"

"Well."

He turned slightly in his chair, the leather creaking, and looked out the window at where a chicken hawk was diving down the air currents.

So peaceful out there on the open land, under the blue, blue prairie sky. All the problems he had, they were indoor problems. Human problems. Left alone with the land and the lesser animals, a man could be happy and know real peace of mind. But human beings, most of them anyway, they just broke your heart if you gave them even half a chance.

He eased his chair back so that he was once again in line with her. "Have you told anybody else about this?"

"No, sir."

"Don't. I want to handle this personally."

"Yes, sir." Then: "In fact, I'm all packed."

"Packed?"

"Two carpetbags full of clothes. I'm headed for Kansas City. I've been in this town too long."

He reached into one of the drawers, took out a small vivid stack of greenbacks.

He counted off four bills and pushed them over to her. "You'll need money."

"I didn't come here for money, sir."

"I know you didn't. And that's why I'm giving you some."

"Sir?"

"Never mind. Just take the money."

"Yes, sir."

"What time does your train leave?"

"Six o'clock."

He leaned forward, the leather chair making noise as he did so. "You going to stay a whore?"

"I'll probably have to."

"That's nonsense. You can make something of yourself better than a whore."

"I'm not educated."

"You're pretty and clever and reasonably well-spoken. There's no reason to stay a whore."

"That's how white men look at Indian girls. Like whores."

"That's an excuse, and you know it. I don't look at Indian girls that way, and neither do most of my friends."

"Yes, sir."

"If you're a whore, it's because you *want* to be a whore."

"Yes, sir."

She realized then that he had tears in his eyes. He said, "It's like my son. He *chose* to do what he's done. Nobody made him."

"Yes, sir."

He was starting to get a little frightening. He was a powerful man physically, and she sensed that he was starting to come undone, might explode suddenly and start smashing things. Physical violence, for all that she'd seen of it, which was a considerable amount given her days on the reservation, terrified her. She didn't want to see this big, sad man start acting crazy. He just might include her in his craziness.

Then he surprised her by turning completely around in his chair so that he was facing the center window behind him.

She couldn't see him at all.

She said, "I'll be going now, sir."

He said nothing.

"Sir?"

Nothing.

She stood up. "I'm sorry I made you sad, sir, about Bob, I mean."

He said, his voice muffled by tears, "I've been sad about my son for a long, long time before I met you."

"Yes, sir."

Then she was gone.

Cass was just coming into the ground-floor vestibule when she saw Barbara walking down the stairs.

As they passed each other, Cass looked closely at the Indian woman, who was not as attractive close up as she was from a distance. Still, there was a quality of sensuality to her features that Cass was sure men would find erotic.

Barbara kept her head down, walking quickly, making no eye contact at all with Cass.

When she reached the second floor, Cass looked downstairs in time to see the Indian woman disappearing into the sunlight.

She still wondered what the woman had been doing with her father.

She knocked once on the door marked TREVOR ENTERPRISES. A muffled voice said, "Come in."

Her father stood at the window, his back to her. One of his favorite pastimes was to look down on the street and see what all his hard work had wrought. God examining his garden.

But when he didn't turn around to greet her, she knew that something was wrong.

"Dad?"

"Yes." Still not turning around.

"Are you all right?"

"I need a minute."

Icy fear stabbed her chest. All sorts of wild dread filled her mind. Was her father suffering from some terminal ailment? Was the ranch going broke as so many big cattle spreads seemed to be doing in these economically inflationary times?

The Indian woman.

That was it.

Something the Indian woman had told him.

Cass closed the door quietly behind her and walked into his office.

She went over to the chair in front of the desk and sat down.

"You'd probably feel better, Dad, if you talked about it."

He didn't respond immediately. Then he said, "I'm not even sure I can tell you."

"Of course you can tell me. I'm not only your daughter, I'm your best friend."

He sighed, and she noticed the old-man way his shoulders suddenly slumped. Whatever the Indian woman had told him, it was enough to decimate him.

"I saw the woman leaving your office."

He didn't say anything.

"This has to do with her, doesn't it?"

He still didn't say anything.

She stood up and walked over to him and slid her arm around his waist and put the tip of her chin on his shoulder.

"You're a very handsome man, do you know that?"

He smiled sadly. "You may be just a bit prejudiced."

"Mom always said you were the handsomest man in the valley, and she was right."

"Right now," he said quietly, "I'm glad she died."

"Father!"

His words shocked and hurt her, and she pulled back from him.

"I don't mean that disrespectfully," he said. "I'm just glad she didn't have to be here to hear all this."

"Hear all what?" Cass said, impatience sounding in her voice for the first time. "Let's sit down and talk about this. Okay?"

She led him to his chair. He was like a dazed man. His eyes didn't quite focus. His words were dull, lifeless.

He sat down, then she went around and sat on the other side of the desk. "What did the Indian woman tell you?"

"Maybe she's lying."

"Tell me, Father," she said, afraid that he was never going to come to the point.

"She hates Bob because of what happened to Jimmy Clinton last night."

"Hates Bob? My God, Jimmy tried to kill him. And anyway, it wasn't Bob who killed him, it was Harry Winston."

Focus returned to his eyes. She almost wished it hadn't. He looked sadder than she'd ever seen him since the time when her mother died.

"I'm afraid your Mr. Coyle is right," he

said quietly. "Jimmy Clinton threw a rock and hit young Coyle in the forehead right at the time he started to draw. It's an old gunfighter's trick. They lose attention, and that gives the other man a chance to get a clear shot."

"My God."

He shook his head. "I keep trying to convince myself that she's lying, that she's just saying it as a way of getting back at Bob. But I always wondered . . ." He paused and looked down at the hands that were splayed flat on the desk. "Bob's never been much of a marksman. I guess there was always a bit of doubt in the back of my mind. About his fight with Mike Coyle, I mean."

"Poor Coyle. I was just pretty mean to him down on the street."

Her father looked up at her. "So you believe it, too? About the gunfight?"

She did not want to say the word, but what choice did she have? Softly, she said, "Yes."

"My own son," he said. "My own son." Then: "But that's not all."

He leaned down, opened a drawer, and brought back up a whiskey bottle and two small glasses. He smiled sadly. "I keep this on hand to relax. But I think I need a shot now. And you're going to need one, too."

He poured a finger into each glass. She reached over and took hers. She wasn't much of a drinker and, in fact, couldn't ever remember her father offering her any alcohol before.

She sipped at it, made a face.

He smiled sadly again. "You don't have to drink that if you don't want it, hon."

She fanned her mouth. "It burns."

"Just leave it, sweetheart. I'll finish it for you." He sat back in his chair and stared up at the ceiling for a moment. He took a sip of whiskey and then looked over at her. "She says that Bob and Harry are going to break into my safe tonight."

"My Lord."

"It may not be true. Remember, right now she'd do anything to hurt this family. I guess I believe the gunfight story. But breaking into my safe —"

"I just can't believe he'd do it. You two don't have a very good relationship, but he loves you. I know he does. And I just don't think he'd ever hurt you that way."

"The safe has got a lot of money in it, the night before payroll and all. And he knows that."

"That doesn't mean anything."

"He also knows that you and I are going over to Nick Grove's for that party tonight."

"That doesn't mean anything, either."

He sipped some more whiskey. "I've thought about it, Cass. I need to know if she's telling me the truth."

"How'll you find out?"

"Tonight, you and I'll leave when we're supposed to. We'll ride away from the ranch and then double back on foot. We can hide in one of the outbuildings and see what goes on."

"I just can't believe he'd do that."

"I hope you're right, Cass, because if he ever did try to get into that safe . . ."

Once again, he was overtaken not by anger but by sadness. She wished he would get angry. It would be easier for her to watch than this. He seemed almost disabled now, unable physically or spiritually to rally himself. Old. He seemed old; vastly old; unimaginably old; heartbreakingly old.

"You'll go along with me tonight?" he said.

"Yes. I'll be there, Father."

"Maybe it isn't true."

She knew what he wanted her to say and she was eager to say it — because she didn't want to believe it, either. "I'm sure she's lying, Father. It's like you said, she just wants to hurt this family. That's all."

But she knew the grim truth. She tried to

hide the spasm of anxiety that passed through her upper body. But her father saw it and looked quickly away. Then his own right hand began twitching, twitching.

Chapter Four

When she saw Coyle standing on the porch of her hotel, Barbara turned quickly around and started walking back down the street.

Coyle caught up with her easily enough, took her elbow firmly in his hand, and steered her back toward his hotel.

"Let me go," she said.

"I want to talk to you."

"I don't give a damn what you want. I want you to let me go!"

She tried to jerk away from him, but he held her elbow firmly.

"I'll buy you coffee."

"I don't want coffee."

He was just tugging her into the diner when he saw Sheriff Graham walking toward them. At first, Graham seemed to be just walking along, not paying much attention to where he was going, a little preoccupied perhaps.

But when he saw Barbara struggling to get free of Coyle, the lawman in him took over.

He walked faster, he squared his shoulders, his right hand dropped to the general vicinity of his Colt.

"Afternoon, folks," he said, amiably enough.

"Tell him to let me go!" Barbara said.

"Are you holding the lady against her will, Mr. Coyle?"

"She seems to think so," Coyle said. "All I want her to do is to tell me what Jimmy Clinton said about the gunfight."

Graham remained the amiable lawman, low-key and just slightly amused. "You may want to talk to her, Mr. Coyle, but it sure doesn't look like she wants to talk to you."

He nodded to Coyle's grip on Barbara's elbow.

"Now, I don't know what the law is where you come from, Mr. Coyle, but around here we tend to frown on men who hold ladies against their will."

"I wasn't hurting her," Coyle said defensively. All of a sudden, he was embarrassed. For all his amiability, Graham was implying that Coyle was the lowest kind of man, the kind who preyed on women.

"Maybe not," Graham said, "but we still don't like it when men hold women back from going where they want to."

Coyle let go of her elbow.

Barbara smirked at him. "Thank you, Sheriff."

"Just doing my duty, ma'am."

She smirked again at Coyle, then walked away.

"You may make yourself some enemies before you leave our pleasant little valley, Mr. Coyle. Do you *like* making enemies?"

"I just want the truth."

"And you think she knows it?"

"Jimmy Clinton was a drunk. Drunks talk. I'm sure he told her the truth about the gunfight."

Graham frowned. "You know, there's something I like about you, Coyle. If there wasn't, I would've kicked your ass out of here soon as I spotted you. Maybe it's because I feel sorry for you. Because of your boy dying and all. But you know what? You're just causing trouble for both of us. And even if you do find out the truth — even if you can prove that it was a rigged fight — it's just like I said to you before: You can't bring him back. No matter what you do, Mr. Coyle, he's still gonna be dead and you're still gonna be just as sad about it as you are now."

"Hey, Sheriff!" a sunburned boy said, running toward Graham and Coyle. "One of the horses got loose over at the livery and they can't get a rope around him! He already kicked Mr. Simpson pretty bad!"

"You see, Mr. Coyle," Graham said, "according to dime novels, all a lawman does is have shoot-outs with villains. But what we really do is stuff like this." He nodded good-bye and then chased off after the boy. "Hold on, Leonard, I'm coming!"

When Coyle started looking around for Barbara, she was gone.

He was a boy again, Harry Winston was, at least for a minute there when he stepped inside the general store and saw the glass case that held all the candy. He was a boy again, and chewing on licorice; a boy again, and tossing a honey popcorn ball up in the air the way he would a baseball; a boy again, making his teeth tingle and smart by biting down the wrong way on a piece of peanut brittle.

A boy again.

Sometimes he wished he was a boy still. He'd do a lot of things different, Harry would, if he was starting over. But maybe there was still time. After tonight, he'd have money to go anywhere he wanted.

He walked up to the stout woman behind the counter and said, "How about a twist of that black licorice?"

"You tried root beer licorice yet?"

He laughed. "That the hot new flavor, is it?"

"The kids love it."

"Tell you what. Why don't you give me one licorice and one root beer?"

"Be glad to."

While the woman got the candy ready for him, Harry looked around the store. He wanted to get the little girl something, but he wasn't sure what.

"Here you go."

Harry walked back to the glass case, remembering a time when he'd been too short to reach over it. He'd had a bitter childhood, actually, but memory had softened the worst of it. In prison, trying to escape the gray and confining reality of his cell, Harry had sentimentalized his childhood, turned it into a sunlight-dappled dreamland where he had fished and hunted and smiled at pretty little girls in bonnets. No drunken, belt-wielding old man; no drunken, sobbing mother. A perfect childhood, at least in his mind.

"I want to buy a gift for a little girl," Harry said.

"You see the dolls over there?"

"Guess I didn't."

She handed him the candy, he paid for it, and then she said, "Let's go look at the dolls."

She led him through the store, through

the smells of spices and strong washing soap and cider and cotton.

A small table was covered with a dozen different dolls as well as tin soldiers and wooden spinning tops. The one she picked up was a rag doll, a sweet little girl with big blue eyes and raggedy red hair. The doll managed to be impish and melancholy at the same time.

"Got a niece who loves it," the woman said.

"The other ones look fancier. The porcelain ones."

"They look fancier," she said, nodding to them, "but they also break real fast."

"Oh."

"This one takes a lot more wear and tear," she said, handing it to him.

"You do a good sales job," he said with a smile.

"Just try to be helpful."

He looked at the rag doll a final time. He could see it in the arms of the little girl. She'd pretend the doll was her sister or her friend or her cousin and they'd spend a lot of time playing together. That was the kind of life he wanted for her, a good and gentle one, the kind all kids should have.

When he handed back the doll, he noticed she was looking at him carefully. "You're the one killed Jimmy Clinton last night."

"I'm the one."

"Harry Winston."

"Harry Winston," he said.

"I knew your pa."

"Oh."

"And your ma."

"Oh."

He expected a scowl, some kind of disapproval of the kind of people they'd been.

"Lot of folks didn't care for them," she said. "Personally, I didn't think they was as bad as a lot of people said."

He laughed. "I guess that's a compliment."

"They liked moonshine," the woman said. "That ain't the worst thing in the world."

She carried the doll back to the counter and started wrapping it.

"You got a bow you could put on the wrapping?"

"Cost you an extra penny."

"Fine."

"I could give you a ribbon, too."

"Good."

"That's an extra penny, too."

"Fine."

"You want blue or green?"

He thought of Ellen's hazel eyes. In some

light, her eyes were green. Maybe the little girl's were, too.

"Green, I guess."

A few minutes later, Harry walked from the general store and started his walk toward Third Street, where Ellen lived.

Every half block or so, somebody would recognize him. Last night had made him notorious. For all the yellowback images of violent frontier towns, most of them were peaceful. Violence was a seldom thing, and when it happened it was talked about and remembered for a long time.

He was a block from Ellen's when he saw Deputy Voss across the street watching him.

Voss turned toward him suddenly, cutting across the street, weaving in between wagons and the horse-drawn trolley.

Voss's tan uniform and campaign hat showed sweat and dirt. He was a big, shaggy, unkempt man who reminded Harry of some of the prison guards. They were dumb but cunning. And sometimes cunning was worth a lot more than being smart was.

Voss said, "Hold it."

Up close, he smelled of heat, tobacco, and piss. "What's that?"

"A present."

"What kind of present?"

"For a little girl."

"Whose little girl?"

"I don't see where that's your business."

Voss snatched the doll away without warning.

Harry was back in prison again. Anything you held dear, the guards seemed to sense. And they had to ruin it for you, break it or burn it or take it for their own.

Harry could see Voss's big, dirty handprints all over the pristine white wrapping paper.

Funny, what a man would kill for. You took one of Harry's women from him, he might slap you around but he wouldn't kill you. Same with his money. But this wrapping paper . . .

Harry felt a terrible fury rise in him, one he wasn't sure he could control.

He wouldn't shoot Voss, he'd beat him to death, which was a more satisfying way than a bullet when you really hated a man.

Voss ripped off the top of the paper.

"You play with dolls, do you?"

Harry didn't say anything.

"That what you did in prison all those years? Play with dolls?"

Voss wanted him to react. And then Voss would break him.

Two ladies and their parasols came strolling by, and this obviously was an ideal time for Voss to play hard-ass.

He pitched the doll onto the grass and then said, "All right, jailbird, hands up in the air."

He said this fine and loud and proud, so the strolling-by ladies would be sure to hear. Deputy Voss was living out a yellowback in his mind.

He patted Harry from shoulder to shoe, clearly disappointed that he didn't find any guns.

Now that the women were gone, Voss didn't need to talk so loud.

"Jimmy Clinton was a friend of mine."

"Yeah?" Harry said. "That's too bad."

"You didn't give him no chance."

"He didn't give Bob Trevor a chance, either."

"Bob Trevor?" Voss said. "Everybody in town knows he was with you the day you held up that stage. Man finked out on me that way, I sure as hell wouldn't save his life, I'll tell you that. Sonofabitch cuts out on you and you save his life. Don't make much sense to me."

But most of Harry's attention was on the doll that had been tossed so carelessly to the ground.

From what he could see from here, the doll itself didn't look damaged. He remembered what the woman in the general store had said about how durable they were. He was glad now he hadn't gotten a porcelain one.

Voss saw where he was looking and then grinned. "Hey, I almost forgot your little gift there."

"Leave it alone."

Voss obviously noted the harsh sound of command in Harry's voice.

"I just musn'ta heard you right, jailbird. You tryin to give me orders?"

"I told you to leave it alone."

The thought of Voss touching it again, soiling it with his sweaty filth, was becoming impossible for Harry to handle.

He was afraid he was going to do something very, very stupid.

Voss reached down and picked it up.

He smiled. "You don't like my hands on this, do ya, jailbird?"

He wiped his hands all over the torn wrapping.

"But what'd really piss you off is if I reached inside like this and pulled the doll out."

Which is just what he did, of course.

"My, my," he said. "You probably had

278

this in prison with ya all the time, didn't you, jailbird?"

Harry's hands became fists. Harry took a dangerous step closer to Voss.

"Hey, now, the jailbird can't control himself no longer, can he?"

Then Voss did it, spit right in Harry's face.

"Now, if that don't make you swing on me, jailbird, nothin' will."

The money. Had to concentrate on the money. He would get the money and he would escape from this town forever. Had to concentrate on that, otherwise he'd give Voss the satisfaction of smashing him in the face. And then Voss would have the satisfaction of locking him up again.

"Aw, c'mon, jailbird, guy spits in your face, you got to haul off and slug him, don't you think? At least once? No? You don't think so, jailbird? Then how about this?"

Voss held the doll up in front of Harry's face.

"You ready for this, jailbird?"

Harry just watched, the globule of spit sliding down his right cheek.

"Watch real close now, like them magician fellas say."

Voss's big hand covered the entire head of the doll. "One, two, three, I'm gonna make

279

it disappear. You ready, jailbird?"

He smiled, and then he did it, ripped the head off right at the shoulders.

"Aw, poor little thing, look what happened here, jailbird."

He tossed the head onto the grass. It looked grotesque, a symbol of a deeper and darker violence than Voss seemed aware of.

The money, Harry thought. The money. I do anything to this redneck pecker, and I'll never get my hands on that money.

"You sure got quiet all of a sudden, jailbird," Voss said. "You sure did."

Another pair of ladies came strolling up. Voss smiled at them, doffed his hat.

The ladies looked from him to Harry and then to the wrapping and the doll's head on the grass.

They hurried on by.

"I got to be gettin' back, jailbird," Voss said. "But you just remember that I'm always around. Even when you don't think I am. And someday, jailbird, I'm gonna nail your ass, and real good, too. You understand?"

And then, the final touch, he spit in Harry's face one more time.

Chapter Five

Twenty minutes after Barbara walked away from him, Coyle tried finding her again.

The first place he looked was her sleeping room. He knocked on the door several times but got no answer. Then he tried to pick the doorknob lock but had no luck.

The walk to Ione's whorehouse took a while, but it was pleasant walking in the Indian summer afternoon.

He passed a graveyard, then stopped. He went inside the black wrought-iron fencing and looked at the headstones. The dead children made him sad. He could imagine the grief these deaths had caused the parents.

He wondered what kind of headstone his ex-wife would get for Mike. She was a religious woman, so she would likely get him something with angels on it.

He stood looking down the graveyard hill. This was a pleasant place to be, quiet except for the sweet birdsong of jay and wren and robin, and empty except for the gray, tail-switching tomcat and the lost-looking basset hound.

Sometimes graveyards spooked him, but up here he felt a real solace. He hoped death would be like this, with the scent of sweet autumn on the air, and the winds down from the birches and oaks and hardwoods in the hills. But he knew better, or feared so, anyway. You see a wagon-crushed squirrel in the road . . . He was afraid a human life was no better, just a dead carcass and utter extinction.

After a time, muttering a prayer to anybody who'd listen that there was some kind of existence after death, and that his worst fears were false, he left the graveyard and continued his steady, dusty walk to the whorehouse.

Not much doing here this time of day.

A whorehouse might get an occasional passing-through cowboy on a day like this, but not many. Going to a whorehouse was fine, but not during the day. By day, it spoke of laziness and self-indulgence and wasn't at all manly.

A black woman opened the door. She carried a broom and wore a vast white apron across her wide hips.

"Yes?"

"I'm looking for Barbara."

"You don't want to talk to me, mister."

"Oh? Who do I want to talk to, then?"

"Miz Ione, she say no menfolks upstairs lessen she's here."

"And she isn't here?"

"Nope, she sure ain't."

"She go to town?"

"Yep, took the good buggy and everything."

"When you think she'll be back?"

The woman wiped sweat from her brow with her sleeve.

"Hour, somethin' like that."

"Then I think I'll just wait here on the porch."

"Could be longer, mister."

"That's all right. It's a nice day for just sitting down and watching things."

"Up to you."

"Thanks."

He did just what he said, parked himself on the top step of the whorehouse porch, leaned back against the pillar, and rolled himself a cigarette.

Then he wondered idly if Mike had ever come to whorehouses like this. He'd known so little about his son when you came right down to it.

So damned little.

Bob Trevor needed to walk off his case of nerves. Could he actually go through with it tonight? What if something went wrong, and his father thought he was trying to steal the money from the safe, not save it?

He walked past the corral, past the bunk-house, and up along the narrow, winding trail that led through timberland and came out near the foothills.

It felt good to sweat in the hot afternoon. He wanted to sweat away last night's liquor and this afternoon's fears.

No, it would go smoothly. For once in his life, he was going to do things right. He was sure of it.

As a boy, he'd always enjoyed playing in the woods. He'd felt hidden here, safe from the disapproving eyes of his family and the ranch hands. In the woods, he imagined himself to be Robin Hood, that being the only storybook he'd ever read all the way through. This was Sherwood Forest, not a mere woods on his father's ranch, this was Sherwood Forest, and it was here that he hid from the evil sheriff, and it was here that he wore his breeches and carried his sword and his bow and arrow.

Now, as he made his way through the woods, the earth smelling of pine and loam and mint leaves, sunbeams fracturing on the canopy of leaves above, squirrels and chip-munks and raccoons and possums taking note of his passage, he was embarrassed by these memories. Making up stories was something a girl did. Not a man — not a serious man, anyway. He should have been stronger when he was a boy. He should have been like his brother Don.

Just as he was thinking this, he emerged from the woods and stood on the small hill that overlooked the swimming hole.

The air seemed to echo with the silver laughter of children splashing and playing in the swimming hole. He could see Mary Kay Kenyon, a girl he'd had a crush on for so long, bobbing in the water and waving to him. He could see the white corpulent body of Tubby Riley as he was about to do one of his fancy tumbles into the swimming hole, water splashing everywhere when his body hit the surface. And he could feel how the water had cooled his summer-hot body in those long-ago days, and how going under for the first time had stung his eyes, and how the palms of his hands and the bottoms of his feet had shriveled up when he stayed in for a long time.

But then these sunny memories gave way to a darker one. His brother Don screaming for help as Bob and Harry continued to drown him. Don had fought all the way, and fought with every weapon at his defense, fist, fingernails, teeth. Both Harry and Bob had been pretty well bruised up by the time it was over with. And then the silence. That was what Bob remembered even more than the screaming. The silence afterward, he and Harry bobbing in the water, looking at each other, and then staring down at the suddenly still surface of the water, Don's body a pale shape deep down as it floated dead below. The silence. Sound had seemed to come back to him one creature at a time: a hum of dragonfly, a cry of owl, a yip and yap of dog, and then Harry's breath, coming in sharp gasps, Harry still worn out from his part in drowning Don.

He stared down at the water now. So much time had passed since Don's death, and yet it was as if no time had passed at all. You would think that in the ensuing years, he would have grown up. But somehow he hadn't. Cass had become a woman but he hadn't become a man, and that was his shame. He was still a boy, and he could see this in the amused glances of the ranch hands, and in the quick smirks of the towns-people. Still a boy.

Killing Don had seemed so sensible a thing to do. The ranch would fall to him, and Harry would be his foreman, and he would ask Mary Kay Kenyon to marry him, and somehow in the process of all this, he would grow up, and everything would be fine. Just fine.

But instead of a full life of hard work running the ranch, instead of that there had been too much liquor, too many whores, too many brawls where Harry and Jimmy had had to save his ass. And then the gunfight. God, he could still remember how scared he'd been when they'd followed Mike Coyle out to the alley, Coyle not knowing they were coming after him. "I'll take care of it," Jimmy had whispered. "You just draw down on him." So Jimmy had taken care of it, as usual, but Bob had been scared as hell. Back in the saloon, he'd had whiskey dreams of getting himself a gunfighter rep. The old man might be impressed with that. But when he saw Mike Coyle lying there dead in the moonlit alley, he realized that this was how he'd end up, too, if he ever got a rep as a gunny. Then he just wanted to forget about the gunfight, have Doc pack up the body and get it the hell out of town, and forget that the whole thing had ever happened.

Remembered laughter again. Mary Kay Kenyon, and how he'd ached to kiss her in reality as he'd kissed her so many times in his dreams, and then her up and leaving town with that soldier boy, moving away to Fort Collins, while all the prim and proper town ladies wondered and whispered if she was pregnant. Eight years Bob had loved her, and she'd never let him kiss her once. Not once.

He was tired then, depleted somehow, feeling ridiculously old. Being around the swimming hole wasn't good for him. He'd never come back here to swim even once, not after that day with Don. It hadn't bothered Harry any. He went swimming here right on up to the day when they took him off to prison.

Bob turned back to the ranch. Maybe he'd lie down when he got back, sort of rest up for everything that was ahead for tonight.

He began walking, slow, the drained feeling still inhibiting his energy.

He was glad for the forest, for the shadow, for the secrecy of this very private world.

He wanted to be Robin Hood again, not Bob Trevor. Robin Hood.

Chapter Six

The bastard was downstairs.

Every few minutes, Barbara would walk to the front of the house on the second floor and look down on the porch.

Ray Coyle sat on the stoop. The colored maid said that Coyle had asked for Barbara but that she'd told him Ione's strict rule about no visitors while Ione was out.

But that still hadn't gotten rid of Coyle.

Barbara paced up and down the hall. All she cared about was tonight, the robbery that would bring all the parties into direct conflict. That would be Jimmy's vengeance, the arrogant Trevor family coming undone.

She didn't give a damn about Coyle or his son. And speaking to Coyle, telling him anything about the gunfight, might get in the way of tonight's showdown. He'd go to the sheriff and the sheriff would start looking for Bob Trevor.

No, she had to keep Coyle out of it.

But what would she do if he paid Ione money to come upstairs and see her?

Ione was greedy. She'd take anybody's money, and she wouldn't give a damn about Barbara.

Barbara went back to the room she used here and sat on the bed. The air smelled of perfume and sachet and douche bag. The colored lady hadn't worked her way down to this end of the hall yet. Ione's door didn't officially open for another two hours yet. The colored lady had plenty of time.

Rolling herself a cigarette, Barbara decided to do what she'd been thinking about since Jimmy's death: get out of this town.

She'd set everything in motion. What was the point in waiting around?

There was a train to Kansas City in three hours. Everything valuable she owned would fit into a single carpetbag.

A knock.

"Miz Barbara?"

"Yes."

"I needs to do your room."

"That's fine. Come in."

Some of the girls didn't treat the colored lady well at all. But even though she had a lot of irritating habits, Barbara tried to treat her decently anyway.

"You can just sits on the bed, Miz Barbara. No need for you to move."

Barbara put her feet up on the bed so the woman could use the dust mop on the floor.

"He still down there?"

"Oh, yes, Miz Barbara, he's still down

there, all right. That's a man that ain't leavin' till he sees you, I can sure tells you that."

The decision to leave town sounded better all the time. Put all this behind her.

"You have the key to the back door?"

"Yes'm."

Ione locked the door so nobody could sneak in or out. If you wanted to go out the back way, you told Ione and she personally let you out. Valuable information it was, who didn't want to be seen leaving the whorehouse. It told you a lot about a person. When the proper ladies started demanding that all fancy girls be driven from town, Ione could just whisper a few words into the ears of her more prominent customers, and the proper ladies would be silenced. Until next year.

"In ten minutes, you come back up here," Barbara said, "and let me out, all right?"

"Yes, Miz Barbara."

"But don't tell anybody."

"No, Miz Barbara."

"And whatever you do, don't let that man on the porch in here."

"No, Miz Barbara."

As soon as she was alone, Barbara started pulling together the few personal things she kept in this room.

★ ★ ★

The store woman didn't have another rag doll, so Harry Winston had to settle for a porcelain one.

This time, on his way to Ellen's, he didn't see Deputy Voss, though a part of him wanted to. He could still feel the hot sting of spittle on his face. For all the indignities Harry had suffered in prison, nobody had ever spit on him before. He couldn't stop thinking about it, the utter humiliation of it, and the impotent way he'd felt just standing there, taking it. He would bear this bitter memory his entire life.

Only when he thought of the money did his mind shift into a happier mode.

The money. Only hours away now. The money. Total freedom for the first time in his life. Only hours away.

The little girl was jumping rope by herself in her front yard when Harry came along.

He stood for a time behind her so that he could watch her skip rope, her calico dress clean and girlish in the slanting autumn sunlight. She was very coordinated, graceful, her feet lifting from the grass at exactly the right moment, the rope clearing her feet with no difficulty. She sang some kind of singsong song he didn't understand. A beagle lay a few feet away, one eye open, watching her.

He walked up to her.

"You do a good job."

She kept on jumping.

"Thanks. But you better not be here, mister."

"Oh?"

"My dad said he'd call the law the next time you came around."

She kept eyeing the gaily wrapped gift in his hand. Much as she'd been taught to fear strangers, she was intrigued by the gift.

"Bet you can't guess what's in here," Harry said, holding the package up for her to see.

The girl was a little breathless now, but she kept on jumping.

And that was when Ellen came out of the front door and stalked down the walk.

"I warned you, Harry," she said angrily. "Now I'm going to go get the law."

"I just brought the girl something, is all."

"I don't want you to bring her anything," Ellen said, "not anything at all."

"Oh, Ma," the girl said, obviously aware that she might not get this gift after all.

"Just because he's your uncle," Ellen said, "don't mean he's got the right to just show up here anytime he wants."

Uncle. So that's how they'd explained him to the girl.

"Here," Harry said, handing Ellen the doll. "You give it to her, then."

Ellen snatched the doll roughly from Harry's hands and then told the girl to go inside.

"Oh, Ma."

"Git, now. And no back talk."

"But Ma."

"I'll see what he brought, and if I think it's somethin' you should have, I'll give it to you."

The girl knew better than to argue past this point. Ellen was small, but she was scrappy and she'd always had a formidable temper.

The girl looked at Harry a final time. "Thanks for bringing me that, mister."

"Uncle Harry," Harry smiled. "Didn't your ma tell you that was my name?"

"I guess so."

"Then call me Harry."

The girl looked at him a long moment, and for a time Harry wondered if she'd guessed who he really was. Though there was virtually no physical similarity between them, maybe blood had a way of telling blood, an almost mystical way.

But then the girl turned shyly away and hurried into the house.

"Good thing my man ain't here," Ellen said.

"Right now, it's a good thing he ain't," Harry said, thinking of Voss. "Right now, I'm not about to take any bullshit from anybody."

"Well, you're gonna take some from me, Harry. I told you I didn't ever want to see you around here again."

"I brought the girl a doll. I'm her father. I've got a right to."

"You ain't her father, Harry, not in the sense you mean, and you never have been. He's her father. You should see how he treats her, and all the time he spends with her. He's her father, you ain't."

The words hurt, and hurt a lot more than he'd have expected, hurt indeed even more than Voss's spittle had, but Ellen here had her own version of him as a cold and heartless man with no feelings, and so he didn't let her see his pain. He said simply, "Later on tonight, I'm going to drop somethin' off here and I need to know where's a good hidin' place."

"Just what the hell are you talkin' about, Harry? Is this another one of your damned schemes?"

"It'll be late tonight. Where can I put it?"

She studied him. "You're gonna git yourself in more trouble, ain't you?"

"That's my business."

"You'll go back to prison. Or they'll kill you."

"Like I said, Ellen, that's my business." Then: "I want to leave something for the girl, and I need to know where to hide it."

Ellen shook her head, but she turned around and pointed to a shed in the backyard. "The shed, I guess."

"In the morning, soon as you wake up, you go out to the shed and you'll find it."

"I don't want no trouble with the law."

"There won't be any. Not if you hide it away where your man can't find it."

"You gonna stick up somebody, huh?"

"Somethin' like that, yeah."

"And you're gonna leave some of it for her?"

He nodded.

"Guilt money," she said bitterly.

"Maybe."

"She don't want stolen money."

"She won't know it's stolen money. Not unless you tell her."

"I don't want it, and she don't either."

"You speak for her, huh?"

"Sure I do, Harry. I'm her mother."

"I want you to hold it for her till she's eighteen and then give it to her."

"He'll find it. I couldn't hide it that good."

"If he finds it, tell him it's none of his business."

"I love him, Harry. Of course it's his business. You never understood that, how married people are supposed to act. You think because he's true to his wife and patient with his daughter, he's less of a man. But he's more, Harry, not less. A good family man, that's the best kind of man there is." There were tears in her voice now, and they were not without their effect on Harry. "You're like an animal that never came up to the fire to warm himself, Harry. You've always stayed out there in the darkness, you and the other ones like you. You don't understand the first thing about how to treat a little girl, Harry." She looked down at the gift-wrapped doll. "I'll give her this, Harry. But the money — you keep it. I don't want no part of it, and neither does she."

Her eyes lingered a few moments longer on Harry, then she made a sad little face and bent down and picked up the girl's jump rope. "So long, Harry."

She walked back to her cottage and went quietly inside.

Chapter Seven

She made a mistake.

She eased out of the back door very well, but when she got to the ground, her toe stubbed against something and made a sound just loud enough to catch Coyle's attention.

As soon as the sound registered, he was up off the front stoop and moving around the side of the house.

He caught a glimpse of Barbara's cornflower-blue dress as the woman ducked down into a weedy ravine that ran parallel with the railroad tracks.

She looked over her shoulder, saw him, and then swiftly disappeared in the ravine.

He was running in the sunny day, the dusty scent of milkweed filling his nostrils, exciting his sinuses, and forcing a .38-caliber sneeze to discharge.

By now, she was scooting up the other side of the ravine.

He ran straight down into the gully, grabbed some weeds for purchase, and then began pulling himself up the other side.

Had to catch her. Had to.

But when he came up the other side and

stood on top of the ravine, she was gone. Vanished.

But where could she go so fast?

Where could she possibly hide?

He started walking along the railroad tracks toward town. The steel rails sparkled in the glinting late-afternoon sunlight.

Where the hell was she?

Far as his eye could see, first in one direction and then the other, she was nowhere to be found.

Maybe the madam taught her girls some stage magic as well as boudoir skills.

He continued his way toward town, feeling foolish that a young woman like that could outsmart him. Coyle didn't have a lot of pride, but he had some anyway.

In the far distance, the beautiful blue slopes of mountains ringed the valley. A part of Coyle just wanted to take off up there, find his son a good burial place where the jays and raccoons and possums could watch over his grave. And Coyle would find a place for himself in the mountains, a good and true and safe place, and live out his life washing up every morning in clean fast creeks, and looking up at the stars at night and feeling a part of something vast and unknowable and bedazzling.

But he owed the truth of Mike's death to

Mike's mother, and so he had to go on.

Then he saw her, up in the meadow, riding a horse bareback, slanting eastward with the wind, toward town.

Somehow, she'd managed to elude him long enough to find her way to the meadow. And then . . .

"Sonofabitch," Coyle said to no one in particular. "Sonofabitch."

He reached town twenty minutes later and went immediately to her room.

He didn't knock, he pounded.

People stuck their heads out of doors to see what the ruckus was.

"Who're you?" an old man with an ear horn said accusingly.

"Who're *you?*" Coyle shot back.

"She left," a plump woman said.

"When?"

"Couple minutes ago."

"She say where?"

"Well, she was carrying her carpetbag and it looked real full, so she's probably leavin' town. You know how them fancy girls are. They come and go."

But by then Coyle was already halfway down the stairs.

He went out back and found that she'd ground-tied the horse she'd taken into town. The mount was a sweet-faced old thing, and Coyle took the time to stroke her neck a couple of times. The old girl was probably confused about everything that had been going on.

Then he set off to find Barbara.

This late in the afternoon there weren't any trains for a while, so the depot was church-quiet. Except for the click and clack of the telegraph, in fact, there wasn't any noise at all.

Barbara walked through the strange silence of the place. She went straight to the ticket window and bought herself a ticket to Kansas City.

"Nice place," said the old duffer selling the tickets. He wore a green eyeshade and sleeve garters and probably considered himself to be a fashion plate.

But Barbara didn't care about his opinions. She just wanted the ticket.

"How long before the train leaves?"

"Hour and a half, I guess."

"I'll be back, then."

"I wouldn't go much longer than an hour, though. Just in case, I mean."

"Just in case of what?"

He shrugged skinny shoulders. "Some of these engineers get worried about bein' late down the line, so they leave a little early here."

"I'll be back in fifty minutes, then. How's that?"

"Fine by me, ma'am," he said. "Fine by me."

Asshole, she thought, and flounced back out to the street.

He checked the stage line first.

A sleepy kid with a cowlick told him that he hadn't seen anybody in there for half a day. "That gat-darned train gits all the bidness these days," he explained around a yawn.

So Coyle went to the depot.

All the passenger benches were empty, the ticket window unmanned.

He went outside, walked around the back, where he found a scrawny old guy with a green eyeshade and sleevegarters chopping up firewood. Despite the Indian-summer weather, he was laying in for winter.

You wouldn't think anybody his age could wield a long ax with such precision and force. Coyle, at least thirty years younger, doubted he could equal the old man's dexterity and strength.

The old man was also a juggler, juggling

his black railroad cap with the shiny bill on his head. The damned thing looked as if it was going to fall off every time the old man bent down to pick up another piece of wood. But somehow it stayed on.

"Excuse me."

The old man jerked to attention. Coyle could see that he'd scared him.

The old man didn't want Coyle to see his fear, so he covered it in a sudden fit of coughing. After he was sufficiently calmed down, he said, "Hep ya?"

"I'm looking for a woman."

The old man gave him an incredibly dirty wink. "We all are, son. We all are."

Coyle had to grin. He wouldn't be surprised if this old fart had a young woman stashed back at his place.

"An Indian."

"Oh," the old man said.

"Short, wearing a blue dress, carrying a carpetbag."

"How much it worth t' ya?"

"What the hell you talking about? I just asked you a question."

"You know how them railroad tycoons got to *be* tycoons? By screwin' little people like me."

"I just wanted to know —"

"So I got to supplement my income some

way, don't I, the pittance them sonsabitches pay me?"

Then he leaned forward and said, "One half dollar for one question."

"This is bullshit."

"One half dollar, take it or leave it, sonny."

Being called "son," he didn't mind. "Sonny" wasn't the same thing.

The old man picked up his ax again, eyed the woodpile for a new piece of wood, and then started to lean forward.

"All right," Coyle said.

"Figured you would eventually."

Coyle dug in his pocket and pulled out a half dollar.

The old man held his hand out, palm up.

Coyle slapped the half dollar into it.

"Now, where the hell is she?" Coyle said.

"I don't know."

"You just charged me a half dollar and you don't know?"

"I know where she's gonna be later, but I can't tell you exactly where she is at the moment."

"Where's she going to be later?"

"Another half hour, she's gonna be right back here."

"At the depot?"

"Yep."

"Catching a train?"

"Yep."

"Bound for where?"

"That's another question."

"What?"

"You didn't listen carefully, sonny. I said one half dollar for one question. I already answered one question. Now you're on to a second one. I'll need another half dollar."

Coyle started to do some serious pissing and moaning but saw that it was no use.

He dug out another half dollar and gave it to the old man.

"Now, where's she headed?"

"Kansas City."

"You're sure of that."

"That's what she told me. That's all I've got to go by, sonny."

Coyle looked around. He could start searching the saloons for her, but by the time he got through three or four of them, it'd be time to be back here.

"I'll just wait inside, I guess," Coyle said.

"Be my guest."

"Not going to cost me anything, is it?"

"No call for sarcasm, sonny," the old fart said and picked up another piece of wood and proceeded to cleave it in half.

Sonny, Coyle thought as he went back inside. Sonny.

You half-dollar sonofabitch.

Cass had never seen her father like this, and she was scared. He had driven the buggy all the way home, she sitting right beside him, in total and utter silence. A neighbor had come past on a horse. Cass had returned the man's wave. Ralph hadn't acknowledged the man in any way. Cass was sure he hadn't seen the rider, he was so lost in his thoughts. Now, as they approached the ranch, he didn't seem any more likely to speak.

The only other time she could liken this particular day to was when she'd told him that she was going to marry Lawrence K. Talbot. Her father had spent a long and bitter night giving her all the reasons she *shouldn't* marry Talbot, and then he'd fallen into a silence that had lasted a week. He let his work around the ranch go. He went for long and solitary rides. He spent an inordinate amount of time up on the hill at the gravestone talking to his wife.

And he spent a lot of time in his bedroom, sitting in the squeaking rocking chair, staring out the window.

He never spoke to her again about Talbot. He gave away his daughter at the wedding, as a father should do; he seemed genuinely thrilled with the prospect of becoming a grandfather when she announced she was pregnant; and he seemed equally sorrowful when she lost the child in miscarriage. He never once — not till long, long afterward, anyway — told her of the stories he'd heard about Talbot, his womanizing, his gambling, his use of the Trevor name in his business dealings. But once Talbot realized that Ralph Trevor was never going to invite him into the inner circle — that he would be, at best, tolerated rather than accepted — he dropped all pretense of being the good and true family man. His excesses got so bad that even Cass, who had clung stubbornly to him, gave up and ordered him out of the house. The divorce came through a year later.

Now she sensed that same introspective sorrow in her father. She had betrayed him with Talbot; and now Bob was betraying him with Harry Winston.

"Dad."

He looked up slowly. She saw no recognition in his eyes.

"Maybe it'd be better if I talked to Bob."

"No."

"If you let him go through with the robbery . . ."

Plans like this frequently went awry.

Harry Winston, whom she'd known since he was a little boy, was an angry and violent man. If Ralph trapped Harry and Bob at the safe —

"I think Bob would tell me the truth."

"You do? Since when has Bob told *either* of us the truth?"

"I could just talk to him, tell him we've heard this rumor."

"No."

He had a variety of ways of saying no, but when he said no in this way, with this particular inflection, then there was to be no more discussion. You proceed with caution from this point.

Ralph said, "We'll have to pretend that nothing's wrong when we get in there." He nodded to the ranch house.

"I know."

"You think you can do that?"

"I'm going to try."

He put a hand on hers. "I don't want you giving him any hints that anything's wrong."

"I know."

"I'm sick about this."

"I know that, too, Dad."

He raised his head, his eyes sweeping the mountains and the dying day. Indian summer was suddenly giving in to real fall weather. Heavy coats would be worn to-night. You could smell the stove smoke from the bunkhouse. It smelled warm and neighborly.

He left her off at the house. "Remember what I said. You have to act as if nothing is wrong."

"I will, Dad."

"Maybe he'll surprise us. Maybe that whore was just making it up."

"Maybe she was, Dad," she said with as much sincerity as possible.

"I just can't believe . . ." He shook his head. "I just can't imagine Bob going this far. Stealing from his own father."

"I can't either, Dad."

"Really?"

This was another one of those occasions when she knew what her dad wanted her answer to be.

"Really," she said, and reached up and took his hand. "This may turn out much better than we think."

Then she turned and walked into the house, and there, standing in the living area, was her brother Bob.

He smiled and said, "Hey, Sis, where've you and Dad been?"

Coyle saw her coming and stepped back

from the depot door before she got a chance to know he was there.

The ticket man was back in his cage, tapping out a telegram, not paying any attention to what else was going on.

Barbara came in a few minutes later.

Coyle let her reach the middle of the depot before calling her name.

"Hey, Barbara."

She spun, a frown already pulling her mouth down.

"You bastard."

"Nice talk."

"That's what you are."

He walked over to her. "We've got fifteen minutes before your train pulls in. I want you to tell me about the gunfight. Exactly what did Jimmy do for Bob Trevor?"

She looked over at the ticket man. "He's bothering me. You're supposed to help me."

The old fart shrugged. "He don't look like he's bothering you to me."

"Well, he is."

To Coyle, the old fart said, "You don't lay a hand on her."

"I won't."

The old guy shrugged again and went back to his telegraphy.

"You heard him," Coyle said. "Let's go outside."

She made a clucking sound. "Why can't you just forget this stuff? Take your kid back home and give him a decent burial."

"You don't want to get even with Harry Winston for killing Jimmy?"

She smirked. "Maybe I already have."

"Oh?"

"That's all I'm gonna say."

"Jimmy threw a rock and hit my son in the head, didn't he?"

"God," she sighed, "you really don't give up, do you?"

"No, I don't."

"Oh, shit," she said. "I guess it don't make any difference now anyway. I mean, Jimmy's already dead."

He nodded to a bench. "Let's go sit down."

He started to take her elbow, to guide her to the bench, but she shook his hand away.

"I can walk. I'm a big girl."

They went over and sat down. She took out a cigarette she'd rolled and put in the pocket of her dress.

The old fart looked up when he heard a match being struck. He didn't look pleased that a woman was brazenly smoking in public right here in the depot. Smoking was something a woman should do in private, like having sex.

"Tell me about Jimmy."

"He did what you said, that's all."

"Threw a rock and hit Mike in the head right before Mike was supposed to draw?"

"Yeah."

"That was Bob's idea?"

"Yeah." She smiled. "Too bad Jimmy's dead, huh? You probably wanted that honor for yourself."

"You said you were getting Harry Winston back. How're you going to do that?"

"No, that part I don't tell you."

"Why not?"

"I don't want anything to go wrong. And anyway, it's not any of your business."

"If it concerns Bob Trevor it is. He killed my son."

She stood up and walked over to the window and looked out at the sky. Night was staining it black. The stars were winter cold, winter distant.

"We were going to go away together," she said softly. "We were going to start everything over. He was going to get a job and settle down. And I was going to quit being a whore."

Her head angled downward; her shoulders trembled slightly. He thought she might be crying, but when her head came up

312

again her voice was strong and clear.

"I'm sorry he helped kill your son, Mr. Coyle. But this one time, I don't want Bob Trevor to escape punishment. That's the trouble. He's never had to pay for anything he's ever done. Harry Winston went to prison for him." She turned and looked at him. "Did you know that?"

"No."

"Yes," she said. And then she explained about the stagecoach, how Bob had escaped punishment.

"I'm surprised Harry wants to work with him again."

"They have another plan," she said. "Jimmy and Harry and Bob always had plans. And they were always stupid plans, too, believe me. They were like little boys. The trouble was, Jimmy and Harry were the ones who paid when they got caught."

He pushed himself up from the bench and walked over to her.

"But you've figured out a way to pay Bob Trevor back, is that it?"

She smiled bitterly. "Oh, yes. This is one time his father won't try to help him, believe me."

She turned around and looked out the window again. "I didn't even have enough to bury him very well. Jimmy, I mean. They just put him in the ground like some animal."

Distantly, Coyle could hear the train coming. He saw Barbara turn her head toward the sound.

"Where're you going?"

"Kansas City," she said.

"Why there?"

She shrugged. "That's where we were going, Jimmy and me. He had some kin there. I'll probably look them up. Though they won't be happy that he was going to marry a 'breed."

"Maybe they'll surprise you. Not all white people hate Indians."

"Not all," she said quietly. "But most."

Then they were silent, listening to the train as it charged up the steep hill that led to the valley here.

The old fart came out from his cage and went over to the door where he'd stacked boxes.

"Train'll be here in a few minutes, miss," he said.

"Thanks."

He nodded and started carrying the boxes out the door. He looked too old for this kind of work. But then Coyle remembered what he'd looked like chopping wood.

Coyle put a big hand on her slight shoulder.

"I want to see Bob punished, too," he said.

"I know you do."

"Then help me. Tell me about your plan."

"You'll go and spoil it for me."

"No, I won't. I promise."

The train hooted now, as it started down-hill into the darkening valley.

She sighed. "There's going to be a robbery tonight."

"Where?"

"At the Trevor ranch."

He instantly thought of the money wagon that he'd seen going to the Trevors' this morning.

"The payroll money?"

"Yes."

"Who's going to rob it?"

"Bob and Harry."

"Bob'd rob his own father?"

"I have to admit, I was a little bit surprised by that, too. This sounds more like a Harry idea. He always hated the Trevors. I'm sure he thinks this is a good way to pay them back."

"How'd you find out about this?"

She told him.

"But that isn't all. I told Ralph Trevor about it."

"When?"

"Late this afternoon."

"What'd he say?"

She shrugged. "Nothing, really. He just looked very sad. He's been going through this all his life with Bob."

"I wonder if Cass knows."

"I'm sure he told her. She's not only his daughter, she's also his only real friend, since his wife died and everything."

He thought a moment. "So Ralph waits for them to rob the safe and then —"

"— and then walks in and finds his own son stealing from him."

"Harry'll put up a fight."

"But it'll be too late. Ralph Trevor will already have a rifle on them. And this time, I'm sure he'll punish Bob the way he should've been punished a long time ago."

She sighed, slumped forward, her forehead touching the cold window glass.

"I'm so tired. That's what hating does to you, it makes you weary."

"Yes, it does."

"But I can't help it. I owe it to Jimmy."

Then she turned away from the window and slid her frail arms around his waist and clung to him with the desperation of a small and very lonely child. "I'm afraid to go without Jimmy."

"You'll be fine."

"I just want peace now. I don't want to be a whore anymore, and I don't want to hate people."

She squeezed him tight. He smoothed her hair, cupping the top of her skull in his hand.

"Thanks," she said.

"My pleasure."

She walked back to the bench and picked up her carpetbag.

"What're you going to do?"

"I'm not sure," Coyle said.

"Let it play out tonight, don't try to stop it."

"I won't."

She smiled sadly. "You would've liked him."

"Jimmy?"

She nodded. "People didn't know his good side. He could be very kind and gentle. And funny. He had a real good sense of humor."

He thought of Mike. He wished he'd known Mike well enough to make the same sort of comments. Mike was his son, but Mike was also a stranger. Coyle hadn't taken the time to know him as a boy; and Mike hadn't taken the time to be around once he'd become a man.

"Good luck with everything."

"You, too, Mr. Coyle."

The old fart said, "Train's just pulling in, miss."

And then the air in the open door was filled with the smells of steam and oil and heat. The huge metal beast that reduced the vast continent to a traversable distance was here at last.

Coyle still felt a small thrill when he saw trains. It was the last vestige of little boy in him.

"Good-bye, Mr. Coyle."

She put out a slight hand, and he took it. And then she turned toward the open depot door, and the new life that awaited down the moon-gleaming tracks in Kansas City.

Chapter Eight

"Where's Dad?" Bob Trevor said as Cass took off her hat and hung it on the vestibule's hat tree.

"Putting away the buggy."

"Oh."

She heard at once how strained his conversation was. Nerves. Fear.

"Esmerelda says roast beef tonight." He tried a boyish grin. "I'm starved."

"I'm hungry, myself," Cass said, following him into the wide living room where Mexican artifacts, including a beautiful blanket hung decoratively on the east wall, gave the room the flavor of historical Mexico. Her father had spent some time near the border and had fallen under the sway of the culture and its history.

"I'm going to have myself some wine," Bob said. "How about you?"

"That sounds good. Thanks."

She couldn't help staring at him. He looked bad, all twitches and gulps and averted glances. He didn't want her to peer into his eyes. He apparently feared she could read his mind.

Ralph came in just as Bob was handing her a wine goblet.

"None for me?" Ralph said, smiling at his boy.

Ralph wasn't having any trouble carrying off the ruse.

"I'll get you some, Dad," Bob said, scurrying back across the room.

Ralph and Cass glanced at each other.

Esmerelda came into the room. "Dinner will be ready in another twenny minutes. I know you want to leave early to go to your frien's ranch."

"Roast beef?" Ralph sniffed the air.

Esmerelda nodded.

"Smells wonderful," Ralph said.

"Sure does," Cass said.

A minute later, the three Trevors were seated comfortably in the living room. Because of the late-afternoon chill, Esmerelda had started a fire in the big open fireplace. The smell of wood smoke was sweet in the nostrils, and the heat from the crackling flames felt good.

"So, Bob, are you going with me and Cass tonight?"

"Thought I'd just hang around here," Bob said. "Guess I still haven't gotten over last night. Jimmy was my best friend."

Bob had spent a good deal of his life soliciting the pity of his father and sister. They'd given it to him in sparing amounts, feeling it would corrupt him. A boy with all his advantages had no reason to feel sorry for himself.

"He sure didn't act like your friend last night," Ralph said.

"No, I guess he didn't."

"You owe Harry a lot," Ralph said.

"Yeah. Yeah, I do."

Bob wasn't looking at them. He stared into his glass of wine as if he were reading tea leaves.

"Sure you won't change your mind?" Ralph said.

Bob raised his head. "Change my mind?"

"About the party."

"Oh, no thanks. I better hang around here."

"Lot of folks over there'd like to see you," Ralph said.

His mood had changed abruptly. Up till now, he had spoken with false bravado, sounding bluff and happy. But now you could hear a slight plea in his voice. He wanted Bob to change his mind, to go to the party, to forget all about the money in the safe.

"You could always go over and have a look and stay a little while, then come home if you didn't like it."

"No, thanks, Dad. I'll just stay home tonight. For one thing —" he manufactured a yawn, "— I'm real tired."

Sensing how difficult the conversation was for her father, Cass started talking about some of the new things she'd seen in town today, including a saddle she wanted for her prize mare.

"I thought maybe I could get my birthday present a little early," she said. "If you're open to bribery, I mean."

Usually, her father would have responded in kind to her kidding tone. But now all he said was, "Get the saddle next time you're in town, honey. Have them put it on my account."

"Thanks, Dad."

Cass was about to force some more conversation on the suddenly silent men, but then Esmerelda was there calling them to dinner.

"I put the carrots and the potatoes in the pot with the meat," she said, as she walked with Ralph to the long, narrow dining room that continued the Mexican motif. "Just the way you like them."

Ralph slid his arm around her broad shoulders. "You're not only a great cook, you're a great salesman. You've got me salivating."

That was the old Dad, Cass thought, happy and talkative.

But within moments, he had fallen silent again, as had Bob.

Grace was said. Dinner put on the table. Dishes passed around.

"This is delicious, Esmerelda!" Ralph said, loudly enough that he could be heard in the kitchen.

Esmerelda peeked around the corner. "I'm glad you like it! We'll be eating left-overs from it for the next three nights!" She laughed, and disappeared.

"Her birthday's coming up, too, don't forget," Cass said, engaging in small talk again.

"That's right," Ralph said. "Why don't you pick out a nice dress for her when you're in town next time?"

"And a nice shawl, too," Cass said.

Ralph smiled. "It's a good thing I have a lot of money, isn't it?"

Nobody talked for the next few minutes. Everything got passed around one more time. Esmerelda ducked in to ask if any-body was ready yet for apple pie. Ralph's dog Teddy, a sweet-natured border collie well into his second decade, came charging into the dining room and stood at rigid attention next to his master, who fed him small pieces of beef.

"I can remember when you told us never

to feed dogs at the table," Cass said with a laugh.

"Old Teddy's different," Ralph said. "He's getting too old to hunt as well as he used to. So I have to help him along, don't I, Teddy?" All the time stroking the dog's small, handsome head. Then Ralph said, "I can remember when Don used to have Timmy hiding down on his lap."

Ralph's eyes gleamed with tears. Every once in a while, he had a memory of his dead son that seemed to overwhelm him. This was one of them. When Don was eight, he had a puppy named Tim. Tim used to sit on his lap during dinner and Don would drop scraps to him.

"Oh, Dad," Cass said, holding out a hand to squeeze his.

"I used to have a dog too, remember?" Bob said. "You never seem to remember that, Dad."

"Of course I remember, Bob."

"He might not've been as smart as Don's dog, but he was mine."

The hurt in Bob's voice was familiar to both his sister and father. They heard it any-time the subject of Don was raised. Bob had spent his life comparing himself to Don, and finding himself wanting, at least in his own mind.

"I'm sorry," Bob said. "I shouldn't have said that. Tim was a good dog."

Esmerelda saved the awkward moment by bringing in more coffee.

"Everybody ready for pie?"

Ralph said, "I sure am."

After Esmerelda left, Ralph took out his pocket watch and said, "Guess we'd better get a hurry on, Cass. You know how they are about people getting there on time. Sure you don't want to go, Bob?"

"I'm really tired. Guess I'm not as young as I used to be."

Ralph said, "You're right at the beginning of your life, son. You can do anything you want." He paused. "Good or bad."

Esmerelda came in with three large slices of apple pie.

The family finished off their dinner with small talk about the ranch. They'd hired two new hands within the past month. One of them was working out, one wasn't.

"Well," Ralph said, patting his stomach the way he usually did when he'd finished a meal. "Guess I'll go wash up and change shirts and bring the buggy around."

"I'll be ready," Cass said.

Ralph stood up. "There's still room in the buggy, Bob."

"No, thanks, Dad."

Ralph nodded and left.

Cass lingered a moment. "I know it bothers you sometimes when we talk about Don. But it shouldn't, Bob. We love you just the same as we loved him." She said this honestly, even though there were times when she could barely stand to be around Bob.

"It doesn't seem like it, Sis. Don's always been perfect. At least in Dad's eyes."

He looked so forlorn when he said this, Cass felt guilty about the way she'd treated him sometimes. Maybe if she'd been more understanding of Bob, maybe he wouldn't have gotten in so much trouble over the years. He'd always been jealous of Don, but had she or Father ever really understood how much this had truly troubled him?

Maybe there was still a way. Maybe he could somehow pay with a short prison term for his gunfight with Ray Coyle's son. Maybe he could somehow start his life fresh.

"He loves you, Bob," she said. "You haven't always gotten along, but he really does love you and care about you. You have to remember that." She paused. "I wish you were going with us tonight. You could always change your mind."

He shrugged. "I really am kind of tired, Sis."

She washed, changed dresses, combed her hair, put on perfume, all as if she really were going to the festivities tonight.

She did all this quickly, so that she was waiting by the front door when Dad pulled the buggy up outside.

The night was chill. She wrapped her shawl around her.

She climbed up into the buggy. Her father was smoking his pipe. In the starry autumn night, the smoke smelled warm and pleasant.

"Don't look," her father said, "but he's in his bedroom window upstairs."

"Watching us?"

"Uh-huh. We're leaving later than he'd planned. He's probably worried about us seeing Harry come out here."

"Oh God, Dad, I feel as if we're betraying him."

"I know. So do I. But we've got to find out if he's capable of doing something like this."

"I know."

He tugged on the reins and the horses pulled them away.

When they were gone, Bob went over and sat on the edge of his bed.

His bed. Sometimes it struck him funny.

He'd had this same single bed since he was six years old. The single pushed against the far wall had belonged to Don.

The same bed. All his life. As if he'd never grown up. Was still a father-protected boy who couldn't fend for himself in the world.

He thought about Harry.

What if Harry passed Dad and Cass on his way out here? Wouldn't they get suspicious, Harry not exactly being a welcome guest in this household?

If they saw Harry, then the whole thing was off. Dad would turn around and come back and find out just what the hell was going on.

A terrible weariness came over him. He lay back on the bed. Looked up at the ceiling. When he was a boy, he used to look up at the ceiling and dream of all the things he'd become when he grew up. But somehow they'd never come to be. He'd developed an early taste for alcohol after killing Don, and the taste for alcohol had inevitably become a taste for trouble. Flanked by Jimmy and Harry, he found trouble everywhere he went, usually trouble he started himself.

But tonight it was going to change.

Tonight he was going to become a hero in

the eyes of his father and sister.

Tonight.

A knock.

"Yes?"

"It's Esmerelda."

"Yes, what is it?"

"You look pale tonight, Mr. Bob. I thought I bring you a little something for your stomach."

"I'm fine."

"Apricot wine. It's good medicine."

"No, thanks, Esmeralda."

"If you change your mind, I'll be downstairs."

If you change your mind.

That was another thing about tonight. The way his father had kept saying, "If you change your mind." Almost as if he knew what Bob was up to tonight. Almost as if he wanted to talk him out of it.

"If you change your mind." But no. He wasn't going to change his mind.

Tonight, he was going to become an honest-to-God hero. For the first time in his life.

Chapter Nine

Coyle heard the horses long before he saw them.

He was nearing the ranch when he heard the sound of horseshoes meeting the hard-packed earth road. A few moments later, he saw a buggy, outlined in moonlight, coming down the road toward him.

He guided his horse off the road and to a hiding place behind a copse of birches.

He wished he'd had something heavier than his denim jacket to wear. At least he'd been smart enough to bring gloves. The wind from the surrounding mountains had the bite of the scent of winter in it. Wouldn't be long now before snow threw a white shroud over everything.

The buggy moved slowly. Took several minutes before it came abreast of Coyle.

He let it get a few yards past him and then moved his horse out into the road.

He rode alongside Cass's side of the buggy.

"Ray," she said. "What're you doing here?"

"Barbara told me what's supposed to happen tonight."

Cass glanced at her father. "She shouldn't have said anything, Ray."

"I just thought I could lend a hand," Coyle said, looking around Cass to Ralph Trevor.

"This isn't any of your business."

"You're wrong," Coyle said. "I want your son to tell me the truth about what happened to my son that night."

Cass said, "Then Barbara told you about that, too?"

Coyle nodded. "Jimmy Clinton threw a rock. Just what I figured."

"What do you plan to do about it?" Trevor said.

"Turn him over to the sheriff. Let the sheriff decide."

"You're not going to kill him?" Cass said.

"Not if I don't have to," Coyle said.

Cass looked at her father again, then back at Coyle. "We're very sorry, Ray. What happened with your son, I mean."

"I appreciate that."

"Bob is . . ." She paused. The steady clop-clop-clop of the buggy horses and the thrum of the wheels and the sound of a distant barn owl disappeared into the deep shadows of the hills.

"Bob isn't as bad as you might think," Cass said.

"I just want him to face what he did," Coyle said. "This is one thing he shouldn't be allowed to get away with."

Ahead, the road veered both left and right. Right led to the hills and the ranches that spread beneath them. Left led to town.

"I thought I'd pull in behind those pines over there," Ralph Trevor said, "and see if Harry Winston shows up. If he does, we'll give him a little bit of time and follow him back to the ranch."

"You're inviting me?"

"I am if you're true to your word. I don't want my son shot."

"But you'll see that he's turned over to the sheriff?"

Ralph Trevor paused, then said, "Yes. I'll take him in myself."

"That's all I ask."

"I don't want any of my hands involved in this," Trevor said. "Not good to get them mixed up in family business this way. So I'm appreciative of having an extra gun along. No telling what Harry Winston'll do."

Coyle nodded and began angling his horse to the right, where the road turned to the hills.

Harry Winston had three quick shots of

whiskey before he left his room to walk to the livery.

All day, his plans to take the money from Trevor's safe had had a nice inevitability about them.

Ride out to the ranch. Get the safe open. Kill Bob Trevor. Ride off with the money.

A prison daydream come true.

But late in the afternoon, Harry's nerves had started to go on him. He found himself dry-mouthed, he found himself twitching a little bit, he found himself suspicious — but about what? Bob wouldn't have any choice but to go along. And Bob couldn't say anything to his father, because if he did, Harry would tell the old man how he and Bob had killed Don that day at the swimming hole.

So why did he feel so anxious?

The livery smelled sweetly of fresh hay and fresh horseshit.

The old black man who worked for the livery owner went and got Harry's mount. Harry saddled the animal himself, then rode out of town.

And felt better.

Prison was the trouble, he decided.

All those gray and wasted years in prison, a man lost his self-confidence.

Now that he was on the road, actually heading out to Trevor's ranch, now that he had his Colt strapped on, he felt much better about tonight.

He was going to have himself a whole lot of money. And he was also going to have the satisfaction of killing Bob Trevor, something he'd dreamed of daily in his cold, dirty prison cell.

He filled his nose and lungs with the chill fresh air of the hills and mountains. Clean air, no prison smells of urine and shit and sweat. Clean air. From now on, that was the only kind Harry was going to breathe.

"Maybe he's not coming," Cass said.

They'd been here nearly half an hour. Cass kept pulling her shawl tighter and tighter about her. She had a blanket thrown over her legs. "Maybe Bob decided not to go through with it. At the last minute, I mean."

"Maybe," her father said, clearly not sharing her optimism.

Since Coyle had joined them, Ralph's mood had grown darker. Coyle's presence apparently confirmed for the old man that the Indian whore had told him the truth. This really was going to happen. His own son really was going to betray him this way.

"Listen," Coyle said.

Hooves striking the ground. Echoing off the hills. Moving in this direction.

"Harry," Ralph Trevor said.

"Yes," Coyle said, his voice hard in the darkness. "Good old Harry."

The buggy horses got restless. Coyle dismounted and steadied them. Didn't want them giving away the position over here.

The horse came to the turn that led to the ranch. Harry Winston was a big man. In the moonlight, he seemed to diminish his horse greatly, as if a giant were astride a pitiful beast of burden.

Harry reached the crossroads and headed west, straight to the ranch.

"It's going to happen," Ralph Trevor said. "Bob's going through with it." He sounded more sick than angry. Mostly, he sounded tired.

"Yes," Cass said quietly to herself. "It's going to happen."

Nerves always got him in the bladder for some reason he'd never been able to understand exactly.

Three trips already in the brief time since his father and sister had taken off. Three trips.

Now, walking back from the outhouse to the ranch, Bob Trevor paused a moment and stared down the long road that led to the ranch house.

The way the moonlight shone on it, there was an almost unearthly glow to the road tonight.

It was exactly then, him standing there staring, when the imposing silhouette of Harry Winston rode into view.

Harry's whole body slanted forward when he rode, so far forward that sometimes it appeared as if he might pitch off his horse.

A dark figure now, Harry too had an unearthly look to him, some creature from the fires below, charred all black, and headed to see Bob Trevor.

That was the funny thing. Harry had taken an incredible amount of shit from Bob all his life. Harry had never understood how much Bob feared him. At any time, Harry could have grabbed Bob and threatened him — and Bob would have done exactly what Harry wanted him to.

Maybe in prison, thinking back, Harry had come to understand that.

This thing about opening the safe tonight, the way Harry had pushed it, absolutely demanding that it be done, obviously Harry had changed a lot in prison. No more bullshit from Bob Trevor.

Harry loomed even larger the closer he got.

Bob wanted to run away. Far away. Fast. He wasn't sure why.

Just that Harry — Harry was more than a man on a horse.

He was — fate somehow.

Bob, who had never been much for religion, had always thought about fate a lot. Maybe that was his religion — fate. You turned the wrong corner at the wrong time, you stopped to pick up a handkerchief a lady had dropped, you decided to go this place instead of that, and your whole life could change.

Fate.

Harry was fate.

Bob's whole life was going to change, and very soon. Very soon.

He wanted to run.

Run fast. Run far.

Run.

And then it was too late, because the hellish dark figure was riding up to the ranch house itself.

Harry was here.

Fate was here.

This was one of those nights Sheriff Jim Graham just couldn't stay home. Tried hard, tried (for instance) reading the news-paper, reading a magazine, playing with his granddaughter, straightening up the back porch, and then playing a couple of hands of cards with his wife, daughter, and son-in-law (daughter and son-in-law living here till son-in-law found a job to replace the other six he'd lost since they'd been married two years earlier). But he was still restless. And it was barely seven-thirty.

"Maybe I'd better go down there and check on Willie," he said after his son-in-law started shuffling the cards for another hand.

"Willie?" his wife said. "Is that a prisoner, dear?"

"No, hon. That's a hunting dog."

"Oh, one of your hounds."

"Right. One of my hounds."

His wife smiled at her son-in-law. She actually didn't like him much better than her husband did, but she was able to put on a much more elaborate pretense.

"I swear, he'd have those hounds sleep in our bed at night if I'd let him."

"Want me to go with you, Gramps?"

Graham's jaw muscles bunched, his stomach tightened, and a tiny stab of pain made itself felt just above his right temple.

His son-in-law, after being asked not to

do so in the politest terms, was calling him "Gramps" again.

Graham was going to say something, and say something real good, but then he looked at the sweet, earnest face of his daughter and knew that he could not. She loved his son-in-law with an intensity that both embarrassed and troubled Graham. She loved him so much she was willing to overlook the fact that his loud mouth had caused six employers to cut him loose, that he owed debts to practically every merchant in town, and that there was a good possibility he was sleeping with Juanita in the church choir (or so Deputy Voss had eagerly informed Graham on several occasions).

"No, I think I'll go alone. Never can tell when something'll come up and I'll have to stay down there for a long time." Graham looked sternly at his son-in-law, who managed to find just about as many excuses to get out of the house as Graham did. "You should be here with your wife and daughter."

At which point, Graham's dimpled, pug-nosed, angel-eyed granddaughter began crying upstairs.

The son-in-law was smart enough to understand that, in the most civil of tones, Graham had just given him a direct order.

Stay in tonight or get your ass kicked around the block the way you did the night you staggered home late with lipstick on your neck. (Graham had not told his wife or daughter of the incident. It gave him a good stick he could use to keep his son-in-law in line.)

Graham stood up. Leaned down. Kissed his wife. He still couldn't get used to her having white hair. Somewhere in his mind she'd always be the red-haired eighteen-year-old he'd met at the county fair all those years ago. Now she was white-haired. But then, she probably couldn't get used to (a) his baldness, (b) his paunch, (c) his liver-spotted hands, or (d) the terrible bouts he waged with flatulence the older he got.

"You sure you don't want some company?" the son-in-law said.

"I'm real sure," Graham said, and two minutes later was walking out the door.

He had trouble with the doorknob.

All his life Bob Trevor had been using the front door of the ranch, but for some reason tonight, he couldn't get the knob to turn.

"You need to calm down," Harry Winston said.

"It's this goddamn door."

"It's you, Bob."

340

Trevor gave the knob another wrench to the left. The knob wouldn't turn.

"Here," Harry said, and pushed past Bob.

He got a firm grip on the doorknob and turned it to the right.

The door opened.

Bob Trevor shook his head, went inside.

Harry used to come out here and just stand in the front room and marvel at what he saw, everything so fancy and decorative and expensive. It was like a sanctuary in here, nothing could get in at you, not Indians, not gunnies, not even the law. You owned the world when you lived in a place like this. At least that's how Harry looked at it when he was a kid. But even rich and powerful people had their woes, as he'd learned. Ralph Trevor, for all his power, had lost a wife and a son.

"We better hurry."

"You got to calm down, Bob, I'm telling you."

"They could come back."

"Why would they come back?"

"Who knows? Things happen."

Harry shook his head and followed Bob through the house to the office in the rear.

The place was filled with pleasing odors — pipe tobacco, perfume, floor wax, and, when they passed next to the dining room, roast beef.

This was the kind of life Harry Winston had dreamed of every day in prison. Sane, orderly, civilized. With just a few whores every once in a while to remind himself that he was still a red-blooded man after all.

"Here," Bob said.

They stopped in front of the office door.

"You think you can handle this doorknob yourself, or you want me to help you?"

"Go to hell, Harry."

Harry smiled. "Just trying to help."

Bob didn't have any trouble with the doorknob.

They went inside.

Harry was impressed by how orderly and neat everything was. This is the kind of office he wanted for himself someday. Sit behind the big desk in the big chair and make big decisions. Have men, powerful men, quake at the mere mention of his name. Have women, beautiful women, feel dampness between their legs whenever they thought of him. Harry Winston, Esquire.

Then his eyes found the black bulk of the safe and it was as if his eyes could bore through the steel walls of it and see right inside, see the stacks and stacks of greenbacks. He'd brought three pair of saddle-bags in with him. He wouldn't be able to get all the money, but he'd be able to get a good deal of it.

"C'mon," he said, "let's get the safe opened up."

"I thought you weren't in a big hurry," Bob said.

"Just get the safe open," Harry said. "All right?"

Bob went over to the safe and knelt down and got to work.

The three of them rode in silence, Coyle pacing the buggy.

Just around the bend ahead, the ranch house came into view.

Ralph Trevor stopped the buggy. Coyle ground-tied his horse and then went over and helped Cass to the ground.

It was cold enough now to see the silver breath of the buggy horses. Even the road apples smelled cold.

They were still silent. There was nothing to say. Ralph's son was in the process of be-traying him. What could a man say to that, anyway?

Cass and Coyle looked at Ralph. Maybe it was just the moonlight, but he seemed older now. Kind of pale. Kind of stooped. Kind of slow. Kind of all trembly and uncertain of gait.

They started down the road to the ranch house. Somewhere in the darkness a coyote cried, lonely and hungry, reminding Coyle of the way he'd heard Indian babies cry all night on a reservation he'd stayed on for a time as part of the Wild West Show. The noise of their crying hadn't kept him awake; it was the *quality* of their crying. The sense of sorrow and need.

Ralph stumbled once. Cass was quick and caught him.

"How's it going?"

"Fine."

"Fine. What the hell you talking about, Bob? Fine. You should've had that sonofabitch open five minutes ago."

Nerves. He was doing something wrong. Needed a little more of this or a little more of that. And then he'd have it. He was sure, Bob was, he was real sure.

And then he heard it.

And Harry heard it, too.

The mechanisms inside opening up.

Harry didn't wait. He threw the three saddlebags on the floor right next to Bob.

"Fill them," Harry said.

And in that moment, Bob realized that

he had miscalculated.

How was he going to shoot Harry when Harry was standing over him with his gun drawn?

How was he going to prove to the old man that his only living son really was a hero after all?

"Hurry up," Harry said. "I want to get the hell out of here."

In a few road ruts where water had settled, ice formed a thin silver skin. Cass stepped on one of these patches once, and the sound seemed to fill the entire valley.

Coyle, the silence bothering him, kept trying to think of something to say. But everything that came to mind seemed stupid. So he just shut up.

They swung west when they reached the yard of the ranch house. Ralph apparently wanted to swing wide of the outbuildings and approach from the rear.

As soon as they reached the barn, Ralph drew his Navy Colt.

"C'mon, c'mon," Harry said. "Hurry up."

The money packed the safe full. Just the way all of Harry's prison dreams had told him it would.

And Bob was jamming the money into the saddlebags real fast. Just not fast enough to suit Harry.

"C'mon," Harry said again. "You're like some old woman."

And Bob thought: How the hell am I ever going to get my gun on him?

How the hell is that going to happen?

Coyle wondered if the old man would actually be able to shoot his own son. He hoped not. Coyle didn't want to know a man who could do something like that.

They stayed in the shadows of the barn, silo, chicken house, and then there was a stretch of open area maybe thirty yards long that led to the house itself, an area bathed in the eerie incandescence of moonlight.

Ralph was still silent.

He stared at the house with a kind of miserable anger, a man who didn't want to believe what he knew to be true.

Cass came up next to him, slid her arm through his, laid her head momentarily on his shoulder, the way a child would.

Ralph didn't seem to feel it.

He just stood there, gun in hand, staring at the house.

"Let's go," he said.

Coyle came out of the shadows, eyed the

darkness beneath the sloping roof of the large Mexican-style house. The coyote cry was fainter now. His fingers were beginning to stiffen from the cold even through his gloves.

Behind the pale curtains of a window, kerosene lamplight could be seen flickering.

The office.

Bob and Harry were at work.

Coyle drew his gun.

"No more room, Harry."

Bob Trevor nodded to the bulging saddlebags stacked neatly beside him.

The safe door stood open, a virgin violated. Bob smelled his own sweat and the tart fumes of the kerosene lamp he'd set on the floor next to him while opening the safe.

"You can pack a little more in that last one," Harry said.

"Harry, this is more money than you've ever had in your life."

Harry smiled harshly. "Being a rich boy, you wouldn't appreciate what it's like to need money. There's always more where that came from for people like you."

He walked over to where Bob was crouched down and kicked him hard in the ribs.

Bob slumped to the safe, pain obvious on

347

his face. He groaned, holding his ribs.

"I think you broke something, Harry."

"Stuff more in there," Harry said. "And right now."

There was a door around the corner, a door that Ralph Trevor had made certain would be unlatched when he snuck back.

They went inside the house, and right into the kitchen. Roast beef and broth and spice aromas filled the air. Esmerelda had cleaned everything up, put everything away. A calico cat squatted on a table, watching them with green and curious eyes.

Ralph led the way through the house. Even in the deepest darkness, he was able to maneuver from room to room without banging into anything.

All Coyle could do was follow him. Now that they were so near, Ralph had obviously grown impatient. Wanted to confront his son. Wanted it over with.

Coyle wasn't in any hurry for what lay ahead. A son betraying a father this way wasn't anything a decent man wanted to witness, that was for sure.

After veering left and bumping his knee against a corner, Coyle found himself lost momentarily in the pitlike gloom of the hallway leading to the office.

"What the hell you doing, Harry?" Bob Trevor said.

Harry laughed. "What's it look like, asshole? I'm going to kill you. You still owe me for prison, remember? Now, pick up those saddlebags and bring them over here."

"Why should I? You're just gonna kill me anyway."

"I should've killed you a long time ago, Bob. You've never been worth a shit to anybody. Not me, not your old man — not even your brother. I shouldn't have helped you kill him that day. You wanted him dead, you should've done it yourself."

Coyle had never heard — or felt — the kind of silence that followed the last words.

He tried to imagine what Ralph Trevor was feeling right now, having just learned that his oldest son had not drowned accidentally after all.

Don had been killed by his own brother.

"Get those bags over here, Bob."

Bob, whining now: "I think you broke my rib. No shit. It hurts to even stand up."

"You little runt."

"You broke it, Harry. I'm not kidding."

"I'll break a couple more, you don't push it over here."

"You bastard."

"Hurry up."

"You bastard, Harry."

Until now, the office door had been open only an inch or so, the lamplight from inside a golden strip between frame and door.

Harry swung the door wide open now, reaching behind him to do so, his back still to the hallway, and that's when Ralph Trevor said, "You put that gun down real fast, Harry, or I'm putting three bullets into the back of your head right now."

"Dad!" Bob Trevor shouted.

Coyle followed Ralph Trevor into the office. Bob Trevor gripped the edge of the safe and pushed himself to his feet, a grimace apparent on his mouth. Apparently, he hadn't been exaggerating about the damage Harry Winston had done to his ribs.

"I told you to put the gun down, Harry," Ralph Trevor said.

Cass came into the office, hurried over to the lamp, and turned it up.

Coyle looked down at the three saddlebags on the floor. They bulged with money. A big dream had ended here tonight.

"Harry," Ralph Trevor said again.

Harry Winston was close enough to the desk to set the gun on its surface. In the lantern glow, the office looked far too orderly and civilized a place for this sort of thing. This was a room of good wood and leather, of sipping brandy and fine cigars, of contemplation and study, not a room of coarse talk and bloodshed.

"Turn around," Ralph Trevor said to Harry Winston.

"What happens if I don't?"

You could hear the smirk in Harry's voice.

"If you don't, I kill you."

Harry Winston was smart enough to know the difference between a real and an idle threat.

He slowly turned around.

Bob Trevor started to move toward his father, but Ralph snapped, "Stay there, Bob! Right next to him, where you belong!"

"You don't understand, Dad," Bob said, sounding as if he was going to cry. "I was going to stop him. I really was. I was going to make sure he didn't get the money. I was —"

"The money?" Ralph Trevor said. "You think I give a damn about the money?"

Cass came up and stood next to Coyle. She looked pale and confused and at least a little bit frantic.

"Was that the truth, Harry?" Ralph Trevor said quietly.

"Was what the truth?"

"What you said about Don?"

The smirk. "What did I say about Don?"

Ralph Trevor took two steps forward and brought the barrel of his weapon down hard across Harry Winston's right cheek.

Harry gave the old man the pleasure of showing pain. And fear. The smirk vanished as soon as hot red blood started snaking its way down Harry's torn cheek.

"I'm going to ask you one more time, you sonofabitch. Was what you said true?"

Harry glanced at Bob, who was only a few inches from him.

"Yes, it was, Mr. Trevor."

"You two drowned my son, Don?"

"Yes, we did, Mr. Trevor." Harry sounded like a frightened young boy.

"But it was Bob's idea," Harry said, "not mine."

"Dad, listen —"

"Shut up, Bob!" Ralph Trevor said. He said this without looking at his son. He hadn't looked at Bob more than twice since coming into the office.

"I'm telling the truth, Mr. Trevor," Harry said. "Bob had the idea and asked me to help him."

"So you drowned him?"

Harry didn't say anything. Just stood there, letting the wound on his cheek bleed.

"So you drowned him?"

A whisper: "Yes, Mr. Trevor, we drowned him."

"You dirty bastard!" Bob screamed, and lunged at Harry.

Harry was ready. As Bob jerked toward him, Harry grabbed the slighter man around the neck and head and wrenched him to himself.

A gun magically appeared in Harry's left hand, a spare he'd concealed somewhere on his person.

Neither Coyle nor Ralph Trevor had had time to shoot.

Harry held the gun to Bob's head. "Cass, you carry those saddlebags out and put them on my horse."

"They'll kill you, Harry," Cass said coldly. "You may as well give up now."

Harry with his famous smirk, said, "You never did like me, did you, Cass? I was never good enough for this family, was I?"

"You killed my brother," she said.

"Yeah," he said. "I did. And I'll tell you something. I enjoyed it, too. He was just as stuck-up as you are. Thought his shit didn't stink."

Bob tried to wrench out of Harry's hold, but Harry only tightened his grip.

"Take those saddlebags out to my horse,"

Harry said. "Or I kill little Bobby right here."

"You killed your own brother," Ralph Trevor said. "Your own brother."

"Dad, we were just playin' with him. We didn't mean to —"

"The saddlebags," Harry said. "Get the damn saddlebags, Cass, and right now."

No more argument from Cass. She went over to the safe, walking wide of Harry, as though if she even brushed against him she might catch a fatal disease.

Harry noted this and duly smiled. He seemed to enjoy the way people despised him.

Coyle went to help Cass with the saddlebags, but Harry waved him back.

"She don't need your help, Coyle."

The saddlebags were heavy. Cass struggled with them for a few minutes. But finally she got them loaded up in her arms.

"Now, get your ass out there and then right back here, you understand me?"

Cass glared at him, then staggered forward under the weight of the bags.

She bumped into the door frame as she went out. At any other time, the collision would have looked comic. Right now, it just looked sad and pathetic.

"Your own brother," Ralph Trevor said again.

There was no anger left in him. Just sorrow.

At least Bob didn't try to talk this time. He was out of excuses and explanations. The act spoke terribly for itself.

Coyle could hear Cass making her way through the darkened house, the occasional noise she made as she staggered and stumbled forward under the weight of the saddlebags.

Coyle was sweaty and needed to piss. He also had the notion that Harry here was not quite hinged right, and might just kill all of them before the night was finished. He was a coldly bitter man, and despite the smiles he was a scary sonofabitch.

When Cass came back, she was sweaty. Her hair had come free of the fancy combs that had held it in place. Her dress was smudged with dirt.

"I got them on your horse," she said. "Now let my brother go."

Harry laughed. "You sure you want him? After what he done to Don?"

"He's still my brother."

"I'm not sure your old man'd agree with that, right, Mr. Trevor?"

Despite his surliness, he paid Trevor the deference of putting a "Mr." in front of his name.

"Coyle," Harry said. "Put your gun on the desk there."

"What if I don't?"

"You don't, and I kill Bob here."

"What if I don't believe you?"

"Goddammit, Coyle," Bob said. "Do it. Harry isn't kidding."

Coyle put his gun down on the desk.

"Now take Mr. Trevor's from him," Harry said. "And put it on the desk right next to yours."

"Your own brother," Ralph Trevor said.

He could no longer be counted among the living. He was back at the swimming hole, on a hot summer afternoon, hearing the screams of his drowning son. Hearing the screams — but unable to help his son at all. The screams would be in his ears forever.

Coyle reached over and gently plucked the gun from Trevor's fingers. Trevor didn't seem to notice. Before, he hadn't looked at his son at all. Now, he couldn't seem to take his eyes off him.

Coyle set the gun on the desk.

"Guess Bob 'n' me'll be going now," Harry said. "Sorry I had to be the bearer of such bad tidings, Mr. Trevor."

His grin said the opposite. He considered it an honor and a privilege to destroy Ralph Trevor the way he had.

"He's gonna kill me, Cass," Bob Trevor said. "He really is. Don't let him take me now."

"Aw, that's so sweet," Harry said. "Askin' your sister to help you. You ever tell her about all the times you used to spy on her when she was taking a bath? The good old Trevors. What a fine, upstanding family."

His grip became deadly. Bob gasped for breath as the strength in Harry's forearm grew even stronger.

"We're walking out of here," Harry said, "and anybody who tries to come after us is gonna get ole Bob here killed. You folks understand that?"

He didn't wait for an answer.

He shoved Bob forward. The gun stayed tight against the side of Bob's head.

In the lamplight, you could see that Bob's buff blue shirt was soaked with sweat. The odor was sour on the air.

Harry turned around quickly, so that he could back his way out of the office. For a brief moment, Coyle thought that there might be some way to jump him. But there wasn't.

Harry backed out of the room, dragging Bob with him.

"He's gonna kill me, he's gonna kill me,"

Bob said, his eyes imploring his sister to help in some way.

Coyle felt embarrassed for him. Bob Trevor didn't have much to claim for himself. He should at least have some dignity.

"You're gonna be fine as long as you shut up," Harry said, tugging Bob out of the office and into the darkness of the hall.

"Remember," Harry said from the gloom, "anybody comes after me, I kill him right on the spot. Understand?"

All they could do was stand and listen as Harry struggled with Bob all the way down the hall and to the front of the house. A number of times you could hear heavy bodies slam against the walls.

Curses, shouts, occasional punches — the darkness was alive with these sounds.

The front door banged open, its echoes swimming through the shadows like eddies of dark fish.

"I'm going after them," Cass said.

"Stay here," Ralph Trevor said.

"But he has Bob."

"He's welcome to him," Ralph said.

"I know what he did, Father. But Bob's still my brother. Maybe we didn't treat him the way we should have. Maybe —"

She didn't have time to finish her sentence. That's when the gunshot sounded.

Only one shot. More like a dog bark than a gunshot, actually. But there was no mistaking what it was. Oh, no.

Cass screamed then, and Coyle grabbed her by the shoulders and pulled her back from the door.

"Let me go first," he said.

He hurried now, grabbing his gun from the desk, pushing on through the doorway into the darkness.

The front door still stood open. He saw a slice of night, all vast heaven and starlight, and then heard a horse riding away hard in a northerly direction.

He rushed to the door.

Bob lay no more than twenty feet from the house. On his back. Arms flung wide. Unmoving.

By now Cass was right next to Coyle, hurrying to Bob's side.

Coyle didn't want to tell her she was too late. Let her have a few more brief moments of hope, anyway.

She flung herself to the figure on the ground, then raised up his shoulders so she could lay his head in her lap. His bloody head. Her gingham dress was instantly imprinted with blood from his wound.

Her reaction surprised Coyle at first. He would have expected her to be as angry with

Bob as her father was — the old man who stood next to Coyle now, staring bitterly down on his dead son.

"Leave him alone, Cass," Ralph Trevor said. "God gave him what he had coming to him. There's no reason to be sad."

"He was my brother, Dad, my brother," she said, her voice trembling with tears.

"He may have been your brother," Ralph said. "But he wasn't my son."

As if to emphasize this, Ralph Trevor walked over to Bob's fallen body, cocked his right leg, then slammed it hard into Bob's ribs, so hard that the body danced an inch or two off the ground on contact.

"You sonofabitch," Ralph said to the dead man. "I wish I could've killed you myself."

Then, to Coyle, he said, "Let's go get Winston. But remember this. I kill him personally."

Coyle knew better than to argue.

While Ralph went to the barn and saddled up, Coyle stayed with Cass.

"I hate what he did," Cass said, looking down at her dead brother. "But I can't hate him. I probably should. But I can't."

And then she fell to sobbing.

And then Ralph was there. And the two men headed out fast.

Chapter Ten

Harry could feel the horse's strain as he approached town. The bags were heavy and Harry was digging in his spurs.

Harry needed a fresh horse. He could steal one from a ranch, but he might be caught and shot. His best chance was to reach the livery before Trevor and Coyle got to town.

But he had one stop to make first.

His spurs dug in harder, deeper.

In shadowy starlight, Harry reached town. He could hear the distant sounds of a player piano in one of the saloons.

He swung east, taking an old trail that circled the streets where the poorest people lived.

There was an alley between the small cottages. He came down it riding hard, stopping by the shed in back of Ellen's place.

He worked quickly, ground-tying the horse, digging in his back pocket to take out a clean red kerchief.

He threw back the flap of the saddlebag. The money felt deliriously real.

He took out four thousand dollars, an

amount it took most people four or five years to earn.

He laid the money inside the kerchief, then knotted the kerchief up good and tight.

His next task was to sneak up on the cottage. Dew glowed wetly in the moonlight. He had to walk cautiously.

When he reached the side of the cottage, the smell of burning stove wood sweet in his nostrils, he got close enough to peer inside.

Ellen and the girl sat at a table in the middle of the cottage's one big room.

Ellen was reading to the girl, who was listening raptly. The dark color of the book identified it as a schoolbook.

He watched them for a long moment in the lamp glow inside.

He could have had this sort of life. Good wife, sweet daughter. He would never have been rich or important, but he would have been respectable, anyway. He certainly would never have served time in prison.

A crooked smile parted his lips.

No, that sort of life would never have been right for him.

Even with prison, even now with the law about to be after him, he'd had the sort of life he'd wanted. There was a freedom in his life, a freedom a workingman would never know.

He watched Ellen and the girl for five minutes. There was no sign of the man.

He decided to risk it.

He walked around the side of the cottage to the front, his boots soaked with dew now, and knocked on the door.

Ellen quit reading.

Her chair scraped back.

She walked softly to the door.

She'd opened it barely two inches before recognizing him. She tried to slam it shut immediately, but he put his foot between the door and the jamb.

"I need to talk to you a minute."

"I'll get my husband, and you'll be sorry you came."

"He isn't here."

"Who is it, Mom?" the girl said.

"Just somebody I know, honey." Trying to sound as if everything was all right.

"I'm in a hurry. I just need a minute."

Ellen glanced back at her daughter. "You read for yourself, hon. I'll be right back."

"Okay, Mom."

Ellen came outside, closed the door softly behind her.

"I'm going to call the law on you the next time you come here."

He smirked. "You won't have to call the law. They're already looking for me."

"Oh, God," she said. "You're in trouble again, aren't you, Harry?"

He said nothing, just brought up the kerchief. "This is for the girl."

Ellen held it. "What is it?"

"Money. A lot. For when she's older."

"You stole this, didn't you?"

"That doesn't matter."

"Maybe not to you, Harry. But it matters to me. And it would certainly matter to her."

"I want her to have it."

She handed the kerchief back. "Get out of here, Harry, and take your money with you."

"It's four thousand dollars."

"I don't care what it is."

"He'll never be able to give you anything like this."

"He gives me something a lot better, Harry, and you just can't seem to understand that. Tonight he's down to church, helping build on the new addition. That's the kind of man he is."

"I was always scum to you," he said.

"Not always, Harry. When we first got married, I thought maybe I could change you. But I learned different very fast."

They stood on the tiny porch of the tiny cottage, the big shaggy man and the small slender woman, and Harry should have been in control, being so big and forceful and all, but he knew now that she really wasn't going to take the money, and that there was nothing he could do for the little girl he'd thought about so much in prison.

"You'd better get going, Harry. I'm sure they're looking for you by now."

The door opened behind her and there in the lamplight stood the little girl. Harry wanted to go over to her and just touch her shoulder. Not hug her, not kiss. Just simply touch her. He'd thought about that a lot in prison. A lot.

He put his long arm out and walked two steps forward so he could reach the girl.

But then Ellen put herself in front of him and pushed his arm away.

"Go now, Harry."

"Is everything all right?" the girl asked.

"Everything's fine," Ellen said, staring at Harry. "He's just saying good-bye is all." Then: "Good-bye, Harry."

A moment later, the door was closed. Mother and girl were back inside.

Sheriff Graham was with his hunting dogs. He'd escaped his son-in-law for the pleasure and peace of his animals.

He'd spent a few minutes in the office,

seeing what had transpired since he'd left four hours before for home, but tonight was slow: a drunk and a small amount of money missing from a cash box, the latter a familiar occurrence. At least once a month, Sam Bowers dragged a deputy out there to say that somebody had stolen money from his cash box. Sam was a gunsmith, and a cranky old one given to a lot of suspicions.

But now Graham was where he wanted to be, out in the pens with the dogs, feeding them and playing with them.

Voss came out. "Riley's back."

Graham sighed. "Good for him."

Voss tucked his thumbs into his gun belt and rocked on the heels of his cowboy boots. The glow from his cigarette defined a granite jaw, a day's growth of beard stubble, and a hatchet nose. Voss was always trying to look the way dime novelists liked lawmen to look.

"You want me to go over and grab him?"

"He do anything yet?"

"No."

"Then why would you grab him?"

"Because we know he *will* do something."

"Not necessarily."

Now Voss sighed. Ted Riley was a rancher who liked to come to town three, four times a year and get drunk. A few years ago, his wife and two daughters had died from influenza. When Riley got drunk, he got sad and then he got angry. He picked fights with people. He didn't carry a gun and he'd never been known to actually *hit* anybody. He just mouthed off. But Voss liked beating him up. He'd done it twice now. Graham wasn't going to let him do it a third time.

Graham was about to say something harsh when the back door was flung back and Ralph Trevor and Coyle came fast down the three steps leading to the dog pens.

"Evening, Ralph," Graham started to say.

But Ralph wasn't here for pleasantries. Not with a Winchester in his hand.

"Harry Winston," Trevor said. "You seen him in the last half hour?"

Harry had to get past the old colored man.

Done with his work for the day, the old man sat in his cardigan sweater, in his rocking chair, in the livery office, a newspaper open on his lap. His head lay against the back of the chair, his mouth was open, and he was snoring. The old bastard worked hard, and Sullivan probably didn't pay him much at all.

Harry had taken his own horse around back. He needed an additional animal. He could divide up the weight of the saddle-bags. It was risky coming into town this way, but his own mount wouldn't get him through the night.

Harry was up front now so he could look at the animals in the livery for the night.

He got up on tiptoes and started into the open area of barn running down the center. The stalls were all filled with sleeping horses. They made a lot of night noises, horses did.

Harry was now abreast of the office. Just a few more steps and —

"Hey, Harry," the old colored man said, eyelids flying open like shades going up on a sunny morning. "How come you came back?"

Harry took out his gun. "How old're you?"

The old man noted the gun. "You drunk or somethin', Harry? What the hell you doin' with that gun?"

"I want a horse."

"All right," the old man said. "You want a horse. You don't need a gun to get a horse. Not from me you don't. You're one of the few people in this town who treats me like a human bein', Harry. I'll be happy to help you."

"There's somethin' else."

"Yeah?"

"Yeah. You don't tell nobody I was here."

The old man grinned. "You're headed back to prison, ain't you, Harry? You done went and screwed it all up again, didn't you?" He shook his head. "It figures. One of the few nice folks in this town and they's sendin' him off to prison."

"Not prison," Harry said. "Hangin'." -

The old man man's tone changed. "Hangin'? Oh, shit, Harry."

"I need to go. Fast. Get me your best horse."

"You bet I will, Harry. You bet I will."

The old man was up out of his chair, moving as fast as he could with his bad arthritis.

Coyle noted that Graham seemed very happy about using his dogs. There probably weren't all that many manhunts in a small, peaceful town like this.

In less than five minutes, Graham, Voss, and two other deputies led Coyle and Trevor to the street. The lamps had been lit. Lamplight mixed with moonglow to turn the street silver.

"He's carrying that much money," Coyle said, "he's going to need an extra horse."

"That's what I was thinking," Graham said. "Let's try the livery first."

They marched down the street, Winchesters and Colts at the ready.

You could tell Voss was enjoying himself. He swaggered instead of walked, and there was a faint smile on his lips. This was the kind of moment a man like Voss dreamed of. A chance to track a man down and kill him, and the law couldn't do a damned thing to you.

Harry heard the dogs coming.

The old man was just leading a big cayuse out of its stall when the barking echoed inside of the high livery roof.

"Graham," Harry said. "I'll have to hide."

"Not here," the old man said. "You'd be too easy to find."

"Yeah," he agreed. "Yeah, I would be."

Then he glanced at the old man. The bastard would tell Graham everything. Colored man like him, how could he resist white law?

"Sorry I have to do this," Harry said. And then he struck the old man with great force across the side of his head, the handle of the Colt coming away with blood and pieces of the old man's iron-gray hair.

Harry ran out the back door, into the starlight. Had to hide the money somewhere so he could double back after a while and get it.

The barking dogs were coming closer, closer.

Hurry, Harry, you sonofabitch. Hurry.

"All right," Graham said when they reached the front of the livery. "Let's stop here. Ralph, you want to go in and see if Rufe is up?"

Ralph Trevor nodded. Coyle went with him.

Ralph went into the office. Coyle looked through the stalls.

Coyle found Rufe in front of the back door. He lay on his back, arms spread wide.

Coyle said, "Back here!"

Coyle felt for a pulse in Rufe's wrist. He felt a faint one. Harry had struck him very hard.

Graham took the dogs on through the barn. By the time Coyle got there, Graham had his dogs sniffing the horse. Harry had been nice enough to leave his gloves on his saddle. Graham gave each dog a long sniff of them.

"He isn't far," Graham said. "Let's spread out."

★ ★ ★

One time, years and years ago, Harry Winston went into the general store and, when old man Whitaker wasn't looking, stole a couple of lengths of licorice. Old man Whitaker, who spent most of his time gossiping, happened to be turning around just as Harry was stuffing the candy into his pocket. Whitaker shouted for his son, who was fat and lazy and astigmatic, to go after Harry, who had by then reached the front door.

Well, he may have been fat and he may have been lazy, but the sumbitch sure could run.

That day, he ran Harry all over town, up and down streets, up and down alleys, in and out of woods, over roofs and under bridges, and the lard-ass bastard kept running like he was never going to run out of breath or strength. The only way Harry ever eluded him was by diving into the river at dam point, which his mother would have kicked his ass for had she ever found out.

Now, all these years later, ducking down dark alleys, cringing at every sound, sweating something fierce and needing to piss so bad he could barely stand it, Harry felt like that same woebegone kid again. Running, running, running — running to,

372

running from, all his life he'd been running — even in prison he'd run internally, lying in his midnight cell, thinking of all that might have been, and all that might yet be. Running. He was sick of running. So damn sick of it.

He'd buried the money out in back of the livery, under a stack of dusty boxes that looked as if they hadn't been moved in years.

Somehow he'd swing back there tonight, get the money, and start the final run. The run to California. And freedom. And the life he'd always dreamed of.

But for now he had to find a good place to hide.

The dogs practically dragged Graham along behind them. They were pure energy, and Graham their helpless slave.

They seemed to know exactly where they were going, and they were taking Jim Graham along whether he wanted to go or not.

A few minutes later, Coyle and Trevor were inching down an alley. Coyle covered the left side, Trevor the right.

The alley ran behind a block of businesses, each of which had small loading platforms built around their back doors.

The moonlight cast the alley into an eerie shift of shadows. A tomcat sat perched on one of the platforms, watching them.

This was a perfect hiding place.

Coyle expected to feel a bullet tearing into his back at any moment now, Harry letting them pass so he could get nice clear shots at their spines.

They went down one, then two, then three blocks of alleys.

No sign of Harry Winston.

No sign at all.

Actually, it was Deputy Voss who found Harry first.

Voss was thinking how great he'd look to the boys in the Red Dog Saloon if he was the one who treed Harry Winston. No dogs. No extra men. Just hisself and that lawbreaking scumbag Harry Winston.

The Red Dog'd be buying him schooners for the next six months. And maybe when that butthole Graham decided to retire — maybe the town council would remember who it was who'd brought down Harry Winston and made the streets of Cooperville safe for children and old ladies and virgins of all ages.

None other than — you guessed it —

good old Deputy Voss.

Right now Voss was making his way down Fourth Street, where there were two boardinghouses favored by transients.

One of the houses had a back entrance that opened on one of the darkest stairways Voss had ever seen. Perfect place for a man to hide. Especially since it was pretty close to the livery.

By now Voss had convinced himself that he was going to find Harry in here.

He took a couple of deep breaths, then reached down for the pint of whiskey he carried in his back pocket. He had himself a couple of nice swigs. Then he crept up to the back door on tiptoes and went inside.

It was even darker than Voss remembered it. Only at the first landing was there light, grimy moonlight through a small, unwashed window.

He stood there, not wanting to admit he was scared, but dark rooms had always scared him. He used to cry out for his ma a lot when he was a little kid. She forbade him to listen to the ghost stories his older brothers were always telling. He got too scared.

Voss imagined he could hear breathing, the way that guy in that Edgar Allan Poe story heard the heartbeat of the friend he'd killed. Louder and louder and louder.

Voss couldn't help it.

Even with the whiskey, he was scared.

Sweat was running down his face, his armpits, his legs, his feet.

He was like to lose ten pounds in here tonight.

Dust motes were thick on the air. He sneezed. Great. If Harry didn't know he was in here before, he certainly knew now.

He decided maybe he'd better go. He tried to convince himself that he wasn't a coward. No, he was going, without exploring the dark two stories of stairs, simply because he was sure by now that Harry wasn't in here.

Not because he was afraid.

He thought of spitting in Harry's face. Twice, he'd done it.

That was the sort of thing a man never forgot. No sir, you never forgot anybody who spit in your face. No matter how old or forgiving you got, you never forgot that.

Best get out of here.

Best get out of here *now*.

He'd find Graham and tag along with him. Graham had the dogs. They'd keep Harry at bay if nothing else did.

He pushed open the door and went outside and stood on the stoop.

Harry Winston put the six-shooter right in his face and said, "You lookin' for me, are you, Voss?"

"Aw shit, Harry," Voss said.

"Aw shit is right, Voss," Harry said.

"I'm real sorry I spit at ya."

"Yeah, I'll bet ya are."

"I got me a wife and kids."

"I'll be doin' them a favor."

"I'm beggin' ya, Harry. I'm beggin' ya. I really am. I'm even shittin' my pants. I can feel the shit right in my drawers right now."

Harry couldn't help himself any longer.

He spat a big greasy goober right on Voss's nose.

And then shot Voss three times in the face before Voss even had the chance to fall down dead.

Harry went over and stomped down on Voss's face with his boot heel. He worked him over a good five minutes before the heel of his boot started dripping blood.

Deputy Voss wasn't going to look real good in his coffin.

Not real good at all.

Harry made a face. One thing Voss hadn't been lying about was crapping his pants. The smell was sour.

Then Harry heard the dogs. The damned dogs. In prison a lot of guys talked about how some lawmen had their hounds trained to tear a man apart when they caught him. Others talked about how the barking sound of the dogs came back to you even years later, usually late at night, how angry and hungry they sounded in the darkness.

By now the posse would have grown. Folks would want to know why Graham had his dogs out this late at night. So they'd tumble out of their beds and grab their clothes and their guns and hurry to the street to find the sheriff and join up with him. Who the hell would want to miss excitement like this, anyway?

Now was the time to double back to the livery. That's the one place they wouldn't look for him.

There was no place else to go.

At the sound of the gunshots, every ragtag end of the posse, Coyle and Trevor included, starting moving fast up toward Front Street, which was approximately where the gunfire came from.

Trevor stumbled once and pitched forward, almost cracking his head on a porch, but Coyle grabbed him in time.

When Trevor was standing up straight again, he said, "I'm sorry for what my boy did to your son."

"I know you are."

"He got what was coming to him."

"I'm not sure I could judge my own son that harshly, Trevor."

"He killed his own brother."

Coyle sighed. "That's the hell of it with life. The older you get, you realize there aren't any easy answers. About the time you're thirty-five, all the easy answers start to sound real stupid."

"I don't have any easy answers," Trevor said, "that's for damn sure. Not anymore, I don't."

They hurried down the boardwalk toward the growing crowd near the Front Street alley.

Harry Winston cut wide, heading in an easterly direction back toward the livery.

He took an alley that let out half a block from the livery. He walked, he didn't run.

Between the small houses, in the open spaces, he could see all the men with carbines and torches moving toward Front Street.

Hell, he was going to make it. By the time Graham and his men decided to check the livery again, Harry would be long gone.

Coyle had seen a few Indian raids. Every

once in a while the raiders had decided to mutilate the faces of their victims.

Voss looked as if a couple of bucks had decided to spend a good half hour on his face.

"Sonofabitch," Graham said. "Sonofabitch."

"Harry always did have a mean streak," one of the posse men said.

Coyle almost smiled. The posse man had a gift for understatement. What Harry Winston had done to Voss represented more than a mean streak.

"Wonder where the hell he went?" one man said.

"Wonder if he's got some of the money with him?" another asked.

"Wonder if he's gonna kill anybody else tonight?" a third said.

"Fan out," Sheriff Graham said. "Half you men walk to the outskirts of town. The other half follow me. We're going back to Main Street."

"What for?" a man said. "Why'd he go back to Main Street?"

"Because he's convinced he's a genius," Sheriff Graham said. "He'll think we'll be too stupid to think he might double back. Now, let's get going."

Coyle decided that sounded pretty sensible, doubling back. He and Trevor went along with Graham and the dogs and a handful of other men.

Cass left the ranch shortly after her father and Coyle did.

She rode fast to the sheriff's office. A freckled deputy who didn't look older than fourteen sat behind the front desk, an unlit corncob pipe in his teeth.

"Where's the sheriff?" Cass said.

When he recognized who it was, he dropped his feet down and sat very straight in the chair.

"Evenin', Miss Cass."

"Never mind that now. Where's the sheriff?"

"Out looking for Harry Winston, ma'am. He took the dogs 'n' everything."

"He's in town, then?"

"Yes'm. Somewhere."

"Thank you."

She started to go outside again.

"Ma'am?"

She looked back at him. "Yes?"

"I'm sorry to hear about your brother."

She nodded. "Thank you."

She went back outside. The posse was coming back this way. The dogs were loud, their bark echoing harshly on the slumbering night. She couldn't see anybody as yet, though. They must be coming down the alleys.

Something —

She looked left, her eyes narrowing.

Somebody —

Somebody creeping out of the alley a block away.

Looking left, looking right.

Apparently in so much of a hurry that he didn't even see her.

Harry Winston.

She recognized his clothes, his particular slantwise way of walking.

Then he was gone, little more than a shadow, hurrying across the street and into the other alley.

All she could think about was her brother Don.

She walked back into the sheriff's office. She'd changed from her dress to denims and a workshirt. But there was one thing she'd forgotten to bring along.

"I need a gun."

"Ma'am?" said the young deputy.

"A gun." She nodded to the Navy Colt in his holster. "Yours'll do."

"Ma'am, I'm not sure —"

She didn't like to pull rank, didn't like to use the Trevor name, but there was no time for anything else now.

"Do you want me to tell Sheriff Graham that you refused to help me?"

"No, ma'am, I sure don't."

She put her hand out, palm up. "Give me your gun, then."

The young deputy gulped. "Yes'm," he said, and handed it over.

"Those dogs're gonna piss off everybody in the next three counties," one of the posse men said. And they were tireless. Bark bark bark.

They were even getting on Coyle's nerves. He just wanted two or three minutes of pure silence.

"Maybe I'll go on ahead," he said to Ralph Trevor, who was walking next to him.

Coyle had expected the old man to tire at some point. But if anything, the old man looked angrier and stronger than ever. He was obviously thinking about what he was going to do to Harry Winston if and when they ever caught up with him.

"I'll go with you," Trevor said. "Those dogs are driving me crazy."

The first thing Harry Winston did was make sure the livery was empty, that Graham hadn't posted a deputy to wait behind or anything.

He checked out the haymow, he checked out the stalls, he checked out the corrals in back. No sign of anybody.

Had to move fast now.

He took two horses from their stalls and proceeded to saddle up one of them.

When he was finished with that, he went over to where he'd buried the money.

Then he set to work.

She wanted to tease him a little bit. Make him think he was doing just fine.

From the front of the livery, Cass watched Harry Winston saddle up his horse and then drag the money bags from beneath the stacked boxes. He threw two of the bags over the unsaddled horse and one bag across the back of the other.

He was working so frantically, he didn't see her at all, even though she wasn't particularly well-hidden.

He was just about to swing himself up on the horse when she started walking slowly into the livery.

She kept her gun trained on his chest.

"You're not going to make it, Harry."

He whirled around, hand dropping to his gun.

"I'm a pretty good shot, Harry. Fact is,

you used to give me lessons sometimes when I was a little girl, remember? Be funny if the same girl you gave lessons to ended up killing you."

All the time she talked, she kept walking straight at him.

"Throw your gun down, Harry."

"I could kill you. You know that, don't you?"

"You want to try, Harry? I'd really like that. At least you'd have a chance. Don didn't have any chance at all. Now, throw your gun down or I'll put a hole in your forehead."

She didn't want to start screaming at him, though that's what she felt like doing. Screaming and kicking and clawing. All she could think of was Don's last moments of life. Desperately trying to save himself from drowning in the swimming hole.

Harry seemed to suddenly understand her rage. He carefully lifted his gun from its holster and dropped it on the hay-covered earth of the livery floor.

The dogs again.

Very close now. Very close.

"Hear them, Harry? Won't be long now."

"I won't go back to prison."

"Nothing to worry about, Harry. They'll hang you before they send you back."

Harry snorted. "Bob was going to take over the spread and run it. You had one dumb brother there, Cass, you know that?"

"You were always the smart one, right, Harry?"

"Smarter'n any Trevor, anyway."

"Then how come I've got the gun and you don't?" she said. "And how come —"

She couldn't control herself any longer. She was close enough to nail him, and nail him she did, bringing a knee straight up between his legs.

His cry filled the haymow. He fell straight down to his knees, clutching his balls.

This time she stood back three feet for leverage, and kicked him straight in the face with her boot. She had the satisfaction of hearing his nose crack. Probably broken.

And that was when he grabbed her.

She was startled by his resilience. In great pain, blood streaming down his face, her with the weapon, he still had the quick animal cunning to lash out with his hand, grab her ankle, and jerk her off her feet.

Then he was scrambling in the hay-strewn dirt for his own weapon.

But she was as angry as he was. She crawled to her feet and hurled herself on his back just as he was crouching to get his weapon.

She hit him several times on the side of the head with her Navy Colt.

Every time he was within a few inches of grabbing his weapon, she hit him again.

Then he threw her over his shoulders, the way a wrestler would, and when she landed on the ground, her gun fired accidentally.

By now he had his own weapon and was running to his horses.

There was still time, he thought. Have to hurry, have to hurry —

But before he was quite settled into the saddle, and before he could quite turn the horses to the alley and freedom, she came bursting out the back door, her gun in her hand again.

They both fired at the same time. The horses in the stalls got gun-spooked.

She slowly sank to the ground, clutching her shoulder. She hadn't hit Harry at all.

He fired off a couple more rounds, but neither of them hit her.

He grabbed the reins of the second horse and started out of the corral area.

And that was when Ralph Trevor appeared, almost ghostlike, blocking Harry's way.

Trevor's gun was pointed directly at Harry's face.

"Hold it right there."

"You sonofabitch."

"You heard me, Harry. You don't know how bad I want to kill you."

"You don't have the nerve, Trevor. You want something done, you hire it done. Just the way your son Bob did. I had to do everything for him."

"Yeah," Trevor said bitterly, "even help him murder my son."

Trevor glanced at Cass. Coyle was tending to her.

"She'll be fine, Ralph," Coyle said.

Trevor looked at Harry. "Get down off the horse, Harry."

Harry's gun was holstered. But both Trevor and Coyle kept watching Harry's hand.

The dogs were no more than a block away now.

And that was when Harry moved, spurred his horse so that it leapt up in front of Trevor before the old man could even get a shot off.

Then the horse's front hooves struck the dirt again and broke into a run, knocking Trevor to the ground, his gun flying from his hand.

Harry found the alley, and spurred his horse to move even faster. By the time he reached the end of the alley, he was becoming just one more shadow.

Coyle saw there was only one thing to do.

He hurried to the second horse, flung the saddlebags from its back, and hurled himself up into riding position.

Then he was galloping after Harry Winston.

At first he couldn't find him. Hiding. That was the only answer. Harry was hiding somewhere nearby.

The first shot grazed Coyle's shoulder. The second shot got the horse in the flank. Hot blood soaked the horse and the leg of Coyle's trousers.

Coyle knew the horse was useless now. He threw himself from the animal before it sank to the ground. Coyle felt sorry for the animal, wished there were time to comfort it, reassure it. But there wasn't time now, that was for sure.

Where the hell was Harry?

Coyle was in a moonlit field, an easy target for Harry, who was somewhere behind four railroad cars that were sitting off on a weedy siding.

Coyle started rolling to the right. Harry's gunfire was instant and came very close to hitting Coyle.

Coyle got the information he needed. Harry was at the far right end of the cars.

Coyle could see the shanks of the horse beneath the boxcar. Harry had positioned himself between the two cars.

Coyle rolled back to the left, until he was even with the last car.

Then there was no time for thinking. Harry had an enviable shooting position, all right. The one problem he had was seeing what was going on down at the far end of the cars.

Coyle rolled even farther to the left. The shots this time were still surprisingly close. Harry was a damned good shot.

Coyle jerked to his feet and started running to the boxcar. He jumped up on the ladder and scrambled to the top of the car.

Then he started moving carefully down the other cars toward Harry Winston.

Harry caught on quickly. Within a minute, he'd climbed to the top of the car where he was hiding and opened fire on Coyle.

There was no place to hide.

All Coyle could do was dive to the surface of the car, roll away from the path of the bullet, and then cling to the car while belly-crawling toward Harry.

Harry's head would pop up above the top of the car every few minutes. Then he'd fire off a few more shots.

When he reached the second-to-last car, Coyle waited until Harry squeezed off a few more shots. Coyle then eased himself down the ladder on the side of the car.

He had only moments to make this work.

When he reached the ground, he moved on tiptoes to the last car. He walked around back.

Harry was crouched at the top of the ladder, waiting to fire off a couple more shots. He still thought that Coyle was up top.

"Maybe you're not as smart as you think you are, Harry," Coyle said.

Coyle knew what to expect, Harry turning on him abruptly, firing round after round.

But Coyle was way ahead of him. He picked his shots, crippling shots, not fatal ones. He got Harry's gun hand and then he got his kneecap and then Harry fell off the ladder and struck the ground with enough force to knock himself out.

In the ensuing silence, Coyle could hear Sheriff Graham and the posse and the tirelessly barking dogs coming closer and closer.

Chapter Eleven

Esmerelda had cooked her very best meal ever. This modest appraisal came from Esmerelda herself as she served the three people in the fancy dining room of the Trevors' ranch house. There was the fanciest of fancy table linen, and the fanciest of fancy silverware, as well.

The two Trevors were each on the mend from last night's activities. Cass's left arm was in a sling, the doc not wanting her to move her wounded shoulder any more than she needed to. And Ralph Trevor had a broken right leg, inflicted when he fell on it beneath the power of Harry Winston's horse.

Candlelight made Cass even prettier. The old man, for the first time since Coyle had met him, seemed to be at some sort of peace with himself.

"She ask you yet?" he said, just as Esmerelda was bringing in dessert, which happened to be peach cobbler.

"Asked me?"

"Dad," Cass said. "I thought I'd wait a little while."

But Ralph wasn't about to wait.

"I asked her to ask you if you'd consider staying on for a while. See if you could get used to ranch life."

"Not right now, I couldn't, Ralph." Coyle looked at her and then at him. "I've got to take my son's body back home for a burial."

"Then what?" Ralph Trevor said.

"Then I don't know."

"You don't want to go back to the Wild West Show, do you?" Cass said.

"It's not so bad. Kind of peaceful in a strange way, I guess. And I like most of the people."

"But you'll think it over? About working here, I mean?"

Coyle smiled. He knew what she wanted him to say. And who knew? Maybe someday he really would like to settle down on a ranch like this.

"Yeah," he said. "Yeah, I'll think it over."

Then Esmerelda came in, eager for more compliments on her cooking.

About the Author

Ed Gorman has been called "one of suspense fiction's best storytellers" by *Ellery Queen*, and "one of the most original voices in today's crime fiction" by the *San Diego Union*.

Gorman's work has appeared in magazines as various as *Redbook*, *Ellery Queen*, *The Magazine of Fantasy and Science Fiction*, and *Poetry Today*.

His work has won numerous prizes, including the Shamus, the Spur, and the International Writer's awards. He's been nominated for the Edgar, the Anthony, the Golden Dagger, and the Bram Stoker awards.

Former *Los Angeles Times* critic Charles Champlin noted that "Ed Gorman is a powerful storyteller."

Gorman's work has been taken by the Literary Guild, The Mystery Guild, Doubleday Book Club, and the Science Fiction Book Club.

The employees of Thorndike Press hope you have enjoyed this Large Print book. All our Thorndike and Wheeler Large Print titles are designed for easy reading, and all our books are made to last. Other Thorndike Press Large Print books are available at your library, through selected bookstores, or directly from us.

For information about titles, please call:

(800) 223-1244

or visit our Web site at:

www.gale.com/thorndike
www.gale.com/wheeler

To share your comments, please write:

Publisher
Thorndike Press
295 Kennedy Memorial Drive
Waterville, ME   04901